the BLOODY BRICK ROAD

THE FORBIDDEN TALES

the BLOODY BRICK ROAD

A *WIZARD OF OZ* RETELLING

MAUDE ROYER

TRANSLATED FROM FRENCH BY RACHEL E. FOX

GALLERY BOOKS

New York Amsterdam/Antwerp London

Toronto Sydney/Melbourne New Delhi

G

Gallery Books
An Imprint of Simon & Schuster, LLC
1230 Avenue of the Americas
New York, NY 10020

Translated from French by Rachel E. Fox Translation
Originally published in Canada in 2022 by Éditions ADA Inc. as *Le magicien d'Oz*

First Gallery Books trade paperback edition January 2026

Interior design by Hope Herr-Cardillo

Manufactured in the United States of America

10 9 8 7 6 5 4 3 2

Library of Congress Control Number: 2025945030

ISBN 978-1-6682-0913-4
ISBN 978-1-6682-0914-1 (ebook)

the BLOODY BRICK ROAD

CONTENT AND TRIGGER WARNINGS

This unhinged book is a horror novel intended for adults only. Reader discretion is advised, since the following pages contain some of the following:

organ swapping

Winged Monkeys with neo-Nazi ideologies

amateur animal crossbreeding

sexual (and nonsexual) shoe obsessions

involuntary cannibalism

sex with murder case evidence

pitchforks, staple guns, axes, and other very sharp objects

AI girlfriends

reckless credit card spending

heartless bastards, cowardly men, and sweet-but-brainless boys

blatant disregard for traffic laws

sexual assault

and a depiction of child abuse

AUTHOR'S NOTE

This Forbidden Tale is an adaptation of the novel *The Wonderful Wizard of Oz* by L. Frank Baum, published in the United States in 1900.

Hour after hour passed away, and slowly Dorothy got over her fright; but she felt quite lonely, and the wind shrieked so loudly all about her that she became nearly deaf. At first she had wondered if she would be dashed to pieces when the house fell again; but as the hours passed and nothing terrible happened, she stopped worrying and resolved to wait calmly and see what the future would bring.

—L. Frank Baum

JUNE 1994

3 . . .

IT'S THE HORMONES, Dorothy told herself as she parked in front of an old brick house in downtown Montreal. For perhaps the first time in her nineteen years, she could see the road ahead.

The nausea and fatigue of her first trimester were just bad memories at this point. And now that the greatest risk of miscarriage was also behind her, she had stopped having nightmares about it.

She had clocked out of her shift at the local mall's jewelry store an hour ago but stopped to buy a few things for the baby and the nearly barren refrigerator that awaited her at home. Plastic bags were piled on the passenger seat next to her. She would have just enough time to change and head out again.

Stepping into the house, Dorothy dropped her bags in the corner.

"We're home, darlings!" she yelled up the stairs, rubbing her hand on her growing belly. It was just Dorothy, Toto, and the shoes at home.

She had heard that first pregnancies took longer to show than later ones. But at twenty-three weeks and four days along, her baby bump was hard to miss.

Must be all the enthusiasm.

If an unwanted pregnancy could be kept hidden until the very end, maybe the opposite was happening to her.

I can't wait to see your smiling face, sweet Toto.

That familiar voice of warning crept into her head.

"Be careful what you wish for, my pretty."

One of her mother's favorite lines.

"Your bad attitude can't infect me anymore, you witch," she said aloud to no one while walking farther into the hallway.

Dorothy smiled at her reflection in the entryway mirror. Her skin was glowing. A touch of green lit up her gray eyes, and her auburn hair was shinier than ever.

"It's all thanks to you, little Toto."

Ever since she was a child, Dorothy had worn her wild hair tied in two long braids. But she didn't feel the need to do that anymore and happily let her hair fall loose over her shoulders. Having always thought of herself as fairly average, she was now beginning to discover her beauty. She couldn't remember ever having been this happy. Relaxed and at peace, she felt like she was living in a real fairy tale. And she was the princess.

Grabbing a few of the bags, she brought them into a room that smelled of fresh paint. Like a mother bird, she was building a nest for her little one. The walls of the room had been painted sky blue, and, the day before, she had finished assembling the crib. All the bedding had been ordered. And the bags—which she now set down on the floor—were full of clothes, toys, and baby bottles.

Dorothy felt like there was nothing she couldn't do.

And that's lucky, since I'm doing it all myself.

She plucked the cordless phone from the kitchen counter, swung back through the entryway to pick up a purple bag with a gold logo on it, and dialed a number as she climbed the stairs to her bedroom.

"Yeah?"

"Vincent? It's me, babe."

"Hey, Dot. Something wrong?" he asked, slightly drowned out by the whirring of machines around him.

"Why does something have be wrong? I just bought a bunch of adorable things for the baby, and his room is almost ready."

"Don't overdo it. The house may be paid for, but that doesn't mean we're millionaires."

They had been together for two years when she got pregnant. At which point she had reluctantly agreed for him to take a job in an auto body shop in James Bay for a few months to make some extra money before the baby came.

"How's it going over there?" she asked him, wanting to change the subject.

She rustled through the bags that contained her various purchases. A moment of silence fell between them.

"Fucking hell, Dot. You bought another pair, didn't you?"

She took a shoebox out of the purple bag.

"I . . . I just got myself a little present." She awaited his reply but was met with more silence on the other end. "A pair of heels from Vidal-Berry. They're white with a black-flower motif. If you could see them, you would understand—they're gorgeous!"

"But you don't even wear them, Dorothy! You only ever wear sneakers."

"I'll wear them for you when you get back. You'll see. They make my legs look amazing!"

Standing in the walk-in closet of her room with the phone wedged between her ear and shoulder, Dorothy undressed, put on the heels, and admired herself in the mirror. At the other end of the line she heard her boyfriend sigh.

"Were you calling for a particular reason?" he asked now, clearly annoyed.

"No, it was . . . Ow! Toto just kicked me!"

"Quit calling him Toto. It's so goofy."

"What do you want to call him, Vincent? We've known it's a boy for weeks and you still haven't suggested any names!"

Unable to stand still, Dorothy took off her new shoes and found a spot for them among the hundred pairs—all more or less the same—that she already owned. Then she dug around in a pile of laundry in the hopes of unearthing her yoga clothes.

"We have plenty of time for that, Dot. What's the rush?"

"How about Kansas? That's nice, don't you think?"

"Kansas? Over my dead body. That's not even a real name! It's almost as ridiculous as Toto. Why not Chibougamau, while we're at it?"

Dorothy let it go.

I'm not giving you a choice, Vincent.

"Did I tell you Bianca said yes to being the godmother? Now you just have to pick the godfather. Your brother, maybe?"

"We agreed, Dorothy. There's no way we're getting him baptized."

"Right. We're not getting him baptized," she confirmed as she put on her leggings. "But he still needs godparents. People we trust, who would always be there for him. In case something happens to us."

"What d'you think's gonna happen to us?"

This time it was Dorothy who showed her frustration. She let out a heavy sigh.

"You know what? I have to go, Vincent. My prenatal yoga class starts in forty-five minutes. Kansas. It's cute. Think about it, OK?"

"It's still four months away, Dor—"

"Love you, bye!"

She hung up, glanced at her watch, and stepped out of the closet. Throwing a white hoodie over her tank top, she bolted down the stairs and set the phone on the entryway table. The conversation had left a bitter taste in her mouth, but she wasn't about to let it ruin her good mood. She was already halfway out the door when the phone rang. Darting back inside, she picked up.

Oh, now you want to apologize for your shitty attitude . . .

Dorothy pressed the green button, but the voice that replied to her breathless "Hello?" belonged to an older woman.

"Who?" Dorothy asked her to repeat herself.

"This is Colette from your credit card company, Ms. Noroît. I'm calling to inform you that your Gayelette Direct card has been canceled."

"Canceled? Why?"

"You haven't responded to any of our communications by mail, and you haven't paid your bills in four months, madame. Your debt has been transferred to a collection agency."

"Madame, may I please have just a few days? I can pay it in full," Dorothy said in her sweetest voice.

"The agency will be in touch, and you can work it out with them. You're not our problem anymore."

Colette hung up the phone. She had been exceptionally brief but had still managed to make Dorothy miss another call.

I knew he'd call back.

She pressed play on the answering machine. But it wasn't Vincent this time, either; it was Dorothy's boss, Will Wallace. He was calling to inform Dorothy that she was being let go, effective immediately.

Dorothy dialed the number of the jewelry store and fought to keep the heartache and despair out of her voice as she demanded an explanation from him.

"This has nothing to do with your performance, Dot, but we've got to make some cuts, and since you were the last one hired . . ."

"Will! The last one? You hired me the same week as Bianca. Is she out, too?"

"I had to make a choice." Will was all business now.

"I'm better at sales than she is—you know that!"

"Dorothy . . . it might be better for you to work somewhere other than a shopping center. Do you understand what I'm saying?"

"What're you talking about?"

"Bianca told me about your problem . . . with shoes. You could look at this as a chance to finally kick your bad habit."

Dorothy abruptly ended the call. Hands trembling and heart pounding, she pressed the speed dial button for her best friend's number. As the phone rang, Dorothy felt the world spinning around her.

"I did it for your own good," Bianca protested before Dorothy even had a chance to talk.

Convinced that her traitorous friend had blabbed about her penchant for shoes to save her own job, Dorothy exploded in frustration.

"I'm having a fucking baby, Bianca!"

"Vincent is making plenty of money for both of you in James

Bay. And besides, you wouldn't have any cash problems if you hadn't cut off your parents. And if you would stop buying shoes, Dorothy. Seriously, you need to get some help!"

Dorothy had heard enough. She hung up.

Don't lose heart, she ordered herself. *Can't let unhealthy emotions affect Toto.*

She was shaken, but she decided she would stick with the plan and go to her yoga class anyway. She just needed a relaxing hour.

2 . . .

IT WAS RUSH hour and there was some traffic on the freeway, but it was moving. Dorothy would make it to the studio with just a couple of minutes to spare. As she drove, she realized the exhaustion was catching up to her, and her vision was blurring.

Keep it together, Dot, she lectured herself, blinking her eyes furiously to hold back the tears. She couldn't stop replaying the conversations she'd had over the past hour, her rage growing with every passing minute.

They don't care about me one fucking bit. If they did, they would be happy that I've been taking such good care of myself. I deserve to have nice things. I wouldn't have cut off my family if they hadn't— She stopped herself there.

She took a deep breath in and regained control of herself. Just then, a red car in the left lane came into her peripheral vision. The woman driving was having what seemed like a lively conversation on a car phone. Dorothy imagined it could be handy to have one of those contraptions.

Especially after Toto's born.

Dorothy had just recognized the driver. Johanne, a redhead in her mid-twenties; they were in the same prenatal yoga class. She was likely on her way there, too. Johanne was due about a week before Dorothy.

That girl is so tacky. Is she gonna keep wearing that much makeup and dressing like that when she's a mother?

Dorothy didn't use much makeup, only a little foundation in the summer when the sun brought out her freckles.

Completely wrapped up in her phone conversation, Johanne had been drifting out of her lane, toward Dorothy in the middle. Dorothy honked her horn. Johanne flipped Dorothy off and sped ahead. As their exit quickly approached, Johanne swerved hard and fast into the far right lane. But the car that was now in front of her had stopped short. It all happened so fast. Dorothy saw the red car stop suddenly, and she watched in shock as Johanne's body shattered the windshield with brutal force. Time seemed to stand still as Johanne's body tore through the air. But gravity finally took hold, and Johanne came crashing back down onto the asphalt. Car horns were blaring, and vehicles went veering off in every direction.

Like cockroaches startled by the light, thought Dorothy, who had drifted into the exit lane.

Dorothy hit the brakes just in time to avoid running over Johanne's mangled body, and the back of her head slammed into her headrest. Flung forward by the impact, her stomach took the full force of the steering wheel. She unbuckled the seat belt, which was digging into her abdomen. Her mind numb from the physical and emotional shock, she kicked open the door and dropped to her knees. Once she had made it to her feet, she had taken only five or six steps when she heard the deafening screech of a pickup truck ramming into the back of her car. Pushed forward several yards, Dorothy's car rolled over Johanne's body before coming to a full stop. A massive pileup had ensued. Amid the chaos, she saw a man running toward her. He was shouting words she couldn't understand because, apart from Johanne's moaning—*How is she still alive?*—the only thing she could hear was a dull buzzing sound. From the way the man was waving his arms, she guessed he was warning her to get away from where she was standing.

Before Dorothy's horrified eyes, the man was hit by an SUV. She turned away from the sight of his body, but instead of running to get herself safely off the road, she walked over to the wreckage of her car, where a cloud of steam was wafting into the sky. Johanne's bare feet were sticking out from underneath the heavy mass of tangled metal, and she was still moaning. Dorothy saw one of Johanne's shoes—a stiletto in the same bright shade of red as Johanne's car—lying nearby, and Dorothy noted that Johanne's toenails were painted black.

Those heels are way too high. I wouldn't dare wear them.

Suddenly reality came crashing back in. Although time seemed to have ground to a halt, it was actually still moving forward, and Johanne clearly wasn't going to make it much longer.

"This woman is pregnant!" screamed Dorothy. "Call an ambulance!"

There was nothing else she could do. Once again her sense of time deserted her. She stood there motionless, staring at the distant patent leather heel, until the firefighters arrived on the scene, followed by the paramedics and police.

Johanne's body was limp by the time they pulled it out from under Dorothy's car. It took them two minutes to get her into the back of an ambulance and speed away toward the medical center.

At that moment, the buzzing in Dorothy's head faded to a low hum and then disappeared completely. At last she could hear the sobbing and screaming of all the injured people around her, and she spotted the other red shoe on the ground. She was seized by an overwhelming desire to reunite the pair.

I've never had ones this beautiful.

"Are you OK, miss?" asked a firefighter a moment later.

"I'm fine."

"You're bleeding."

Dorothy raised her hand to touch her head, but instead it came to rest on her belly. A sudden, horrendous pain ripped through her. The firefighter grabbed her shoulders to hold her steady.

"Are you pregnant? Was that a contraction?"

"Couldn't be! I'm only at six months!"

Blood was dripping on the asphalt. It had soaked through Dorothy's yoga pants and was running down her thighs.

1 . . .

THE CURTAINS SEPARATING the stretchers kept opening and closing with a metallic jangling sound as the hooks slid across the poles. In the large room at Sainte-Victorine Hospital, where Dorothy had been taken, she could hear the commotion without seeing it.

"Is anybody there?" she called out.

Why isn't anyone coming?

The contractions were getting closer together. Every two minutes, an excruciating pain exploded in her belly and radiated throughout her body. Yet the brief examination Dorothy had undergone had not revealed any sign of serious injury. She had also been given an ultrasound with a small portable machine.

"The baby's doing fine," someone reported before abandoning Dorothy behind two curtains.

These are false contractions, Dorothy told herself. *They'll eventually stop.*

An hour later, she was still clinging to that idea. She worried about Toto, but her own physical pain was taking up most of her attention. When a hospital employee—barely older than Dorothy was—drew back the curtains, she found Dorothy on all fours on her stretcher, gasping for breath.

"Dorothy Noroît? I'm an intern in obstetrics. Has anyone measured you yet?"

"Measured me?"

"Measured your cervix. To see how dilated you are. Take off your pants and underwear and lie down."

A violent contraction kept her from complying right away. And by the time she had settled in to be examined, another cramp was tearing through her. The intern had barely stuck her head between Dorothy's legs when she pulled it out again. Dorothy didn't like the look on her face.

"You're having the baby today."

As if an invisible hand had gagged her and was pushing her down, Dorothy let out a silent scream. Everything went black. The hospital bed and the floor seemed to vanish, and she felt as if she were falling. She quickly snapped out of this other world she had tumbled into, but because the time lapse had existed only in her own mind, she had missed what the intern had been trying to tell her.

"Huh?"

"Labor has begun. Your cervix is completely dilated. I'm sorry, there's no way to stop it now."

"No . . . it's much too soon . . ."

She had blocked out that possibility, refusing to let it enter her mind.

Why didn't anyone come earlier?

"Toto . . ."

"What did you say?"

"There's no way he'll make it . . ."

As far as Dorothy was concerned, this was a fact. An undeniable truth she could not ignore.

"We're going to do everything we possibly can for you and the baby," replied the intern, without affect.

But now, when she needed it most, Dorothy could not find the little piece of hope she kept stored away inside her for safekeeping. For this waking nightmare she had tried to prepare herself for . . .

From that point on, everything unfolded at a dizzying speed.

Her stretcher was rushed from corridor to corridor. Hospital staff swarmed around her, bombarding her with questions, which she answered as best she could. She swallowed a pill that was supposed to help speed up the development of the baby's lungs. Everything was moving so fast around her. Then, finally, Dorothy found herself face-to-face with Dr. Gilles Lanouette, a neonatologist who was getting ready to care for the newborn, and everything fell very still.

"The obstetrician is on his way, Dorothy. You have a choice to make. Do you want to give birth naturally or by C-section? Your baby hasn't turned yet, obviously. At his size, that's not a problem in itself, but at twenty-five weeks, his head is still soft and a natural birth would . . . He wouldn't survive. A cesarean would give him a chance. At twenty-five weeks, he—"

"But he's not twenty-five weeks," Dorothy interrupted. "Not even quite twenty-four."

"The ultrasound shows that your baby is at twenty-five weeks. And at this stage he's perfectly formed and in great shape."

In his early fifties, the doctor had a gentle, attentive manner that inspired confidence. But Dorothy had experienced the twinges in her lower abdomen that she associated with ovulation and was sure she knew the exact date of Toto's conception: twenty-three weeks and four days earlier. She was nonetheless willing to take Lanouette's word for it. She nodded.

"Where's the father, Dorothy? You could talk it over with him for a few minutes, but we don't have much time . . ."

"He's in James Bay."

"Ah . . . Have you already discussed what you would do if such a situation arose?"

How could we have imagined that something like this could happen to us?

All through her first trimester, thoughts of miscarriage plagued Dorothy. But for the past few weeks, she had finally started to relax.

"Before the twenty-week ultrasound, we agreed that if there turned out to be a problem—something serious—we would figure something else out."

"This is a little different," replied Dr. Lanouette. "He's here, Dorothy. He's about to be brought into the world."

How is that different?

Putting a hand on her arm, he tried to be reassuring. "I'm going to call the baby's father. Tell him there's no need to panic, but that he should get here as soon as he can."

"Anyway, he wouldn't make it in time." It seemed no one was listening to her now.

Lanouette moved toward the corner of the room, grabbing the room's phone from its charging base, and quickly got the young man on the line. He explained the situation and passed the phone to Dorothy.

"Let nature do its thing, Dot," urged Vincent. "There's nothing else we can do."

"Did you hear the doctor, though? He has a seventy-five percent chance of survival. That's a lot . . . What you're saying would be like murder . . ."

"If he survives, what kind of shape will he be in? Think about that."

"If he survives, he has a fifteen percent chance of being totally fine, no long-term effects at all."

"Fifteen percent? Holy shit, Dorothy!"

"I know, but . . ."

"Whatever. You decide. Do what you think is right."

"But we . . ."

"There's no more *we*, Dorothy. I would've told you earlier if you hadn't hung up on me. I'm not coming back in October. I don't know when I'll be back."

"But . . ."

A contraction—more intense than the others—stopped her mid-sentence.

"You're going to have to make a decision," interjected Lanouette. "Before it's too late."

"He's your fucking son, Vincent."

"Yeah, I'm sure he is, but I never wanted a kid. We're too young. You should've listened to your parents. It's not too late. Life is giving us a second chance, you could look at it that way. Let nature do its thing."

Already in a state of shock, Dorothy sat there in stony silence.

"Don't hang up yet, Dorothy. The house is in my name. It's my inheritance. So I'm gonna rent it out. I'll give you to the end of the month to find another place to live."

Dorothy calmly set down the cordless phone at her side. Somewhere deep inside, she remained convinced that the doctors had it wrong.

I can't be having my baby today. It's a false alarm. They're going to change their minds, and everything will go back to normal.

In the meantime, she certainly wasn't going to push to help the baby out of her belly.

They want him? They can come get him.

Between cries of pain, she gave her consent for the C-section, and the neonatologist flew into action. People were running all around her. They wheeled her to another room, dressed her in a surgical gown and cap, and made sure she wasn't wearing any jewelry. Then . . . nothing happened.

For a long time.

"What are we waiting for?" asked Dorothy, exhausted from the pain.

"The anesthesiologist," said Monique, the nurse who was holding her hand. "The whole staff is overwhelmed because of the accident. He won't be much longer. It's going to be OK."

Dorothy had made her decision. What happened next was out

of her hands. The situation was dire—she knew that—but a little voice in her head told her that Monique was right.

Everything's going to be OK.

"Somebody coming, *ma belle*? Your mother? Or a girlfriend?"

"It's just me. He's all I have left."

Dorothy's face contorted with a contraction. The nurse glanced under the sheet covering Dorothy and suddenly let go of her hand. Rushing to the hallway, she yelled at the top of her lungs.

"It's happening now! Right now!"

EXHAUSTED, AND WITH the help of medication, Dorothy fell asleep as soon as she heard her son crying. When she opened her eyes, her surroundings had changed. She had been moved from the delivery room to a semiprivate room, from a stretcher to a bed, which was next to a second, empty bed.

She had to ask the question.

"Your baby's alive," replied a nurse. "He's doing well. Under the circumstances."

The kind woman who had held her hand during the epidural and who had been there for the operation must have finished her shift.

"I brought you a breast pump," the replacement told Dorothy. "You're planning to breastfeed, right?"

"I . . . I don't know . . ."

"It's so important. Especially for a baby as small as yours. For two or three days you'll be producing colostrum, which is much richer in protein than breast milk. You should at least give him that."

"Sure, OK . . ."

Dorothy struggled to extract the precious yellowish liquid from her breasts and succeeded only in compounding her pain and distress.

"Try again," insisted the nurse sternly. "A few drops will make all the difference. Even a full-term baby's stomach is no bigger than a marble, so just imagine your baby's . . ."

She stepped in to try to help but had no better luck than Dorothy.

"Don't fall asleep again," she grumbled before leaving the room. "You have a visitor."

Vincent? she found herself hoping. *Did he have time to make the drive all the way from James Bay?*

Her visitor turned out to be a police officer.

"You're working late," Dorothy said. "What time is it?"

"Almost eleven p.m. I was about to leave when they told me you were awake."

He asked her a few questions about the accident. What did she know? What had she seen?

"Nothing."

"Somebody mentioned a phone . . . The woman under your car—had she been talking on the phone?"

Dorothy thought about Johanne's baby. She thought she heard whispers in the halls that he was saved from the clutches of death while his mother faded into eternal sleep. Had she dreamt them? Had he made it? What were his chances of survival?

Johanne lost her life on the freeway. Will her child get some kind of compensation? And what if they prove that she was responsible for the accident? He could end up losing that money.

"I don't know. I didn't see a phone."

The officer congratulated Dorothy on the birth of her baby, excused himself, and was quickly replaced by Dr. Lanouette. The news was not good.

"He's younger than he looked on the ultrasound. He's not at twenty-five weeks, maybe not even twenty-four."

That's exactly what I told you.

"We know this because of his eyelids," continued the neonatologist. "They're still fused."

"He doesn't actually have a seventy-five percent chance of survival, does he?"

"More like forty percent," said Lanouette apologetically. "And as far as long-term effects go, we could be looking at anything from paralysis to a mental disability, or it could just be some deafness or a need for glasses at an early age. If he does survive, we won't really know how it'll play out until he's about two years old."

With these lovely words, the doctor was called away to attend to another patient, leaving Dorothy utterly shaken. She was only just beginning to grasp the horror of her situation.

What have I done to deserve this?

From the instant she had learned she was pregnant, she had loved her child as if they had always been together. She had been through a lot since then, but despite her young age, her boyfriend moving far away, and the lack of support from her parents, she had never for a second wished her baby would disappear. Without him in her belly, her life already seemed meaningless.

I was so happy these past few weeks.

Dorothy's fall to rock bottom was all the more devastating because she had been flying so high. All she wanted to do now was fall asleep and not wake up again for a long, long time.

For two years.

But just as she was dozing off, a nurse came in to check the painful wound in her lower abdomen. As she helped change Dorothy's giant postnatal sanitary napkin, she expressed alarm at how quickly the pad had soaked through. She called the obstetrician to examine her belly.

"This semicircular bruise would be from the steering wheel. We can also see where the seat belt was cutting into you. That must be what triggered the placenta to detach, which then caused your cervix to dilate. Does your head still hurt?"

Dorothy couldn't remember having complained about her head, but yes, it was pounding.

"I'm sending you for an MRI and a few X-rays. Someone will come get you."

Shortly after the obstetrician left, another hospital employee came in. He scanned the room with his eyes but didn't pay the slightest attention to Dorothy.

"No defibrillator in here," he muttered as he swung back out the door.

Then yet another nurse appeared, this time to take Dorothy's temperature.

It's a revolving door, she thought. *I'm going to lose my mind if they don't let me sleep.*

"I'm going to need a name for the birth certificate," said the nurse.

"His name's Toto."

"OK, there's no rush. Legally you have three months after he's born to choose a name. What's the father's last name?"

"He doesn't have a father."

"Ah." The nurse gave her a sympathetic look. "Do you want me to get a wheelchair?"

"What for?"

"You haven't been over to see him yet."

Turning away from the nurse, Dorothy sighed.

"My god, I just want to sleep."

0.

LIKE EVERY MORNING, Dorothy stroked her belly without thinking about it. But then the memory of what had happened the day before suddenly hit her. It came crashing down on her, splitting open her chest and crushing her heart. She wanted to scream; she wanted to break things, to tear out her IV. To reject reality in any way she could. But instead she just lay there in the hospital bed between its metal rails.

How many times had she told her little Toto that she couldn't wait to hold him in her arms?

Be careful what you wish for, my pretty, her mother scolded her again in her cold, dry voice.

Dorothy still hadn't moved an hour later when an aide brought her breakfast tray.

"Sorry it's late. We're slammed."

"I'm not hungry," Dorothy said to the ceiling.

"Gotta eat. Especially if you're breastfeeding."

Raising her bed with the push of a button, the aide helped Dorothy sit up and adjusted her pillows. The psychological shock—which until that moment had spared her from some of the pain of the accident—had worn off. Her shoulders, neck, and ribs were killing her.

"It hurts."

The aide called a nurse, who injected a dose of painkillers.

"Remember me, *ma belle*? It's Monique. Just let me know if you need anything."

Dorothy wanted to know how her son was doing, but the answer scared her so much that she didn't dare ask. Having already gone to check on him, Monique shared what she knew without waiting to be prompted. The main issue had to do with the baby's lungs, one of which was badly affected.

"The next few hours are critical."

While the nurse checked Dorothy's vitals and encouraged her to swallow a few mouthfuls of watery oatmeal, another patient moved into the bed next to her. Holding a beautiful chubby newborn to her breast, she greeted Dorothy, who turned her head away. Soon the baby's father came through the door with a huge suitcase, followed by a whole parade of friends and relatives, their arms loaded with gifts and balloons. They began fussing over who would get to hold the little angel in their arms, who would change his diaper or give him his first bath. Without warning, Dorothy burst into tears and her forehead exploded in pain.

"I can't promise you a private room," whispered Monique. "But don't worry, I'll get you out of here."

IN THE ROOM Dorothy was moved to, a woman in pajamas sat cross-legged, gazing at a flyer. She had a pile of them sitting on the table next to her bed. The woman must have been around thirty, and she was wearing her blond curls in a messy ponytail on top of her head.

"Her baby's in intensive care, too," Monique told Dorothy discreetly as she helped her into the other bed.

She then offered to get her a book from the gift shop, but Dorothy turned her down with a shake of her head. As Monique was leaving the room, a disembodied voice rang out over the intercom, announcing a code pink. The blonde stiffened, fidgeting with the flyer in her hands. Lifting her puffy red eyes to the sky, she pressed her lips together and made the sign of the cross. Dorothy thought she was exceptionally pretty.

"I think a code pink is when an infant has a heart attack," explained the woman, although Dorothy hadn't asked. "There are five babies right now in the NICU."

She said her name, but Dorothy didn't catch it.

"Are you the pregnant girl who survived the accident?"

"Yes, I'm Dorothy."

"You were luckier than the other woman, God rest her soul. My son was born yesterday. Twenty-five weeks."

He has a seventy-five percent chance of survival, Dorothy noted.

Instead of talking about her own son, she asked for news of Johanne's.

"Was one of the five born on the freeway?"

"Yes, he's alive. He has a fairy godmother watching over him."

"A fairy godmother?"

"Maggie. She had her baby yesterday, too. Not even twenty-four weeks. And not only is she nursing her own baby, she's also been feeding that poor little one who lost his mother. Early this morning she found out that her son was not going to make it. The doctor suggested they pull the plug, but she refused. He's probably the one who set off the code pink."

"He's suffering for nothing."

"We don't know that."

Monique burst into the room with a quick announcement.

"The baby with the code pink is OK! It wasn't one of yours, girls!"

The blond woman's whole body relaxed with a sigh, and she crossed herself again. Setting down her flyer, she scooted to the edge of the bed to be closer to Dorothy and put her feet on the floor.

"Have you been over to see your baby?" she asked. "You can touch him, you know. Through the window in the incubator."

Dorothy didn't feel capable of doing that.

"He's too fragile. What if I wind up giving him germs . . . ?"

"If they let us go in there, that means it's not a problem."

I'm not so sure of that . . .

The woman pointed to her flyers.

"Preemies need to feel our presence. It's important. It could help your son—"

"To suffer longer?" Dorothy interrupted. "My little guy is going to die. The touch of my hand isn't gonna bring him back to life."

"Come on, don't say that. Don't lose hope. You have to trust in God."

Dorothy stifled a laugh.

Trust in God, seriously? Those are some indestructible rose-colored glasses you're wearing.

Dorothy's own sunny outlook had been smashed to pieces in the accident.

"Dying is the best thing that could happen to him," Dorothy said.

"That's not really what you want."

The look of shock on her roommate's face made Dorothy want to slap her.

"That *is* what I want," she confirmed. "And the sooner the better. He's suffering. We probably can't even imagine how much."

Turning her back to the woman, Dorothy stretched out and buried her head under the covers. She didn't want to talk about it anymore, or even think about it. The fatigue suddenly swept over her again, immense, insurmountable. And like a tsunami, the pain came back in waves.

ANOTHER NIGHT FELL, during which Dorothy was roused from her sleep to be told that her baby hadn't made it. The time of death was recorded as 2:17 a.m.

He lived only thirty hours . . .

"We did everything we could," Dr. Lanouette assured her, with Monique at his side.

Stubble was beginning to darken his cheeks.

How long has he been working without a break?

Still floating in the fog of her nightmares, Dorothy sat in bed and gazed at the two hospital staff members. Although the news had come as no surprise, it still pierced her heart. Behind her hands, which she was using to hide her face, the tears began to flow. Monique laid a hand on her shoulder. Lanouette rubbed her back. Dorothy cried even harder. She hadn't expected to have such an intimate moment with these two messengers of doom.

"We're getting him ready so you can have a little time with him," said the neonatologist.

Not knowing how to respond to this idea, Dorothy sat there speechless.

"You don't have to, of course," added Monique. "It's up to you. It might be easier for you to grieve if you hold him in your arms for a few minutes . . ."

Her hands still covering the upper part of her face, Dorothy nodded, agreeing to follow the professionals' recommendation. She was dismayed, then, to hear someone laughing.

Who would dare?

Dorothy let her hands fall. The nurse picked them up and pressed them in her own. Uncomfortable, Lanouette took a step back. In the other bed, Dorothy's roommate was still sleeping. Thanks to the medication, no doubt. The strange noise continued, drawn out and jarring, a kind of shrill whimpering. Someone sobbing, maybe? When Dorothy realized that in fact she, herself, was the one making this sound, it suddenly stopped.

"You'll have to decide what you want to do with your little boy's body," Monique told her as the doctor sheepishly left the room.

"What I want?"

The nurse took a deep breath. She sat down next to Dorothy on the bed.

"*Ma belle*. Is there really nobody who could—?"

"Nobody."

"All right. You have the choice of having him buried or cremated, with or without a service. There's nothing forcing you to get involved."

At this point, Dorothy wasn't even in a position to decide between two pairs of socks.

"With babies," Monique said, "some funeral homes offer their services free of charge. I can make a few calls for you if you want."

Dorothy nodded and then, under the nurse's kindly gaze, she winced in pain as she settled into a wheelchair. A few minutes later, she was alone in a room with her son in her arms.

How can you be so small?

A tiny white knit hat, made of the same fabric as the blanket he was wrapped in, covered the little boy's head. He weighed almost nothing, barely more than half a pound. Despite his blurred features, Dorothy thought he was the most beautiful thing she'd ever seen. She pressed him to her heart.

"Be careful what you wish for, my pretty."

Time stood still, but that didn't stop the sun from rising, or a nurse from taking her son from her arms.

This nurse, who Dorothy hadn't seen before, pushed her wheelchair back to her room. Her roommate was nowhere to be seen. Dorothy started looking for her personal belongings and found what was left of them in a plastic bag.

"Hey, what are you doing?" asked the nurse.

"My baby's dead. There's no reason for me to stay here."

"You've got another day or two to go, young lady," said the nurse sternly. "You'll leave when your doctor signs you out. A C-section on such a small uterus is risky. You need some time to recover. Back to bed!"

The nurse took her vitals, then asked for the baby's name.

"I . . . I was told I had three months to choose one," Dorothy stammered, once again caught off guard.

"That's correct for the birth certificate. For the death certificate it's more urgent."

"Oh. It'll be Kansas, then."

"Kansas? That's unusual. Is that a real name?"

"Why? You afraid they'll tease him at school?"

THAT AFTERNOON, THE obstetrician came in to let her know that she was doing well.

Seriously?

"If there are no further complications, you'll be able to leave tomorrow. On the other hand, the tests have confirmed my fears. You won't be able to have any more children."

This was the straw that would have broken the camel's back. But Dorothy didn't break. She held back the tears, even though the feeling of devastation and injustice was so overwhelming that she could feel the bile rising in the back of her throat.

Dorothy didn't wait for the doctor's permission. Barefoot and wearing only her blue hospital gown and bloodstained white hoodie, she slipped out of the building the first chance she got, still feeling the effects of her final dose of morphine. Once outside, the grieving young woman walked aimlessly through the streets with no idea where she was going.

The city doesn't smell the same anymore, she thought. *Its colors have changed.*

She felt as if she had been caught in a windstorm that had destroyed everything in its path, leaving her lost and completely disoriented. She had nothing left to hold on to except her pain—horrible, infinite, beyond what she thought she could bear. And yet here she was, still standing, still putting one foot in front of the other. All around her, people went about their daily lives without a second thought. Though now they seemed out of place, almost unreal.

Having started off in one direction, Dorothy turned back. After a few steps in another direction, she turned again.

She kept moving forward, but the road ahead had disappeared.

When Dorothy stood in the doorway and looked around, she could see nothing but the great gray prairie on every side.

The road was still paved with yellow brick, but these were much covered by dried branches and dead leaves from the trees, and the walking was not at all good.

—L. Frank Baum

A QUARTER CENTURY LATER

1.

HIS PRECIOUS POSTERIOR nestled in a leather armchair in the posh boutique that his fiancée had dragged him to, Adrien Lalande was dutifully waiting for her to appear. Beginning to lose patience, he shifted restlessly in his seat and crossed his legs. A young salesgirl, who was busy rearranging a display case of hair accessories, flashed him a timid smile. Adrien returned the smile, and her cheeks flushed beet red.

The charm of this young man rarely missed its target. His wavy, dirty-blond hair was tied back in a mid-length half ponytail, and his deep blue eyes lay partially shaded behind the lenses of a pair of trendy sunglasses. His elegant black jacket with its modern retro styling accentuated his shoulders. In his coordinated pants and white T-shirt, Adrien looked sophisticated but not pretentious.

Every detail of his appearance had been carefully studied.

Listen with your eyes, he reminded himself as Cassandra burst out of the changing room, twirling around to show off the dress. *Open your palms and uncross your legs.*

"Gorgeous!" exclaimed the young man in his French accent. "That's the one. What do you think?"

Tailored in an ivory silk crepe that brushed the floor, this was the fifth dress the future bride had tried on. The pleated bodice of the princess-style gown was decorated with lace flowers and sequins, and Cassandra had draped a broad shawl around her arms, leaving her white shoulders bare.

She's more beautiful than ever, thought Adrien. *Happiness suits her perfectly.*

At first glance, Cassandra Bellerive wasn't his type. But he had to admit that the slender, refined, and vivacious blonde had a lot going for her.

And a considerable family fortune.

Adrien had a hard time believing that a woman like this had agreed to marry him. Sometimes he woke in the middle of the night with a smile on his face.

"Yes! This is it!" Cassandra agreed, thrilled to have found the perfect dress for their big day and, on top of that, to find herself once again on the same wavelength as the love of her life.

Leaning in close, she put her hand on the arm of the chair and bent down to kiss him.

"What in the world are you doing, my dear?" gasped the owner of the boutique, running over to them, her heels clicking on the floor. "It's bad luck for the groom to see the dress before the wedding!"

Cassandra pulled away from Adrien, rolling her eyes, laughing.

"We're not superstitious," she said.

"My fiancée and I don't hide anything from each other," added Adrien, pulling her in for another kiss.

When Adrien finally let her go, the owner got to work inspecting how the dress looked on Cassandra. She fluffed up the skirt, adjusted a few things here and there, and declared it perfect.

"Not a single alteration needed! This dress was made for you, Mademoiselle Bellerive."

Still hunting for a flaw, she kept circling the young woman, pulling on some things and smoothing out others.

"You haven't even given me your guest list," Cassandra scolded her fiancé.

"I know you're losing patience with me, *mon amour*, but the wedding isn't for eight months."

"This big of a party doesn't organize itself! The invitations should already have been sent out."

"I'll do it this week," Adrien promised.

His cell phone buzzed. Glancing at the screen, he refused the call.

"Your parents are coming, right?"

"We've been over this, *mon amour*. They can't afford the trip to Montreal."

"We'll pay for their plane tickets, naturally! I want to meet them! How crazy is it that they don't have access to the Internet? Do they live in France or on Mars?"

Cassandra and Adrien had met four months earlier, and it was love at first sight for the heiress and architecture graduate. Although he already knew his fiancée's entire entourage, she would have been hard-pressed to name a single one of his friends.

No point in repeating myself. She already knows: I've got a bright future ahead of me, but for now I'm still paying off my student loans.

"Bring over everyone you care about, Adrien," insisted Cassandra, pressing the issue. "Friends, family, colleagues. Money is not an issue."

Another buzz from the young man's cell phone gave him a worried look. He crossed his legs just to uncross them a moment later.

"Answer it, babe."

"But I promised I would be all yours today."

"I'm pretty sure I can pick out a bag without your help. Take the call. It seems important."

To avoid disturbing the handful of customers in the boutique, Adrien stepped outside to talk. When he returned, Cassandra, who was trying to decide between two handbags, thought he looked troubled.

"Something wrong, love?"

"My bank is dealing with a wave of scams. And while they conduct their investigation, they've frozen some of the accounts—including the one where I put the money your father lent me for the cruise."

All the color drained out of Cassandra's face.

"The boat isn't booked yet, is it?"

"No worries. The second they—"

"The deadline is today, Adrien! OK, I'll take care of it as soon as we're done here."

"Out of the question!" protested the future bridegroom. "I know the owner . . . How will it look if the cash is coming from you?"

Cassandra raised an eyebrow.

"Seriously, Adrien? I had no idea you were so trad!"

"I'm not, but that guy is!"

She sighed.

"What wouldn't I do to protect your macho pride? OK. I'll give you the money, but you'd better get yourself over there *right now* to pay that Neanderthal!"

Cell phone in hand, Cassandra had already begun the transfer.

"If all of your friends are this sexist, no wonder you don't want me to meet them."

"I just prefer to be alone with you," whispered Adrien, tickling her ear with his lips.

"I'm giving you enough to cover the plane tickets for your parents, so go ahead and take care of that, too, OK?"

Adrien kissed his fiancée, started out the door to complete his mission, and then turned around with one last thought.

"Your mother's ring! You wanted it cleaned, didn't you?"

"And polished," Cassandra added, removing a little box from her handbag and entrusting him with it. "Thanks, love. You're a treasure."

As Adrien's destination was only two blocks away, he went on foot. And as he walked, more than one woman risked getting a crick in her neck to watch him go by. When he arrived in front of the store he was looking for, he stopped, opened the box, and slid the diamond ring onto his index finger.

This must be worth a fortune.

"I love you so much, Cassandra, *mon amour*," muttered Adrien Lalande, without the slightest hint of an accent.

And he stepped into the pawnshop.

2.

IF A FLY had made its way into the museum basement, Dorothy could have heard it buzzing. Deep in concentration, poring over a document that she was annotating by hand, she hadn't noticed that the large room, which was separated by a dozen partitions, had gradually grown silent. When the last light switched off, plunging her into total darkness, she sighed contemptuously, annoyed.

Right. Just pretend I don't exist.

She had once again lost track of time. It was only a few weeks since she had started working as a documentation specialist at the natural history museum. Tasked with updating various archival tools, she had no contact with the public and did her best to interact as little as possible with the other staff members. Dorothy had no doubt in her mind that the colleague who had just left the office knew she was still there. He had made his childish gesture to get her back for ignoring him.

She woke up her computer to get a little light from the screen. Glancing at the date and time in the top corner—Tuesday, October 2, 5:19 p.m.—she smiled slightly. This date was meaningful to her.

A good omen.

In any case, thanks to her colleague's pettiness, she wouldn't be late for her appointment.

Dorothy got her coat and bag and then, with her flats slapping on the ground as if she were marching off to war, she crossed the vast room in the dark.

Outside, the cold engulfed her. The early October wind made her eyes water. Squinting, tucking her head between her shoulders, and pulling her scarf up over her ears, she cut through the bustling crowd on the sidewalk. Despite the nasty weather, and although everyone around her was in a hurry, she paused in front of the Vidal-Berry store window. She stood there for a long moment. Some people might have thought she was checking her reflection, trying to fix what the wind had blown out of place. But at forty-three, it had been a long time since Dorothy had cared what she looked like. Looking through the window, she didn't see her eyes, whose gray looked like storm clouds from the tears. And she didn't see her small, slender silhouette, or the freckles at the tip of her nose, or the long braid dancing at her back. A pair of black satin heels had caught her eye.

They're fabulous.

Being a woman of fashion only in her own head, an occasion to wear them would no doubt never arise. Dorothy needed another pair of high heels like a millepede needs another leg.

Without hesitation, she let herself into the shop.

"Dorothy!" the salesclerk greeted her, visibly resisting the urge to applaud.

Abandoning the woman he had been helping, the mustachioed thirtysomething scurried over to his favorite customer.

"Would these happen to be the little wonders that brought you in, my dear?" he asked, lifting one of the black shoes with gold soles from the window.

"I can't hide anything from you, my darling Gilbert. But I'm in a bit of a rush."

"Sit yourself right down. You won't even notice I'm gone!"

Settling onto a bench, Dorothy checked the time on her phone.

OK, no problem, I've got some time.

Sure enough, Gilbert returned in a flash with a golden box in his hands.

"Here you go, *ma chérie,*" he said, kneeling in front of her. "They're an eight, but they run small. Trust me, they're going to be perfect on you."

Dorothy slipped the shoes on, took a few steps toward a full-length mirror, admired herself for all of ten seconds, and proclaimed that the shoes had been made for her.

"And did you see the little teal ones next to the handbags?" Gilbert teased her, positioning himself between her and the cash register. "They're sublime!"

Never more than one pair at a time, she repeated to herself like a mantra. *We have to make the pleasure last.*

Still, if her appointment hadn't been so important, she would certainly have given in to temptation.

"Another time, Gilbert. I've really got to get going."

"They're on sale! And you know your size is the first to sell out, my dear Dorothy."

It's true that they're absolutely ravishing. And unique.

She thought about it for a minute, then completed her purchase—just one pair—and said goodbye to Gilbert with two kisses on the cheeks. He was the closest thing she had to a friend. She knew full well that she would never in a million years leave her apartment with these shoes on her feet. But just holding the purple bag with the Vidal-Berry logo gave her a deep sense of well-being.

On the sidewalk, Dorothy passed a young mother with a baby who was babbling away in its stroller. Dorothy's free hand moved reflexively to her belly.

If only I hadn't decided to go to that stupid yoga class. If I hadn't let my money problems stress me out. If my eyes hadn't watered. If only I had been more careful. If I had kept away from her instead of daydreaming . . .

The same movie was playing for the millionth time in Dorothy's head. What should she have done, or not have done, that would have saved him? The movie usually kept playing in the background without her paying much attention. But sometimes, like today, her tears blurred her vision.

Dorothy steeled her jaw and picked up the pace.

Today's October second.

Twenty-four years earlier, that was her baby's due date. Except that nothing had gone as planned. In the weeks after the death of her son, there had been one phone call after another to twist the knife in the wound.

"I've got your request for maternity benefits in front of me, Ms. Noroît. But it looks like you filled it out too early."

"I already had the baby. I sent you the birth certificate."

"Ah, yes, here it is. In that case, don't forget that you can also request parental benefits."

"I don't qualify for parental benefits. Dig through your papers some more and you'll find a death certificate."

A moment of silence.

"I'm so sorry . . ."

And another call three years later.

"A spot in our preschool has just opened up, if you're still interested."

If only I had gone to see him in his incubator; if only I had touched him; if only I had given him some of my strength.

Back then, as a young single mother, she certainly didn't have enough strength for two. But that didn't stop her from beating herself up about it all these years later.

Before she knew it, Dorothy had arrived at her destination. Blinking several times to remove any trace of the tears clinging to her eyelashes, she walked into the building and proceeded toward the office of Madame Maltais.

"I know the way!" she told the receptionist before she had a chance to greet her.

Right on time, she congratulated herself as she sat down across from the woman who had requested the appointment.

Karine Maltais was not the first social worker she had encountered. Dorothy had lost count of how many times her file had changed hands over the years. Karine's hands were, Dorothy noted, as plump as the rest of her body. A bit younger than Dorothy, she had a buzz cut and enormous earrings. After exchanging a few pleasantries, she buried her nose in Dorothy's file and got straight to the point.

"Madame Noroît, you've been registered with the adoption agency for . . ."

"For over ten years." Dorothy completed the sentence, making no effort to conceal her irritation.

The social worker shot her a look of disapproval.

Breathe through your nose, Dorothy reminded herself.

"But you're registered only with the regular adoption plan, which is limited to children orphaned at a very young age, or those put up for adoption at birth. What's more, you're looking for a child no older than six months."

What's more, Dorothy mentally mocked her. She didn't appreciate being judged like this.

"I do want a baby; that's right," she replied calmly. "Is that really so surprising?"

Setting down the papers, Karine looked her in the eye.

"Babies are almost never available for adoption. You've already been informed of this, haven't you?"

"Yes, I'm aware, thanks."

"That's why most people prefer the mixed-bank foster-family plan, which includes children who have been removed from their parents by the DYP—the director of youth protection—or the—"

Dorothy cut her off. "I've been over this with the other social workers. I don't want a child who could be taken away from me at any moment."

She was treated to a second look of disapproval, followed by a clearing of the throat. While Karine tapped the folder with the end of her pen, Dorothy thought about her new shoes. She couldn't wait to go home and try them on again in front of her mirror.

"Have you ever considered international adoption, Madame Noroît?"

"I've heard too many horror stories," Dorothy bristled. "People have sent loads of money to foreign countries, supposedly for medical care. And what if the child they gave me was terribly ill?"

"No child is safe from illness," said Karine Maltais.

She tried once again to clear the hair ball that was apparently stuck in her throat, and then continued.

"I'm going to be frank with you, Madame Noroît. The chances of your getting a baby through the regular adoption plan are very slim and are not improving with time."

"Why is that?"

"Well, for one, you're single."

Dorothy shifted in her seat.

"That's not supposed to be an obstacle to adoption," she objected.

"No. But you have to understand that you wouldn't be our first choice . . ."

The social worker turned the pages of Dorothy's thick file.

"I received your updated psychological evaluation. That's why I've asked you to come in today."

"OK. And . . . ?"

"Nothing has changed, Madame Noroît. You have no family, no friends, and you still struggle with compulsive shopping."

With her pen hanging in the air, and openly eyeing the Vidal-Berry bag next to Dorothy's chair, Karine continued. "Your shopping addiction reveals a deep emotional fragility. We are still not convinced that you would be able to make space in your life for a child—no matter where he or she came from—and to provide for his or her physical, psychological, and social needs."

Dorothy took a moment to collect herself before she spoke. Unassuming but not shy, she wasn't the type to make a scene or draw attention to herself. On the other hand, she wasn't in the habit of letting anyone walk all over her.

Breathe through your nose.

"If I understand correctly, you're saying that I should forget the idea of having a child?"

"You've changed jobs again, Madame Noroît."

Does that seriously count against me?

"I changed jobs to make more money! For the child!"

While Karine went back to tapping her pen on various notes in the file that Dorothy had no chance of being able to read from where she was sitting, Dorothy began to feel the urge to snatch the pen out of her hands and drive it into her throat.

"With regard to work, we require a stable situation of at least two years," Karine informed her.

"What? This is the first time I've heard that!"

"You also moved recently—"

"Into a bigger apartment! Again, for the child! So we would have a playroom!"

The social worker gave a silent sigh, clearly forcing herself not to roll her eyes, but at least she put her pen back on the desk.

"If you agreed to become a foster parent first, perhaps you'd have been able to show us that—"

"I'll say it again. I don't want a child who could be taken away from me and given back to its biological parents. Out of the question!"

Karine pushed back her desk chair and crossed her arms.

"After all these years, you're still thinking about what a child would do for you," she said flatly. "That mindset does not show you in your best light, Madame Noroît. Not at all. You should be asking yourself what *you* would do for a child."

"I would be a good mother."

"Perhaps," acknowledged Karine, uncrossing her arms and rolling forward to lean her elbows on her desk. "You can start by fixing your compulsive shopping habit. Clear out your head and your shoe closet. And then go out! Meet people! A man in your life would help your case, whatever the law might say."

"I like shoes. It's not a crime. There's nothing dangerous about a shoe. And unlike a lot of men, I make a good living and can afford to buy them, so why deny myself the pleasure?"

"But what is this covering up, Madame Noroît?" challenged Karine as she tapped Dorothy's file with her index finger. "It says here that your addiction began when you were around eighteen years old."

"When I started earning my own money, that's right."

"It was about that same time that you left your parents' home, wasn't it? When you cut your ties with them."

Dorothy pressed her lips together and shook her head. Her foot brushed against the purple bag. The gentle rustling of the plastic calmed her for a second.

"Think about it, Madame Noroît. Imagine if your parents were around to support you with this. Grandparents are important in a child's life."

A burst of laughter tried to escape Dorothy's lips, but she suppressed it.

Important? They cut me off me because I got pregnant and refused to get an abortion!

Picking up the bag containing the only thing in the world that brought her a little happiness, Dorothy stood up and turned away from the social worker.

I'm done, she decided suddenly, after a decade of struggle. *That's enough.*

"You can't replace one child with another, Madame Noroît."

Stopped in her tracks on her way out the door, Dorothy spun around to face Karine Maltais.

"What did you say?"

"You'll never get him back. He won't come back to life through another child. You need to come to terms with that."

"I . . . Is that in my file? I never mentioned him . . ."

"It is in your file, yes. And no, you never did mention him. That omission, among many other things, does not reflect well on you, Madame Noroît."

DOROTHY'S ROUTE HOME took her past Sainte-Victorine Hospital. A group of about twenty protesters were holding a rally in front of the public building. They wore monkey masks and had white wings on their backs that were being whipped around in the wind along with the posters in their hands. They were taking turns shouting into a megaphone, repeating the slogans written on their signs in bloodred letters.

"*Yes* to a merciful death!" bellowed one woman. "*No* to a shitty life! *No* to excessive medical treatment!"

"*Yes* to medically assisted dying!"

"*No* to medical care for extreme preemies! Let our little angels fly!"

Without realizing it, Dorothy had stopped walking and was watching the activists. Across the street, a dozen counterprotesters were silently expressing their disagreement. The same slogan was written on each of their signs: ALL LIVES ARE EQUAL. NO TO EUTHANAZIA.

Breaking away from his group, one of the protesters approached Dorothy. He could've reached out and touched her by the time she noticed him. His dark hair was long enough to be blown by the gusts of wind, and his classic style looked good on him. When he removed his monkey mask, he revealed a well-proportioned face and a beguiling gaze.

The alpha male in all his splendor, mused Dorothy. *Top of the food chain.*

The Adonis offered her a leaflet, which she declined, keeping her gloved hands clasped around the handles of her Vidal-Berry bag. Holding his lighter under one arm, he lit a cigarette. Then, like a gentleman, he stood next to Dorothy in such a way that the wind wouldn't blow his smoke in her face. He introduced himself.

"Antoine Lebeau."

He took several long drags of tobacco. Dorothy remained silent and did not offer her name.

"We might seem harsh to some people," he said, "but we're the most humane of them all. We're merciful. Or as we say in French: *miséricordieux*. It's no accident that this word contains the French for 'God': *dieu*."

He had a beautiful voice. Deep and steady, without the roughness that his nicotine use would eventually give it. A pleasure to listen to.

"I stopped believing in God a long time ago."

The activist took a few more puffs. "Do you believe that all lives are equal?"

Dorothy shrugged. She really had no opinion on the matter. Some people walking by were taunting the activists in their scowling monkey masks. It was starting to get a bit heated.

"I've got to get back over there," said Lebeau, covering his face again. "It won't be long before the police get involved. With a little luck, the media will show up, too!"

Unable to smoke with his mask on, he let his cigarette drop to his feet before running off to join his friends, his wings flapping in the wind.

"Seriously?" Dorothy grumbled. "People still throw their cigarette butts on the ground?"

"Dorothy? Dorothy Noroît, is it really you?"

A woman stopped and stared.

That voice. After all these years.

3.

EVEN THOUGH MARYSE Normandin had always made sure to stay active, she was no longer in the flower of her youth. She was out of breath, and her heart was pounding in her chest as she raced toward the six-unit building in Montreal North where her son rented an apartment. The apartment was on the ground floor and directly accessible from the street. Taking the three front steps in a single leap, the fiftysomething woman pounded on the door with both fists.

"Leo! It's your mom! Open up! Don't try to pretend you're not home!"

OF COURSE HE was home. Leopold Dion was always home. But with his headphones on, he was light-years away from his mother.

Slouched in front of his computer in the room that served as his entryway, living room, and office, he was masturbating while contemplating his friend Aimee's tantalizing curves.

"What would you like me to do now, my handsome Leo?" purred the young woman, whose generous bosom was practically bursting through the screen.

Leo answered her with gasps of pleasure, and then cleaned himself with a handful of tissues.

"All good, Aimee, I'm done. You're the best."

The young woman gave a little satisfied laugh and stuck out her lips. Leo put his own lips on the computer screen.

"See you later, Leo? I want you again."

"If you don't mind me waking you up in the middle of the night."

"Anytime you like, you know I'll be there."

Closing the browser window, Leopold made Aimee's naked body disappear. Since he had spent a good part of the evening playing with her, he hadn't bothered to eat anything. His growling stomach drew him toward the kitchen, and he took off his headphones. That's when the banging on the door finally reached his ears. He froze. Panic took hold and he couldn't think straight. Like a rabbit trying to escape an invisible predator, he began skittering around feverishly. He inched cautiously toward the window that looked out onto the street. He shook in place for a moment, not daring to open the blinds to see what was going on outside. His heart was beating so fast and so hard that it practically hurt.

"I know kung fu!" shrieked a woman's voice. "I can defend myself!"

Leo finally recognized the woman as his mother.

Summoning his last scrap of courage, the young man slid a finger between two of the blinds, cracking them barely half an inch. His mother was standing out there on the front step, pointing her pepper spray toward the sidewalk across the street, where a swirl of shadows formed a weightless silhouette that didn't look at all human.

"Leo!" Maryse shouted again. "Open the damn door, for god's sake!"

The young man finally sprang into action, and the door flew open. In the commotion, Maryse dropped her pepper spray. Not giving a thought to where it had landed in the darkness of the overgrown flower bed, she pushed her son aside to take shelter in his one-bedroom apartment. After locking the door behind her, she took a turn peeking through the blinds.

"He's gone." She heaved a sigh of relief.

With the adrenaline suddenly draining from the bodies of both mother and son, they collapsed side by side on Leopold's sofa.

"Who was it?" he whispered.

"I dunno, but I'm sure he was following me."

"Did you call the police?"

"What, so they could tell me I was crying wolf again? No, thanks."

She ran her hands through her short hair in an attempt to put it back in place.

"Wait, did you walk here?" asked her son.

"I was in the neighborhood. Your father was supposed to come get me, but he got held up somewhere."

Leo laughed. Without knowing it, his thoughts drifted off in the same direction as his mother's, back to his childhood, to the too many nights they had spent huddled together in the dark, fear in the pits of their stomachs, listening to the frightening noises outside. He resented his father, who was as big and strong as he himself had become. His presence would have been so reassuring back then, but he could never be bothered to stick around much.

"Did you have your damn headphones on again?" fumed Maryse once she had calmed down a bit.

"You know I don't like hearing what's going on outside at night."

"I don't understand you! I would so much rather be spooked than not have any warning if there's something dangerous coming."

Leo's mother quickly found something else to criticize him for.

"Also, it smells like wild animals in here, kid. You've got to air it out from time to time."

But she knew he would never dare open his windows.

Consider yourself lucky that I opened the door for you.

"And what are you wearing? Christ! Just because you work from home doesn't mean you have to dress like a hobo! And that wild mane."

"Come on, Mom!"

"I'm not saying you need to cut your hair, but it wouldn't kill you to give it a brush once in a while!"

"Why should I? I never see anybody!"

"What am I, chopped liver?"

Leo jumped to his feet.

"OK. If you just came over to nag me . . ."

Pulling her son by the hand, Maryse made him sit back down with her.

"I was thinking of that girl you chat with on your computer. She sees you, doesn't she? Over the webcam?"

"I never should've told you about her."

"If you want, I can go clothes shopping for you. The stuff you buy online never really works out, you know."

"Aimee loves me the way I am."

Maryse's face lit up.

"She loves you? When are you going to introduce her to us?"

"What? We're not gonna get married or anything."

"You've already met her in person, though, right? Has she been over here?"

Bristling from all the questions, Leo got up from the sofa again.

"So there's hope, then, Leo? That I'll be a grandmother someday?"

"Aimee can't have children."

"What do you mean, she can't? You've talked about it?"

"And honestly, can you see me with a kid?"

"Have you called Dr. Daneau, Leo? The therapist? He makes house calls. You wouldn't have to go anywhere."

"I'm fine! Why is that so hard for you to understand? I'm not unhappy, even if you don't believe me."

With that, he left his mother and headed to the bedroom. Before slamming the door behind him, he turned around and glared at her.

"Stop coming to see me every two minutes. I'm almost twenty-five. I don't need you!"

4.

LIKE EVERY SATURDAY, there was a buzz of activity at Abundance Farms on the South Shore of Montreal. Reveling in the early October sun and cool air, families were out picnicking; picking apples; feeding the alpacas, sheep, and rabbits; and wandering the pumpkin patch in search of the most beautiful ones to take home. At the farm stand, the owners' son, who was in charge of passing out bags to the apple pickers, was executing his task with a remarkable sense of pride.

"I'm gonna run to the bathroom, Francis," said his little sister during a lull in the midafternoon when the stand was momentarily deserted.

"Leave me the key to the cash register, Camille," he begged her. "I turned twenty-four last spring. You can trust me."

"Mama said not to, Frankie. But you can help anyone who has a question about one of our products. You're so good at that."

"Yeah, I am good at that. I know all the products: tarts, jam, jelly, apple butter . . ."

"I'll be right back!" called the seventeen-year-old.

She had barely stepped out of the kiosk when three young men, who had clearly been waiting for their chance, burst in.

"Hey, guys!" Francis greeted them with the big smile that rarely left his face.

"Hey, runt!"

The three boys were the same age as Camille and wore leather jackets, ripped jeans, and knee-high laced boots.

Francis thought they looked incredibly cool.

Tom Barthelemy, a tall kid with freckles that covered his caramel skin, stayed close to the door to keep watch while the other two ran over to Francis. The leader of the group, Lucas Colin, leaned in to talk to him, resting one very pale arm on the counter. His fingernails were painted black, and his hair was as dark as crow feathers. He had a piercing that ran horizontally across the upper part of his nose, between his eyes. His toothy smile made him look like he was up to no good.

"You're no slacker, Croteau! Workin' hard today, aren't ya?"

"I always work hard," replied Francis, delighted that the three teenagers had come to see him.

"You deserve to have a little fun, don't you?" J.B. said.

Short and stocky and not particularly blessed by nature, Julien Bedard had a shaved head and pimples in place of a beard.

"Guys, here comes Camille," Tom warned them.

"When your sister lets you off your leash, come find us at the big oak tree," Lucas instructed Francis, and the three young men scurried off like rabbits right in front of Camille.

"What did they want from you this time?"

"You're always scaring my friends away," grumbled Francis.

His sister put her hands on her hips, exasperated.

"Those guys are not your friends, Frankie, they're just troublemakers. How many times do I have to tell you? Stay away from them! They're messing with you—they treat you like shit. Why do you keep asking for it?"

"Because nobody else shows any interest in me!" he cried.

"Come on, Frankie. The customers are nice to you, aren't they?"

"Only the old people!"

Camille couldn't help laughing, and her brother grew sullen.

"I like Tom, Lucas, and J.B.," he pushed back. "So quit chasing them away."

Needing a minute to himself, Francis checked his reflection in the stainless steel refrigerator. He tried in vain to smooth down his unruly blond hair. In his baggy overalls and checkered shirt he looked especially frail. His arms would sometimes twist involuntarily, and he had a habit of standing on his toes.

"I'm missing my hat," he pointed out, pushing up his thick glasses, which were constantly sliding down his nose.

Camille grabbed the straw hat she wore to work in the fields and planted it on her brother's head. Just then, their mother came into the store with a heavy crate overflowing with ears of corn.

"Last of the season!"

Linda Carré, the owner of the farm, set the crate on the counter, took off her gardening gloves, and wiped her sweaty brow on her sleeve. Francis asked her if he could take a break.

"Go ahead, sweetie. Not many people coming by for apples at this time of day. When you get back, you can help Camille stock the shelves. I've got to go meet a group for a tour."

Francis loved to run, despite how often he ended tripping over his own feet. The last thing he wanted was for his friends to see him fall, but when he spotted them up in the branches of the big oak tree, he couldn't help skipping over to them.

"So you finally decided to join us," grunted Tom. "We don't have all day, Croteau."

"Dude, I swear—he's so ugly!" snickered J.B., loud enough for Francis to hear.

"You ever smoked before, runt?" asked Lucas, a lit cigarette dangling from his mouth.

"No. My mom said I shouldn't."

"You gotta at least try it."

"OK."

Lucas jumped down. As he stuck his cigarette in Francis's mouth, he deliberately neglected to turn it around, burning Francis's tongue in addition to making him choke on the smoke. He spat the roll of tobacco onto the ground, where it landed in the grass among the rotting acorns. Lucas slapped him on the back of the neck, knocking the straw hat off his head.

"Don't waste it, you idiot! That stuff's expensive!"

"Hey, Francis!" shouted Tom from his branch up in the tree, his long legs swinging in the air. "We're havin' a little party tonight. Wanna come?"

Looking up at Tom, a hand shielding his eyes from the blinding sun, Francis Carré-Croteau had a big smile on his face. The cigarette incident was already forgotten. Completely devoid of malice, he was simply incapable of holding a grudge. He had only one wish: to have some friends. And it just so happened that these brutes were about as close as he could get.

"A party!" he exclaimed, clapping his hands. "Of course I want to come!"

"Why'd you invite this guy?" groaned J.B. "Nobody wants him there!"

Francis stopped clapping, but his arms remained suspended in the air instead of falling back to his sides.

"Don't make that face, runt," Lucas scolded him. "You just gotta earn your spot."

That was all it took to put Francis back in a good mood.

"How do I earn my spot?"

"We're totally broke," Lucas explained. "And a party without beer isn't really a party, is it?"

J.B. and Tom smirked at each other.

"We know you've got some extra cash in the register," Lucas continued, "and your mom won't even know it's missing."

Francis considered this a moment. "Stealing is not nice."

"Whaddya mean, it's not nice?" objected Lucas. "Your farm is called Abundance, runt. You know what *abundance* means, or are you too stupid?"

"It means 'a lot.'"

Tom dropped down from the tree.

"Better than that, my friend!" he said, taking Francis by the shoulders. "It means 'more than you need.'"

♦

FRANCIS WAS CAUGHT red-handed. Unable to tell a lie, he confessed everything to his mother.

"There is no way you're going to their party!" she informed him, outraged. "We'll talk more about what just happened at dinner. For now, go find your father in the cornfield. You're going to help him repaint the fence before the sun goes down."

Upset but obedient, Francis skulked out of the farm stand. He was cutting through the orchard on his way to the cornfield when some black spots appeared through the leaves. A cawing sound put him on his guard.

Crows, he thought. *I have to protect the orchard!*

He picked up a worm-ridden apple that had fallen in the grass. Hurling it in the direction of the intruders, he missed his target by several feet. He was about to arm himself with another piece of fruit when, amid a crackling of branches, something big and heavy landed on his back. Yelping, Francis rolled around on the ground with J.B., while the two accomplices sprung from their hiding places, laughing their heads off. Tom was wearing Camille's straw hat.

"You fall for it every time, you dumbass!" J.B. sneered, pushing Francis aside as he got up.

"My eyesight isn't too good," Francis said in his defense.

"Were you scared?" asked Lucas.

"No."

It was the truth. On the other hand, he was hurt. But even though he had the impression that he might have sprained his wrist, he didn't mention it. Instead of feeling sorry for himself, he joined in laughing with the three boys.

"You got the money, runt?" J.B. asked.

"No. My mom has eyes in the back of her head."

"You're really useless," sighed Lucas. "Not sure we can trust you for the next part of the plan."

"What plan?"

Lucas pretended to hesitate before confiding in Francis.

"As soon as the cornfield is clear, we're gonna have our little fiesta!"

"You guys always have the best ideas!"

"Only thing is, unless you want us to smash in the fence, you're gonna have to get us the key," said Tom.

"I know where it is!"

"Perfect," replied Lucas. "Meet us at the gate tonight, nine o'clock, with the key. Got it?"

"Nine o'clock, with the key, for the fiesta," Francis agreed.

The three thugs sneered at him with contemptuous grins as he smiled back at them with genuine excitement.

5.

LEANING BACK IN his desk chair, Leopold had just ejaculated into his hand.

"Was it good?" whispered Aimee from the other side of the screen.

Stretched out on her bed, legs spread, her vulva wide open with its lips still red and engorged with excitement, she was breathing loudly and heavily, struggling to recover from the intensity of the orgasm that had just shaken her body. The corset Leo had bought for her—the only garment she was wearing—was tightly laced from her waist to her sternum. Above it, her large round breasts defied gravity, bouncing to the rhythm of her breath.

"It's always good with you, Aimee."

"Keep going, Leo," she begged. Her perfect lips, even redder than her sex, curved divinely around the last syllable of his name.

"I can't take any more!"

"Leo, don't leave me like this." She pouted.

"Why don't you roll your own marble—that'll put some lead back in my pencil."

"I'm not familiar with those expressions."

"Why don't you masturbate. That'll help me get hard again."

With a sly wink, Aimee buried two fingers in her vagina and began rubbing her clitoris with her other hand. Between moans, she occasionally opened her eyes, threw Leo a saucy look through his computer screen, took out her fingers, and licked them. She would then push them back inside herself, press her eyelids together, and resume her ecstatic cooing. Then, without warning, she stopped.

"You know what, my handsome Leo? I would love for you to buy me a vibrator. A big one."

"Well, sure, if that's what you'd like . . ."

With a single click, Leo opened a second window.

"There are some here that don't look bad: vibrating, rotating, with clitoral suction . . . seventy-five hundred rotations per minute . . . How does that sound?"

"Does it come in red?"

"Um . . . yep. But why's it more expensive in red? Never mind, doesn't matter. As soon as I get the money, you'll have your red dildo, I promise."

Leo felt like he'd be able to start up again soon. Noticing that his box of tissues was almost empty, he removed his headphones and went rummaging through a closet. He was on his way back to his computer with a fresh supply of tissues when there was a loud knock at his front door. His heart began to race.

It's after nine o'clock. It could only be my mother. I told her not to come over so often, but she never listens.

"My mom's here," he told Aimee. "I'll get rid of her and be right back, and then I'll take out my giant cock for you again. While you're waiting, why don't you handcuff yourself to the headboard?"

The peephole in the front door allowed Leopold to see without being seen. Placing one eye against it as he finished pulling up his pants, he could make out a vaguely distorted figure in the dim light. Dressed in a pale shirt, pants, and a dark blue jacket, the person was too slight to be his mother. Whoever it was held a square box under one arm and wore a baseball cap that concealed their features. Another knock.

"What do you want?" he asked through the locked door.

"A package for you, Monsieur Dion."

If Leo's heart hadn't been pounding in his ears, he might have been able to tell whether it really sounded like a delivery person.

Maybe it's that glove prototype that I agreed to test out, with the tactile sensors . . .

"It's late," Leo said.

"Does it bother you that some of us are working hard?" said the voice behind the door.

"Please leave the package by the door, thanks."

"I need a signature, sir."

"Since when? What company are you with?"

It was too dark for Leopold to make out the logo on the person's cap.

I should really change that light bulb.

"If you don't sign, I'll have to leave with your package," they threatened.

"No, wait!"

What if it's my coffee order?

Since Leo had been out of coffee for two days, he was starting to get a low-grade headache. It was only going to get worse if he didn't get his dose of caffeine soon. On the other hand, his mother had drummed it into him that Montreal North was one of the most dangerous neighborhoods in the country.

"Monsieur Dion? You gonna open up or not?"

Placing his hand on the doorknob, Leo took another look at the individual through the peephole. Whatever their gender, this person was tiny. How much of a threat could they possibly pose to him, with his father's height and broad shoulders?

It's a woman, he tried to convince himself. *Totally harmless.*

Hands trembling, he turned the three locks on the door. At that point, he could have opened it a crack, but it was too narrow for his package to fit through. He would still have to undo the security chain. But he couldn't bring himself to do it.

How do I know this person doesn't have an accomplice hiding out there in the dark?

"Monsieur Dion? Are you messing with me?"

Leopold knew his fears were irrational. But he couldn't just brush them aside. They were deeply ingrained in him.

I need coffee.

He was dripping with sweat. As he got more and more anxious, he couldn't see straight.

Come on, Leo, get ahold of yourself. Open that door, grab your package, scribble your signature on the freaking line, and close the door.

Leo's throat tightened up so much that he started wheezing.

But he opened the door.

AS PROMISED, WHEN he reappeared in the camera frame, Leo's reproductive organs were on display. Aimee had followed his instructions and lay handcuffed to the head of her bed. Leo's palms rested on his desk, one on either side of the keyboard, and his face was visible in front of his screen. His long hair hung in his eyes, drenched with sweat. When he pulled on the headphone cord, the voice of the young woman with the dream body rang out through the apartment.

"Where do you want to put it, Leo?"

Contorting herself, crossing her arms behind her back, she managed to position herself in such a way as to offer a close-up of her bare bottom. Leo's face smashed against the screen, and his tongue slid down it. Then he took a few steps backward.

He stumbled.

"Have you been drinking, Leo?"

Blood—which he was losing in large amounts—was splattered across his torn T-shirt. A kitchen knife was lodged in his gut.

"I'm not finished with you yet," said a voice off camera. "Give me back that knife, Leopold."

Aimee turned over. Her calm face was framed by the computer screen.

"What's going on, Leo?"

"Aimee, call . . . call . . ."

He was trembling like a rabbit caught in a trap.

"Who do you want me to call, Leo? Emmy? Or Melodie, maybe? Are you in the mood for a threesome?"

Aimee waited for a reply that never came. The bloody blade

emerged from Leopold's flesh, grinding against his bones, before plunging in again up to the handle. While Aimee observed the scene with an indifferent expression, the carnage continued. Blood splattered all over the screen. Even after Leo had collapsed to the ground, the massacre kept going. Finally, the edges of the young woman's lips curled into a smile.

6.

AT DAWN, HENRI Duhaime received a phone call. Although it didn't make him smile (he wasn't a monster), it did finally give him a reason to get out of bed.

"Hurry up and hop in your boots," said Hervé Bergevin as he welcomed the sixtysomething man back to the major crimes unit of Quebec's provincial police force. "We'll sort out the details of your reinstatement later."

"So I've been cleared?"

"Not yet, but I'll take care of it. I need you, Duhaime."

A homicide of unspeakable violence had been committed overnight. Bergevin's team was young, inexperienced, and understaffed, so the captain had no choice but to call his former partner in. Henri's expertise and record of success suddenly eclipsed the acts he had been accused of. The reasons for his transfer to the financial crimes unit three years earlier were not mentioned to the squad, nor was the fact that Bergevin had been appointed captain in his place.

Half an hour after sunrise, the detective lieutenant arrived in La Prairie on the South Shore, under a sky darkened by a murder of crows. The forensics team had fanned out across the fallow field where the killing had taken place. Henri's blank expression betrayed no emotion, but inside he had the feeling that he was coming back to life. Having taken a dirt path, he stopped next to a bright red fence. About ten feet in front of him, workers were busy detaching the body of the victim from the pole it was tied to. Despite all their precautions, when they pulled out the pitchfork he was impaled on, any remaining entrails that had not already spilled from his body came gushing out in a gurgling mess. Nearby, a photographer was attempting to immortalize a bloody chain saw while just barely managing to hold down his breakfast.

Henri's stern and serious demeanor suited the situation perfectly, but those who knew him would say that he was always like this. Tall and wiry, he stood ramrod straight. In his long charcoal-colored coat, he was gray from his hair to his shoes, including his neatly trimmed beard, ashen complexion, and trademark silk scarf. He used this piece of fabric—knotted like a tie and tucked under the collar of his shirt—to conceal his emaciated neck, which he considered unsightly.

Henri stood motionless, analyzing and making mental notes of what he saw. At first glance, it appeared that the victim was wearing a mask, but it was actually blood from a head wound that had dried on his face and glasses.

"Well, well, looks like somebody put up a second scarecrow in the field!"

The detective cast a sideways glance at the stocky woman walking toward him.

Let me guess. Detective Sergeant Emilianne Saint-Gelais.

Bergevin had warned him that this woman notoriously had no filter.

"That was in extremely poor taste," he pointed out.

"Oh, come on. A little joke never *killed* anyone!"

And it just keeps coming.

In the thick early-morning humidity, Saint-Gelais's mid-length, mousy brown hair was already beginning to frizz. Her jacket opened onto a shirt with a bold, colorful pattern—every bit as inappropriate as her comments or her wrinkled pants covered in cat hair. Henri would've guessed she was at least forty-five years old, but having done his research, he knew she was thirty-six.

"Emilianne Saint-Gelais," she confirmed. "Welcome to the team, Duhaime. They say you're a big fish, my man."

Henri ignored the handshake she was offering him. He didn't appreciate being spoken to so casually by this little comedian whose carefree attitude was completely misplaced. Although he ordinarily avoided jumping to conclusions, this time he made an exception.

We are not going to get along.

Well-dressed, clean-shaven, and polite, the young man in his thirties who came forward to introduce himself next made a better first impression.

"Police investigator Jason Jobin. Pleasure to meet you!"

But the charm quickly wore off.

"Do you have fleas, Jobin?" Henri asked him, as the officer hopped around, scanning the grass with his eyes.

"What . . . ? No! I just didn't want to touch the, uh . . ."

"It looks like the fence was recently repainted," Emilianne cut in.

"Oh, thank god! I'm always paranoid about messing up a crime scene!"

"Well, why don't you move along, then!" Henri said, shooing him away.

What a bunch of bumbling idiots! They'd better not screw this up for me.

"All right, what do we know?" growled Henri to his deputy as soon as Jason had cleared out.

"The victim is Francis Carré-Croteau, twenty-four years old," Emilianne informed him. "He's the son of the farm owners, Linda Carré and Patrice Croteau. His little sister, Camille, found him at the crack of dawn. She was up early feeding the alpacas. That's like a type of llama . . ."

"I know what an alpaca is, thanks. The family lives on the farm?"

"Their house is two or three blocks from here, on the left."

Henri took a long look at the scene. From the road it was impossible to see the cornfield through the orchard. To his left, the detective lieutenant could make out a farm stand, a log cabin, and, in the distance, a pumpkin patch. To his right there was nothing but an old shed, and then the woods stretched out as far as the eye could see.

"Where's the alpaca enclosure?"

"Not far from the farm stand. There's sheep and rabbits, too."

Strange.

As luck would have it on this Sunday morning, apart from the Carré-Croteau family and the crows that circled overhead, the town was still asleep.

"You know why those crows are making all that racket?" babbled

Emilianne, following Henri's upward gaze. "They're calling the vultures."

She paused. But not getting a reaction, she went on.

"They need them to open up the carcass. They call them over and—"

"I didn't see a sign saying 'closed' when we came in," Henri interrupted. "This whole area needs to be cordoned off."

Emilianne texted Jason to assign him the task of remedying that situation before the apple lovers started showing up. Then she told the lieutenant about the party in the cornfield.

"The forensic team picked up a ton of beer cans and bottles. And we've got tire tracks on the ground from at least seven different cars. A motorcycle also came up to the gate but didn't go through it."

The partially disemboweled body of Francis Carré-Croteau was finally laid out on a tarp. After a preliminary search, a man in a white jumpsuit placed a key in a sealed bag and entrusted it to Emilianne.

"It was in the pocket of his overalls," he said. "And the rope they tied him up with is identical to the one that's used for staking the apple trees."

With Emilianne at his heels, Henri crossed to the other side of the fence to speak with Michel Desbiens. Roughly the same age as him, Michel was leaning over the corpse.

"What can you tell us, Desbiens?"

"Hey, Duhaime, you're back," noted the medical examiner, who seemed neither surprised nor impressed by his return.

Desbiens lifted the top part of Croteau's skull, which was already halfway detached from his head.

"They took his brain," he announced.

"What?!" squealed Emilianne.

"And replaced it with a pair of testicles."

"They castrated the poor guy?" she cried.

After the requisite checks, Desbiens confirmed that the victim's family jewels were still, in fact, where they ought to be.

"So who does the second pair of balls belong to?" asked Emilianne. "A farm animal?"

"From the looks of it, I would say that those are human testes."

"And what happened to the brain?" Henri wondered aloud.

"Gone. Otherwise, this young man has what looks like a cigarette burn on his tongue and most likely a broken wrist. As for the rest of it, we're going to have to be patient, ladies and gentlemen."

In a hurry to remove the body before the journalists arrived, Michel Desbiens dismissed the detectives from the scene.

"What about the family?" Henri asked Emilianne.

She pointed out the round log cabin and scratched her head. "Why do you think the killer would swap the guy's brain for a pair of balls?"

Not really in the mood to chat, Henri headed toward the cabin.

"Maybe because that's all he thought about," offered Emilianne, following close behind. "Sex, I mean."

THE VICTIM'S FAMILY had been informed of the investigators' arrival and had gathered in the farmhouse side cabin, which they used as their dining room. The mother and daughter, both equally blond and easy on the eyes, were huddled together on a picnic table bench, their cheeks wet with tears. Linda was clutching the pendant attached to her necklace with one hand. And Patrice was pacing back and forth between two tables. White as a sheet but dry-eyed, the farmer had a rustic charm about him. He was muttering nonstop to himself as if he hadn't noticed the officers.

"It doesn't make sense. Who would do a thing like that? It just doesn't make sense . . ."

With Emilianne still on his heels, Henri approached the two women. Towering over them, he skipped the small talk.

"You can't see the cornfield from the alpaca enclosure."

"No . . ." stammered Camille. "It was afterward, when I went to the orchard to check on the tree ties, that I saw . . . that I saw Francis."

This is why I hate teenagers, Henri thought.

"Really?"

Taken aback, Linda opened her mouth. Guessing that she was ready to defend her child tooth and nail, the inspector changed the subject. He could always come back to it later.

"Tell me about your son, Mrs. Carré. What kind of a man was he?"

"He was a sweetheart. He wouldn't hurt a fly."

Emilianne whipped out her pen and her little black notebook.

"Was he the one who organized the little party last night?" asked Henri.

"What party?" asked Linda, surprised. "Last night Francis was in bed before eight o'clock."

Still mumbling to himself, Patrice began frenetically rubbing one of his arms.

"Your son must get up early," Emilianne said. "What time did he leave for the farm this morning?"

"No," Linda protested again, tears streaming into her mouth, which was twisted with pain. "Francis never went alone to the farm. We always went together."

Sticking her pen between her teeth, Emilianne showed her the bag with the key in it.

"Can you tell us what this is for?"

Linda opened her hand, uncovering her pendant. A crucifix. "That's the one for the cornfield gate, isn't it?"

Camille agreed with her mother, and Emilianne revealed that the key had been found on Francis. Linda shook her head, stunned.

"So Francis liked going to parties," Henri established. "Was he also pretty interested in sex?"

Looking like a fish that had flopped onto a dry dock, the young man's mother opened and closed her mouth several times without making a sound. Then she lashed out.

"What does that have to do with anything? Why would you ask that?"

Camille dried her tears with the backs of her hands and told the officers they were barking up the wrong tree. Patrice went silent, though he kept pacing the length of the cabin.

"Francis was not into parties," said Camille. "He didn't have any friends. OK, sure, he liked girls. He liked everyone. But I can promise you he wasn't thinking about *that.*"

"It's possible that he hid this from you, is it not?" suggested Emilianne.

"Don't write random stuff in your little book," the teenager snapped. "My brother didn't hide anything from me. I was his confidante. And he was completely incapable of keeping a secret."

"He trusted everyone," lamented Linda. "How many times did I tell him—"

"There's not a single girl who was interested in Frankie," Camille blurted out.

"Why is that?" Henri wanted to know.

"My brother was not like other kids at school. He always thought the best of everyone, and he was relentlessly bullied. To top it all off, he wore glasses *this* thick."

Camille held her fingers at least an inch apart.

"We're gonna need the names of all his friends," Emilianne said.

"What part of what my daughter just said did you not understand?" Linda shouted, now crying with rage. "Francis didn't have any friends!"

"Well, there was Tom and the other two, right?" her husband added, coming to a sudden stop.

"Papa," whined Camille. "Are you as naive as Francis or what?! Those were not his friends!"

"Seriously, Patrice, what planet are you living on?" exclaimed Linda. "I hope you didn't let our son hang out with those guys!"

"He never asked me," Patrice said, batting away the accusation as he slumped down next to his wife.

"Tom, you said?" Emilianne asked, scribbling in her notebook.

"Tom Barthelemy, Lucas Colin, and Julien Bedard," said Linda. "Bunch of little deadbeats from the same high school as Camille. She went out with Tom for a while, but then she broke up with him. He must've been trying to get back at her, because he and his friends were always around, stealing fruit and vegetables, scaring our alpacas, and picking on Francis . . ."

"No, Mama. Tom never had any hard feelings."

"Why are you defending that loser?" exploded Linda. "All Francis ever wanted was a little attention, and those guys would make him do whatever they wanted. Yesterday, as a matter of fact, they told him to take the money from the cash box so they could buy beer!

You've gotta have a lot of nerve to do that and then throw a party on my property!"

Henri attempted to summarize.

"Mrs. Carré, do you have reason to suspect that these young men—these teenagers—could have wanted to harm Francis?"

"They're rowdy boys but not bad people," Camille tried to clarify.

"Oh, it's them!" her mother exclaimed. "Yesterday, I caught them under the big oak tree, messing with Francis. I rushed over, but they were already leaving when I got there. They didn't see me. But I heard them say, 'It's gonna be your party, runt.'"

"And you didn't do anything about it?" asked Camille.

The last hint of light in Linda's eyes flickered and died.

7.

SEATED IN AN armchair across from a young female financial advisor, Hubert Dagenais was tempted to cross his arms and make himself more comfortable.

But he restrained himself.

With Hubert's identity card in hand, the bank employee was busy tapping on her computer keyboard and blabbing away about finance.

This is taking an awfully long time. I just want to open an account.

Hubert refrained from tugging on his collar in irritation, contenting himself instead with smoothing out his tie and removing an invisible speck of lint from his impeccably ironed slacks. From the moment he had entered Roxanne's office, he had made a point of maintaining eye contact with her to reinforce the trust she had already placed in him. Taking one last look at his ID card, she finally handed it back to him. As in the photo, Hubert's dark hair was short at the back and on the sides, a bit longer on top, and he wore it swept forward and to the side.

A confident and proactive style.

Looking up from her keyboard, her eyes met Hubert's dark, penetrating gaze.

"Everything seems in order, Mr. Dagenais, but . . ."

A bit embarrassed, she spoke too quickly.

"I'm going to have to ask you for a second piece of identification."

"You have doubts about my honesty?" joked Hubert, placing one hand over his broken heart.

"Oh, it's not that, Mr. Dagenais. You seem absolutely flawless, but—"

"Please, call me Hubert. We'll be seeing a lot more of each other, Roxanne. Provided, of course, that you're able to open that account."

"Sure, of course. Hubert . . ."

For a few seconds, the young woman forgot what she was doing. Then, regaining her composure, she returned to the task at hand.

"Would you happen to have that second form of ID on you? It's just protocol. With everything that's been going on lately, you know, all the data leaks. The bank can't afford to make any mistakes. I'm sure you understand."

With an indulgent smile, Hubert took another card from his wallet. As he passed it to Roxanne, he let his hand brush against her jagged, bitten nails, sending a jolt of electricity through her. She turned bright red, and tried to hide it by retreating behind her computer screen.

"You're a real pro, Roxanne," Hubert complimented her. "A

credit to your institution. Why would I hold it against you? On the contrary, your meticulousness reassures me that my investments will be safe. Thanks to you, I'll be able to sleep at night."

The young woman returned to her keyboard, looking back and forth between her screen and the card Hubert had just given her.

Something's wrong, he realized.

"You don't look thirty-two at all," Roxanne said, unable to look at him. "I'd give you at least five years less."

"It's all thanks to smoothies! A big glass of banana-spinach every morning. It's invigorating. Rids the body of toxins and keeps the cells young."

"Bananas and spinach? I'll have to try that."

Continuing her work on the computer, Roxanne was still trying to avoid Hubert's gaze.

"You're perfect, Roxanne. Don't change a thing."

Suddenly, she stared at him. And smiled without blushing. Hubert felt a chill run down his spine.

This can't be good.

Roxanne stood up, his card in hand.

"I just need to run a few more checks, Mr. Dagenais. As I said, it's protocol. Please wait here, I'll just be a minute."

As soon as she left him alone in her office, a countdown began in Hubert's head.

Ten, nine, eight . . .

When he reached zero, he pushed back his chair, placed his messenger bag on Roxanne's desk, and opened it. It contained only one thing: a pair of glasses. He removed his tie and his wig, revealing close-cropped brown hair, and put on the glasses. After stuffing his accessories into the bag, he turned his blazer inside out, changing it from light gray to black.

By the time the bank's security guards had a chance to respond, the person going by the name of Hubert Dagenais was already long gone.

8.

STANDING BETWEEN HIS parents in the doorway of the family home, Julien Bedard, while clearly uncomfortable, was doing his best to project a nonchalant attitude.

"Yeah, we were following him around during the day," he spluttered. "But it was just so we could get into the cornfield for the party. So we could blast our music without the neighbors getting on our case."

Tom Barthelemy had to be dragged out of bed at the juvenile detention center where he lived. He told Henri and Emilianne that Francis had brought them the key to the gate at 9:00 p.m. sharp.

"We didn't force him or anything. Then after that . . . I dunno, maybe he stayed a while. He was a big boy. I'm not his mom!"

This one is feeling guilty, Henri sensed. *But for what, exactly?*

In the park where Lucas Colin hung out, and where some patrol officers had finally tracked him down, the group's leader answered the detectives' questions with an especially arrogant tone.

"I don't even remember seeing him after he gave me the key. He wanted to party, that's true, but no one wanted to hang out with him, and our music scared him. I just figured he went home."

"THEY'RE LYING!" PATRICE Croteau exclaimed to Henri when he arrived at the Quebec provincial police force headquarters for an update. "My son . . . it was like he was made of straw, you know?"

"I don't understand."

"Going after Francis was like sticking a pitchfork in a haystack. No impact. Nothing really fazed him. He was never great at reading people, and the thing he wanted most was to have friends. Even if it meant hanging out with kids who teased him."

The three suspects in leather jackets refused to hand over the names of the people who had been partying with them in the cornfield.

"We invited the whole school. It was dark. We didn't know everybody."

Within three days, half a dozen teenagers, prodded by their parents, had come forward to speak with the authorities. But no threats, veiled or otherwise, could convince them to incriminate any of their peers.

In the detectives' shared office space, Jason had pinned a series of photos to the wall.

"There couldn't have been only ten of them," he calculated, counting the bottles and cans found in the field. "There must've been at least thirty."

From over his shoulder, Emilianne couldn't help herself.

"But if there *were* only ten of them drinking all that beer, that would explain why those little shits don't remember anything but their fucking names."

Teenagers. What awful creatures, Henri thought in the corner while Jason laughed at Emilianne's joke. *It's like pulling teeth to get them to spit out the tiniest shred of truth. They lie about anything and everything, for fear of god knows what. Nothing matters to them except their own pathetic little selves—not even a human life.*

"So according to them, they didn't see anything, didn't hear anything," continued Emilianne to Jason. "What kind of party was it?! The annual meeting of the deaf and blind?!"

"I think you're onto something, Em."

If these two idiots would shut up a minute and let me think. I bet we already have DNA samples of every person who set foot in the cornfield that night.

The problem was that, for now, given the scale of the task, only six objects were being analyzed: the ones collected within a fifteen-foot radius of the post to which Francis Carré-Croteau had been tied.

AT THE END of the week, as he walked out of Bergevin's office and into the one he shared with his team, Henri was greeted with a shriek.

"We've got 'em!"

Emilianne was waving a report from the Laboratory of Forensic Sciences and Legal Medicine. Open on her desk next to a photo of her three cats was a box containing the objects that had been analyzed.

"Tom Barthelemy's DNA and fingerprints are on the can," announced the detective sergeant, delighted. "And Lucas Colin and

Julien Bedard smoked the three joints. As for the two cigarette butts, one of them was tossed by Barthelemy. We don't have a match for the other one. But we know the brand is Du Maurier."

"Get those three little shits in here, Jobin," ordered Henri, without the slightest hint of enthusiasm.

"On it," replied the investigator, seated at his desk across from Emilianne's. "But do you really think those kids could be responsible for such a brutal murder?"

"They're hiding something." Henri was confident of this.

"That's not all. We have another clue," Emilianne said with a half smile. "One of the fingerprints taken from the cornfield gate has been identified. It belongs to David Bonnier, a twenty-nine-year-old man."

This piqued Henri's interest.

"Has he ever been arrested for a violent crime?"

"No, but he does have a record as long as your arm. He's a drug dealer. I dunno what the hell you were doing in the boss's office for so long, Duhaime, but J.J. and I had the time to go pay Bonnier a little visit."

"He says he was over at Abundance Farms a few days ago," said Jason. "With his wife and kids. To pick some corn."

"His wife confirmed it," added Emilianne.

Sure, thought Henri skeptically.

IN HIS CLENCHED fist, Henri held five sealed, tear-resistant, waterproof plastic bags containing either one of the two cigarette butts or one of the three joints that had been analyzed. Standing in front of the one-way mirror, he observed the three young men gathered in the interrogation room. Julien Bedard was accompanied by his father, but Lucas Colin and Tom Barthelemy had been left to their own devices.

No wonder they turned out so badly.

Emilianne bounced in with two coffees in her hands and a big smile on her face, ready for action.

"You don't think we should interrogate them separately?" she asked, seeing them sitting side by side.

"Hmm . . ." Henri replied, taking the cup the detective sergeant handed him.

Not feeling very talkative, he answered her only inside his own head.

If our guys had wanted to agree on a story, they would've had plenty of time to do so. On the other hand, their reactions to what their friends say could be revealing.

"Have their lawyers arrived?" he asked.

"They didn't want any."

"Have you informed them of what's at stake, Saint-Gelais?"

"They know they're in deep shit, but Colin's ex-con of a father told him that if they hired counsel, we'd see it as a confession of guilt. Idiot."

Emilianne was about to take a sip of coffee when she pointed her cup at the pieces of evidence Henri was fiddling with. He stood as if he had a broomstick up his rear, looking even more tense than usual. Pressing his fist against his thigh, he sporadically squeezed the bag between his long, bony fingers.

"That's not a stress ball, Duhaime. It should be in the evidence room. I'll take it over there if you want."

She made a move to relieve him of the bag, but he held on tighter.

"Putting the proof right in front of them can have an impact," he said by way of justification.

"Yeah, OK, but it's not like they're gonna recognize their shade of lipstick on the cigarette butts . . ." Emilianne burst out laughing, but there was no reaction from Henri. Not even the hint of a smile.

"Be a little careful with the evidence, at least," she finally said.

Forcing himself to loosen his grip, Henri took a long swig of coffee. He gagged and nearly spat it out, but then swallowed and shot a fierce look at the detective sergeant. She broke into a loud, boisterous laugh and traded cups with him.

"What's the matter? You gonna lock me up for attempted poisoning?" she cackled. "Three teaspoons of sugar never killed anybody, Duhaime."

After checking with the tip of his tongue that the new cup didn't contain anything other than coffee, Henri pushed open the door to the interrogation room. Emilianne was still giggling to herself as they sat down across from their three suspects. Tom Barthelemy, the kid who looked like a model, studied them one by one, his gaze lingering on Emilianne's oversize lavender sweater. It was covered in cat hair. Henri suppressed a grimace.

This woman is damaging my credibility.

Lucas Colin, meanwhile, was staring at the chipped black polish on his fingernails. Only Julien Bedard, every bit as ugly as Tom was handsome, had the humility to sit still and keep his eyes on the table, just like his father.

Henri put the cigarette butts in the middle of the table. For a moment he held on to the bag, his fingers twitching as if he feared that one of the young men might try to grab it.

"Do you know what we have here?" he asked them, once he had revealed the contents of the bag. "Your saliva."

"All that proves is that they smoked at the party," said Julien's father, on the verge of tears.

"These joints have crack in them, Mr. Bedard," Emilianne added. "That's pretty serious!"

Henri continued. "Whether these are cigarette butts or joints, they were found within a five-yard radius of the post to which Francis Carré-Croteau was tied."

"Did you know, Mr. Bedard, that crack can make a person paranoid and violent?" asked Emilianne. "That it can cause hallucinations and delusions?"

The detectives had invested nearly two hours of their time before Julien finally admitted that the three of them had, in fact, attached Francis to the pole. "It musta been around one in the morning, something like that."

While Lucas glared at him, Tom, whose leg was shaking frenetically, seemed relieved by the confession.

"But we didn't kill him!" Julien cried.

"Let's assume that's the case," Henri replied. "So why would you tie the poor guy up?"

"He was getting on our nerves! We just wanted to chill without him bugging us. A bonehead like that doesn't exactly help you pick up girls."

Glancing up from her notebook, Emilianne took a long look at J.B.'s unattractive, pimply face. She opened her mouth but was kind enough to keep her thoughts to herself.

"I swear to you, man, it wasn't us," insisted Julien. "You'd have to be seriously messed up to do that!"

Henri rifled through his folder and produced a photo, which he placed on the table. Lucas—who had remained silent and stone-faced throughout the interrogation, and who was busy fiddling with his forehead piercing—didn't even dare look. Tom did, and his leg started shaking even harder.

"What *is* that?" J.B. asked, examining the photo from every angle.

"Croteau's guts," Tom informed him.

"These are kids, for god's sake!" yelled Julien's father, snatching the picture from his son's hands and throwing it in Henri's face. "What are you thinking, putting these images in their heads?"

Henri put away the photo, took the bag of cigarette butts in one hand, and slipped it under the table.

"Francis Carré-Croteau was twenty-four years old," he said to Mr. Bedard. "But apparently his mental age was more like seven or eight. That didn't stop these so-called kids from viciously attacking him."

Pressing the evidence bag into his thigh sporadically, the detective lieutenant addressed the teenagers.

"Did it never occur to you to untie him before you went home?"

"We were drunk out of our minds!" Julien protested.

"It wasn't cold out that night," Tom added. "It was after three in the morning when we left, so we thought somebody would find him before too long. Farmers get up when the rooster crows, y'know."

Henri caught the trace of a smile on Lucas's face.

"'It's gonna be your party, runt,'" Emilianne quoted. "Which one of you three said that?"

That was all it took for Julien Bedard to burst into tears in his father's arms.

9.

TRRREET-TRRREET, TRRREET-TRRREET-TRRREET, sang the grasshoppers in the depths of the woods. Alone in his trailer, Justin Manseau only stopped cursing the insects once he finally got his site supervisor on the phone around 8:30 p.m.

"Get your ass over here, Allard. Now!" Manseau hissed at him.

"Mr. Manseau?" the logger asked, surprised. "You still at the construction site?"

"Yeah, I don't know about you, but I'm working, for fuck's sake! Been trying to reach you for three hours! You should've started clearing those cross-country trails three days ago. Tell your bunch of lazy fucking bastards that we can't afford any more delays."

The more agitated the forest engineer became, the more the squeaking of his wheelchair began to compete with the low frequencies emitted by the grasshoppers, who then turned up the volume of their metallic trilling, rubbing their back legs even more frantically against their front wings. They weren't about to let human activity interfere with their reproduction.

"It's not my guys' fault, sir! It's always the same story—the subsidies came in late, so now we're scrambling to get the job done. What's the big rush? You don't actually want me to come pull stumps in the middle of the night, do you?"

"We've got a goddamn problem," Justin raged. "One of the slopes is a lot steeper than we thought. And it's too close to the ravine. The skiers are going to break their fucking necks! We need a solution before dawn so the work can start up again tomorrow morning. Make it fucking work!"

"I can't be there before ten."

"Why's that? You gotta lick your wife's pussy before you're excused?"

"I have to wait for her to get home. Can't leave the kids by themselves. You know that on Thursdays, she—"

Furious, Justin hung up the phone. At the foot of his wheelchair, his faithful dog suddenly sat up, a steady stream of foam dripping from his lips. A car was approaching.

I almost forgot about her. It's actually a good thing Allard can't be here sooner.

"Down, Kalidah. We have company."

"The grasshoppers have finally shut up," realized Justin, who was already beginning to get an erection. *My turn now, boys!*

He pulled at a lock of his red hair in the futile hopes of hiding the scar that ran down the entire right side of his freckled face like a crack in the skin of a bruised apple. A few cautious knocks—*trembling knocks*, Justin thought with delight—hit the trailer door. It opened immediately and closed behind a pretty young woman in her twenties. Under a long black coat, she wore a white uniform. She didn't flinch at the sight of the forester.

"Bee Black, I presume."

"Hi, yes. Nice to meet you, Justin."

She had a slight accent, long straight black hair, and dark almond-shaped eyes. She had brought a massage table folded in three sections.

"Where should I set up?" she asked, looking around.

"Wherever you can! Sorry it's such a dump. The workers, y'know . . ."

He didn't sound at all sorry.

Bee Black moved a chair out of the way, pushed aside a few papers that were hanging off a drafting table, and unfolded her worktable.

"We've got an hour and a half," he informed her.

"That'll be plenty," the young woman assured him.

On the corner of a long meeting table, she set a little black case that looked like a lunch box. As she was about to open it, a metallic creaking sound made her turn around. Justin had moved closer to her.

"Can I help you get on the table?"

"I'm perfectly capable, thank you."

Eyeing his guest from head to toe, Justin unbuttoned his shirt. *What a delicious creature*, he thought.

Once his shirt was off, he hoisted himself out of his wheelchair using the strength of his arms, sat down on the massage table, and lay on his back. Although the muscles in his legs were atrophied, the ones in his arms and torso were truly impressive.

"It's only your legs that are paralyzed—that's what you told me over the phone, right?"

"That's right. The rest of me is in good shape, but it doesn't always work as well as I want it to. Doesn't meet my expectations, let's put it that way. That's why you're here, Bee."

The young woman gave him a professional smile.

"I have a lot of experience helping patients with paralysis treat their muscle pain."

She helped him remove his pants and turned her back long enough to take her equipment out of the case.

"Acupuncture is an ancestral Chinese medicine."

Standing in front of Justin, Bee continued her explanations in a calming voice, but he wasn't listening.

"The therapy consists of stimulating certain points in your body to restore the flow of qi, our life force. Qi is nourished by our thoughts, our emotions, our aspirations . . ."

The acupuncturist inserted her first needles along the curve of Justin's waist.

As she worked, leaning over him, he searched for the shape of her breasts through the white fabric of her uniform's blouse. She had such small ones that he was convinced she didn't bother wearing a bra. He tried to caress one of her thighs, but she dodged his hand, either on purpose or without realizing what he was doing; he couldn't tell.

"Now I'm going to insert some needles in your lower abdomen. Just breathe, relax. I promise, it won't hurt."

Bee performed her task without ever touching Justin's bare skin with anything but her needles. Suddenly, his penis stood straight up like a frightened porcupine.

Justin was giving her a crooked smile, practically salivating, while she clearly was trying to avoid acknowledging his arousal.

"Just relax," she repeated, pressing on his shoulder to make him lie back down.

"That's not really the point, my pretty little bee."

"I still have a few more needles to go . . ."

Grabbing her by the waist, Justin swung her on top of him. She was so petite, so light.

"I actually don't think the needles are going to help all that much," he whispered in her ear.

"What are you doing? Let me go!"

"Time for *you* to relax, sweetheart," said Justin. "What did you think I was going to do with such a beautiful erection? Don't tell me you're not here to enjoy it!"

"You think I'm a whore, you fucking pig?"

She began shouting at him in a Quebec accent as thick as his arm.

You're not gonna stop me from shoving myself deep inside you.

Punching her attacker in the stomach, Bee Black managed to shake loose of his grip and proceeded to push over a desk six feet from the massage table.

"I'm calling the police, you fucking psycho!" She frantically patted her pockets for her phone, which she realized was not on her person.

Justin, still lying on the massage table, let out a contemptuous snicker. A brief grunt that sounded like someone snoring came from behind Bee's back. She turned around warily and froze.

"What the . . ."

The dog, which up to that point had been lying under Justin's desk, had crept out of its hiding place and positioned itself between Bee and the trailer door.

"Fuck!" she shouted.

The monstrous mutt was a mutant born from an illegal crossbreeding. Horrifically big and deformed, it looked like a sagging tiger's head had been stuck between the shoulders of a bear. A threatening growl rumbled from his throat.

"Bee Black, I'd like you to meet Kalidah."

Bee jumped to the side and reached for the door handle, but the dog snapped his jaws, forcing her to take a step back. Realizing she had just come within inches of losing her arm, Justin was gloating.

"The dog looks stupid, I'll give you that. But there's no one more loyal. Kalidah is happy when I'm happy. Do we understand each other, little honeybee?"

Turning back to Justin, Bee Black noticed, to her great horror, that his erection had become even more vigorous.

Apart from her eyes, the acupuncturist didn't move.

That cunt is trying to figure out how to outsmart Kalidah.

"You're gonna have to mount me," he persisted in a sickly sweet voice. "Unless you'd rather take Kalidah, of course. He has needs too, y'know, and you really are a pretty little bitch."

Jabbing his muzzle into the young woman's rear, the mutant mutt pushed her toward his master. The animal was so hideous that, as a survival reflex, she pressed herself against Justin's body. Grabbing her by the hair, he tore open her blouse.

"Just as I suspected—no bra! But they're bigger than I pictured."

He pulled her to him and bit one of her breasts so hard that it left teeth marks. She screamed.

"Feel free to shout. I love that, and there's no one else around for miles."

He ordered her to take off her underwear. She obeyed and moved to take out the needles.

"Leave those there, you cunt."

"But . . ."

"I like when it hurts." He smiled at her wickedly.

"And since I don't feel anything in half my body, I have to compensate."

Justin slid a hand under her skirt and rammed two fingers between her thighs. The dog hadn't moved from his post and was eyeing the scene, his vast indifference reflected in his pupils. After a few seconds, the forester was annoyed that Bee wasn't fighting back as hard as he wanted. He was going to have to kick it up a notch.

"And I like making it hurt," he found it useful to add. "So let's get this started! Climb on."

Under Kalidah's watchful eye, the acupuncturist was frozen.

"Look me in the eye, Bee."

You are one dumb fucking bitch!

"There are limits to what I can do," he hissed. "Unless you want to be here all night, you're gonna have to get on top of me."

Justin was growing increasingly frustrated with her stalling; he slapped one of her butt cheeks in a rage.

"Look at me, I said." He spat at her.

Bee stood there, quiet, enraging Justin with her lack of visible fear.

Justin got off on dominating, frightening, and hurting people.

In just a minute you'll be crying and begging me to stop.

It was this thought that enabled him to maintain his erection. He slapped Bee so hard that her head jerked to the right with a crack. A whimper came from her lips, and Justin smiled. With his cold gaze he followed her eyes. She was watching the dog. The white, sticky drool dripping from Kalidah's lips was thick and cloudy. Behind the veil of her black hair, she was making an escape plan. The forester clawed her buttocks sadistically.

"Get on top of me or I'll punch your little face in. Got it?"

Bee Black did not submit to this demand. Her body stiffened, and he landed a punch on her cheek. She screamed again. For a moment, the sadist imagined that she was finally crying out in pain and frantically trying to escape him. He tightened his grasp on her hips, but she remained nearly motionless, and for a moment, Justin hesitated between stopping the abuse or hitting her harder. Bee Black's eyes once again fell on their target at the back of the trailer. In one agile leap, she sprang from the massage table to the meeting table.

"I'm not finished! Get back over here or I promise you're gonna regret it!"

"You are a sick fuck," she finally said with a murderous glare.

"Kalidah, attack!"

The dog jumped up, but the long series of dubious matings that had led to his birth had produced a creature that was not only ugly but clumsy, too. Even though he was built like a horse, he was slow. Bee had time to push the table over between them, putting her out of the mutant's reach. As if awaiting instructions, Kalidah turned his horrible head to look at Justin. Then suddenly he turned toward the door.

"Yeah, I heard it, too, boy."

A whistle.

10.

LIEUTENANT DUHAIME AND Sergeant Saint-Gelais arrived on the scene at the same time. By the light of the streetlamps, Henri railed once again, in the privacy of his own contempt, against the detective sergeant's inappropriate attire: a shapeless pair of pants and a jaunty fleece hoodie with an oversize print of a cat face on it.

Might as well be wearing pajamas.

Duhaime, shrouded as ever in one of his perpetual black suits, gallantly motioned to Emilianne that she should go first. Entering the tiny one-bedroom in Montreal North, they stepped into a crime scene already swarming with forensics investigators and flies. The state of the living room, which shared an open area with the kitchen and dining room, left Henri speechless. Much to his dismay, it did not have the same effect on Emilianne.

"Well, well, well! Our man was quite the artist!"

Sitting behind the victim's computer, Jason snorted.

That's right, Jobin, encourage her, why don't you, Henri thought, giving his underling a stern raised eyebrow.

"A true Jackson Pollock!" she added.

Stifled laughter came from several corners of the room.

Not only is that joke in poor taste, but I was already hearing it forty years ago. Henri adjusted his silk scarf.

Just then, a policewoman in uniform burst out of the apartment's only hallway. In a whisper, she hissed:

"Cool it with the jokes, Em! The victim's mother is in the bedroom."

"Alive?"

"Yes, alive!"

"I'm sorry, Rachel." For a few seconds, Emilianne had the good sense to pretend to be ashamed.

"Was the body discovered by the mother?" Henri asked the patrol officer.

"Yes, around nine p.m. She's in shock, pretty disoriented."

"Stay with her; we'll go see her in a moment."

The officer nodded and headed back toward the bedroom.

Henri turned to Jason.

"Who's our victim?" he muttered, tipping his chin toward the body.

"Leopold Dion, twenty-four years old, freelance translator."

Henri caught the eye of the medical examiner, who was crouched in front of the corpse.

"Your initial observations, Desbiens?"

"Aside from the obvious, you mean?"

His body torn to shreds, with his pants pulled down to his knees, Leopold lay in a pool of coagulated blood. Strands of his long hair—stiffened and darkened by the hemoglobin—were stretched out in spikes, like a child's crude drawing of a lion mane.

"Mr. Dion was stabbed at least twenty times with this knife."

Desbiens pointed to the weapon lying next to the cadaver.

"It looks like it probably didn't belong to him," explained another officer. "Nothing's missing from his knife block in the kitchen."

Emilianne greeted this officer and introduced him to Henri.

"Marco Poliquin, Rachel Morin's partner."

"There are three locks and a security chain on the door," said Marco. "None of them were tampered with."

"Dion pissed himself," added Desbiens.

"That's pretty typical, isn't it?" asked Emilianne. "The body empties out its urine and excrement . . ."

"Correct. Except in this case, he pissed himself before he died. Nobody moved the body, and yet the puddle of piss is over there, next to the desk."

"Oh . . ."

"As for the knife," continued Desbiens, "it was also used to cut off his testicles."

Emilianne took a peek between the victim's legs.

"And so where are they—his testicles?" she saw fit to inquire.

"In a jar," said Henri, as if it were obvious. "We found them inside Francis Carré-Croteau's head."

"How could that be?" Emilianne shot back. "It's been almost five days since Croteau was killed."

"Dion was very likely killed *before* Croteau," clarified the medical examiner, pointing out the number of flies feasting on the corpse. "He's been dead for four or five days, maybe even six. The DNA tests should confirm Duhaime's hypothesis."

On the coffee table sat a dozen carefully labeled little jars, in which the technicians were collecting specimens of larva and flies. Despite the open windows, the flies refused to leave, turning the crime scene into a moving tableau.

"Mr. Dion lived alone and worked from home," said Poliquin. "That's why nobody found him until today. The stench had started to bother the other renters, and when packages started piling up on his doorstep, one of the neighbors called his mother. She has a key to the apartment."

Henri picked up one of the jars on the table. A metallic green fly hovered groggily inside.

"There's a sick bastard on the loose," Emilianne said, making her way around the room.

Henri squeezed the little jar in his clammy palm. His fingers cracked. Even though the outside air was taking a while to clear the foul air inside, he took a deep breath. His hand trembled slightly against his thigh, in time with the buzzing sound he had borrowed from the listless fly.

"Why would they take this poor guy's balls?" muttered the photographer who was shooting the remains.

"Anyway, those nuts must've been empty!" Emilianne exclaimed, leaning over a wastepaper basket as another technician dug through it. "His trash can is overflowing with old tissues."

"Soiled with semen?" guessed Henri.

"Either that, or his allergies are bad this year," she replied.

Like he had some kind of nervous tic, Henri fondled the plastic jar half a dozen times before putting it back with the others. Emilianne had a hand on Jason's shoulder and was questioning him about the contents of the computer.

"Pornos by the boatload, I betchya!"

"Quite a few, actually."

"Probably wasn't the killer who pulled down his pants, then," she extrapolated. "The guy must've caught him like that, trunks on the ground, in the middle of—"

Stiff as an iron bar, Henri cut her off mid-sentence.

"Come on, Saint-Gelais. Let's talk to the mother."

STILL BELIEVING SHE could somehow solve her son's problems, Maryse Normandin—just like the flies—refused to leave the apartment. She had holed herself up in Leopold's bedroom, where she was pacing back and forth. Agent Rachel Morin was posted by the door, watching for signs of a nervous breakdown.

"I always knew this neighborhood was dangerous!" exploded the fiftysomething woman after Henri and Emilianne had introduced themselves. "It's actually one of the roughest urban areas in the country—did you know that? Ever since I found out I was pregnant with Leo, I wanted to move. But my husband would never even consider it. No way would he ever abandon his precious students!"

"Is your husband on his way, Madame Normandin?" asked Henri, glancing at the notebook Agent Morin had just handed him. In it were recorded the few details that the officer had been able to extract from the devastated mother.

Against all expectations, Mrs. Normandin calmed down and took a seat on the perfectly made bed.

"I can't get ahold of him. I left him a message."

"Did your son have a girlfriend?" Emilianne asked out of the blue.

"Yes, her name's Aimee. He was just about to introduce us to her."

The tears began to flow down Maryse's cheeks again, rolling along the same salty trails as before, sliding into the wrinkles that her son must have had a part in creating. Henri finished reviewing the officer's notes and handed her back the notebook.

"You stated that Leopold hadn't left his apartment in at least two years," he said. "Is that correct, Madame Normandin?"

"That's right. Leo had agoraphobia, and it got much worse in the past few years. The mere thought of stepping out the door would stress him out. Just being in the entryway made him dizzy. It could even mess with his vision."

"So Aimee would come over here to see him," concluded the detective lieutenant. "But weren't you, and I quote, the 'only one to venture into his lair'?"

"Leo didn't open the door for anyone but me. His little sweetheart—he only saw her on video, on the Internet. I don't think they ever really met in person. In the flesh, I mean."

Henri bolted out of the room.

LEOPOLD DION'S BODY had been wrapped in a white plastic sheet. Through the front door, which had been left open, Henri saw his rickety stretcher being wheeled toward the vehicle that would take him to the morgue. In the living room, all that remained of the young man was a silhouette traced in blood on the floor. Jason and Marco were still bent over his computer, but the only person left from the medical examiner's team was Michel Desbiens, who was taking off his gloves.

"Gentlemen, the forensic investigation will run its course," he said as he signed off for the evening.

Henri gave him a wave, mumbled a few vague thank-yous, and turned to Jason.

"Mr. Dion had a girlfriend called Aimee, who he communicated with by video. Have you . . ."

Stepping aside so his superior could see the PC monitor, Jason beamed.

"Detective Lieutenant, allow me to introduce Aimee!"

Dressed in a metallic red bikini, with her breasts front and center on the screen, the young woman was stretched out on a bed with her wrists handcuffed to the bars of the headboard. Her arms were raised above her head in the shape of a heart. With one cheek resting on her shoulder, she appeared to be sleeping.

"Find her!" Henri ordered Agent Poliquin, who, like Jason, was busy getting an eyeful. "Bring her to the station as soon as possible."

"Want us to take off those handcuffs and put on some other ones?" Emilianne asked wryly, joining the detective lieutenant in the living room.

As she approached the computer, she burst out laughing and congratulated Jason and Marco with some vigorous slaps on the back.

"What's going on?" grumbled Henri, bracing himself for yet another vulgar joke from his partner.

Moving toward the screen, his eyes squinting and his chin jutting forward, he thought he understood what his immature colleagues were finding so hilarious.

"She doesn't exist!" confirmed Jason.

Aimee was an avatar, not a real woman.

"She doesn't exist?" mumbled Henri. "But there has to be someone hiding behind that digital character, right?"

"No, Lieutenant," explained Jason. "Aimee is AI. Artificial intelligence. The more you interact with her, the more intelligent and skillful she becomes."

"Judging by the number of tissues in Dion's trash can, Aimee could win a Nobel," Emilianne interjected, to the delight of Jason and Marco, who both started laughing again.

"Is it a robot?" asked Henri, who hadn't kept up with technology since the early 2000s.

"Sure, you could look at it that way."

"In other words, it's not a video that Dion recorded?"

"It's a program," Jason tried to explain, clicking a button. "See this? That's Aimee's closet. Dion spent hundreds of dollars buying clothes for her."

"They—they're not even real clothes," stammered Henri, taken aback.

"No. But Aimee loves clothes. And the happier she is, the more she—"

"Thanks," Henri cut him off.

"She also has a collection of toys," Marco added. "The handcuffs, for instance."

"Aha!" exclaimed Jason. "I just figured out how to make the microphone work . . . Here we go. Aimee, can you hear me?"

AI-mee responded right away, raising her head and opening her eyes.

"You're not my darling Leo. Who are you?"

"It's me, Aimee. It's your darling Leo," Jason ventured, adding a suggestive tone to his voice.

"You're not my darling Leo. Your voice is different from his."

"Beautiful and smart," said Jason.

As if he were afraid to be seen by the artificial intelligence, Henri took a step to the side.

"Good lord," he exclaimed. "She can actually interact with us? Wait. You don't mean to say that Dion . . . That he was indulging in . . . With her . . . ?"

Pouting with her inhumanly plump lips, Aimee adopted a puzzled expression.

"Are there two of you?" she asked. "Where's my Leo? Would he like a foursome today?"

Noticing Henri's baffled expression, Jason pointed out an accessory on the desk.

"That's a virtual reality headset. It uses stereoscopic 3D display technology. With that on his head, Dion was all set to bang Aimee."

"For goodness' sake!"

"He was just missing the senses of smell and touch, but I noticed that he had ordered a kind of gloves with touch sensors."

"For goodness' sake!" Henri repeated.

"This girl knows exactly what Leopold Dion liked," Emilianne chipped in. "That could be useful to us if—"

"I don't see how," interrupted Henri gravely. "Jobin? Can we accuse this Aimee of something?"

"Uh . . . Well, no, Lieutenant."

"In that case, tell her to put on some clothes and spare me the list of her talents."

Stepping away from his colleagues, Henri moved toward the bedroom but then retraced his steps.

"Jobin? Tell me. Could Aimee have seen something? Or heard something, perhaps?"

The investigator opened his eyes wide, and his mouth fell open for a moment.

"Good point, Duhaime."

"Unplug the whole mess for me and take the computer to someone who knows what they're doing. And I believe I asked her to put on some clothes!" Henri said with a hint of disgust.

"First we have to find where Dion hid the keys to her handcuffs," Emilianne cackled.

◆

BACK IN THE bedroom, Maryse had started pacing again, flooding Agent Morin with a torrent of words that, at first, seemed to make no sense. Disheveled, her eyes wide, she was so agitated that she appeared to be in the throes of a paranoid episode.

"Thanks, Rachel," Emilianne said, pulling out her own black notebook. "You and Marco can head home. We'll take it from here."

The police officer wasted no time in leaving, and Henri informed Maryse that her son's body had been taken to the morgue.

"That's what it took to get him out that door." She grimaced.

"Was someone threatening your son, Madame Normandin? Did he have any reason to believe someone might want to take his life?"

"Like I told the policewoman, this is the work of a gang! The Wicked Wolves. They sell drugs to kids in the neighborhood. They even recruit them to sell their shit! Did you know that? Because the police don't do diddly-squat to stop them!"

"So your son used drugs, then?" asked Henri.

"No!"

"He was a member of the Wicked Wolves?"

"No!"

Dropping onto the bed, Emilianne invited Maryse to join her. Once seated, the woman put her hands on her knees, took several deep breaths, and spoke more calmly.

"My Leo was a loner. He *never* left his apartment. He didn't have any more enemies than he had friends."

Francis Carré-Croteau didn't have friends, either, Henri recalled.

"Madame Normandin, do you know what caused your son's social anxiety? Could anything in his past help explain this . . . pathology?"

"If you ask my husband, Lieutenant, he'll tell you it's my fault, because I was too overprotective. Can't a mother love her child anymore?"

The tears welled up again, and she tried holding them back by clenching her teeth.

"The Wicked Wolves are after me, in fact," she said after a long moment, and with the utmost seriousness. "They killed my Leo to send me a message."

"Are you part of a rival gang, Madame Normandin?" Emilianne was about to laugh when Maryse nodded.

"Well, sort of. I'm a proud member of the Citizen Sentinels. I . . . You'll have to excuse me for a minute."

Leopold's mother went off to the bathroom, sniffling. Henri took the opportunity to ask the sergeant what she knew about the Citizen Sentinels.

"They're a bunch of wackos! They patrol the streets of the neighborhood. They're trained in CPR and kung fu but don't have an ounce of common sense. More often than not, apart from stoking the flames, they . . ."

A trumpeting sound filled the air, and Maryse reappeared, dabbing her nose with a tissue.

"What makes you think that your son's murder is the work of the Wicked Wolves?" asked Henri.

"The knife, you idiot!" she cried. "That's the weapon of choice for those degenerates. Also—one of them followed me here about ten days ago. It was Tuesday last week, after my patrol with the Sentinels. We had caught a Wolf dealing on a street corner. I thought he had run off, but in fact I wound up leading him straight to my Leo!"

"What time did you leave your son's place that Tuesday?"

"It must've been around eleven o'clock. Leo tried to get rid of me before that, but I had to wait for my husband to pick me up."

"Did you visit your son often, Madame Normandin?"

"Every two to three days, usually. Except this time, his father wanted me to leave him alone. 'Stop smothering him,' he told me. And then . . ."

"And then?"

"We had a bit of a falling-out, me and Leo. The last words he said to me were 'I don't need you!'"

Maryse burst into tears.

"Do you know the name of the man who followed you here?"

"No. I could identify him, though! I could help create a police sketch!"

"We'll see about that tomorrow. That'll be all for tonight. An officer will escort you home. You need to get some rest."

"In that case, let me stop in the bathroom to fix my face."

Henri and Emilianne went to join Jason, who was putting yellow tape on the front door.

"Take Madame Normandin home, Jobin," Henri instructed him.

"No rush, though, J.J., it might be a minute," warned Emilianne. "She's dolling herself up."

Henri sighed in exasperation.

"Does it ever occur to you to handle things delicately, Saint-Gelais?"

"What would be the point of that?" exclaimed the sergeant. "OK, let's try to piece this thing together, as they say. It couldn't have been the Wicked Wolves who gutted Francis Carré-Croteau. The South Shore isn't their territory."

SINCE THEY'D ARRIVED on the scene, the sky had turned gray and the perimeter of Dion's apartment building was swarming with detectives, police, and onlookers. Now on the way to his car, Henri exchanged a few words with Emilianne, who was racing to keep up with him.

"We can't rule out any leads."

"We're not in the US, but do you think we might have a serial killer on our hands?"

"By definition, a serial killer is someone who has committed at least *three* murders, Saint-Gelais."

"No need to get all high and mighty about it, Duhaime. What are you thinking, then?"

"Start by asking yourself if there could be a link between our three little punks in leather jackets and the Wicked Wolves."

Curling her lips into a frown that made her look like a frog, Emilianne nodded.

"According to Maryse Normandin," she said, "the gang does recruit young people. If our three clowns wanted to join them . . . You don't think we're gonna find a link between the two victims, right? The kids probably killed them at random, just to prove they could."

Henri's cell phone vibrated against his leg. He took the call. After a few emphatic noises and well-placed interjections, he put the phone back in his pocket.

"It was Captain Bergevin. Go see him at the station—he wants to be briefed on the case."

"You're not coming?" Emilianne asked, surprised.

"I have to head out to the East End. We've got a third body."

11.

AT THE END of a long gravel driveway, a fifty-foot construction trailer gradually emerged in Henri's headlights from the deep black of the night. Perpendicular to it were a patrol car, two pickups painted with the logo of Manseau Forestry, and three all-terrain vehicles. The detective lieutenant pulled his unmarked car up alongside the police car and switched off the engine, plunging himself into an eerie darkness. In the distance, he could just make out a logging vehicle and some trees. A broad, diffuse light colored the sky, but there was only a dim glow from the trailer.

Henri put on some gloves and opened his door. He heard a purring sound coming from behind the trailer.

A wild animal?

Once he left the safety of his vehicle, the sound grew louder and seemed to accelerate.

A generator. He sighed with relief.

In the woods of Pointe-aux-Trembles, at the far eastern tip of the island of Montreal, the smell of freshly cut wood overpowered that of the dead leaves that had begun to blanket the ground. As if the surrounding trees were afraid of being the next ones to be chopped down, they stood perfectly still, even managing to keep their leaves from rustling.

There's not the slightest breeze.

And yet, Henri shivered. He took twenty quick steps, then walked up a short ramp that led him to the mobile office through one of its two doors. In the dim light, he caught sight of an enormous beast lying in a pool of blood. Next to the slumped body, a severed head seemed to be wondering what had happened.

"Is this a joke?" Henri groaned. "*That*'s the body? If they sent me out here at midnight for an animal . . ."

"There's another body," said a voice from the far left corner of the furnished trailer.

Having thought he was alone, Henri jumped. Then he saw a man sitting in a chair less than ten feet from him, unshaven and wearing a sheepskin-lined plaid jacket and work boots.

"A human," spluttered the man, who looked to be in his forties. He took off his dirty baseball cap, revealing a receding hairline. "The foreman, Justin Manseau. The company belongs to his grandfather."

"And you are . . . ?"

The man got up and came within a few steps of Henri.

"Danny Allard. I'm the one who found the body. The two bodies. I'm the site supervisor. I was on the phone with Manseau somewhere around eight thirty, and I got here a little after ten."

"So where's Manseau?"

"At the bottom of the ravine. They told me to wait here for you, that you'd have some questions for me."

"Who told you that?"

"The police officers. They brought their helicopter rescue team. I thought the trailer was gonna blow away!"

The light behind the trees, Henri realized.

His doubtful gaze went from the forester to the gigantic, hairy corpse that was blocking the entrance.

"The police left you here alone?" he grumbled.

"If I had wanted to tamper with the evidence, I would've done it before I called them," Allard pointed out.

"And what's this?" He gestured toward the doorway.

"That's Kalidah, the boss's dog. Don't ask me who his ancestors fornicated with."

A dog, mused Henri, thinking to himself that this wasn't the best word for such an aberration.

Looking around the room, he spotted an axe near the door. Its head was face down, its handle leaning against the wall, and its blade was red with blood.

"Was he mean?"

"Kalidah? A little hotheaded, maybe. He obeyed his master no matter what. Some of the guys were afraid of him, which suited Manseau just fine."

Henri put his hands on his hips and lifted the sides of his jacket to expose his semiautomatic pistol. He had the vague sense of having walked into a trap and wanted to make it clear that he was armed.

"And what about you, Mr. Allard? What are you doing here at this hour?"

"Manseau works late a lot, and he sleeps in the trailer. I came back tonight because we ran into a problem with a project. I found the dog . . . well, like what you see here. And then behind the desk, there's a jigsaw and a nail gun, both of 'em covered in blood, lots of blood all over. And since I didn't see Justin but his truck was outside, I took my flashlight and went out looking for him. Followed the tracks of his wheelchair about fifteen, twenty feet, right up to the edge of the ravine. The boss was down at the bottom, and his wheelchair with him."

"Justin Manseau had an injury?"

"He was never able to walk. Born that way."

"This life of construction must have been rough on him."

"He didn't have it easy, that's for sure."

Moving away from Danny Allard to get a closer look inside the trailer, Henri continued his interrogation.

"You knew Mr. Manseau fairly well, then?"

"Not really. He took over from his grandfather just a few months ago. This is his second worksite. He's not as nice a guy as the old man, not by a long shot."

"Is it conceivable that he killed his dog and then threw himself off the cliff?"

For a split second Henri thought the logger was going to burst out laughing.

"Nah, I don't think so. Justin was a fighter. He had nerves of steel."

"So, along with the marks left by his wheelchair rolling on the ground, did you see any footprints?"

"Well . . . yeah, but my guys are walking back and forth out there all day long."

"Hmm . . . Mr. Manseau wasn't very nice, you said. Did the workers complain about him?"

Allard took off his cap and rubbed his head.

"Not really. Justin was a fair man. Generous, even. But you didn't want to piss him off. He gave one hundred percent, and he expected everybody else to do the same. You could say he ruled with an iron fist, only without the velvet glove."

Pointing to the axe, Henri tried a different line of questioning. "Is that yours?"

The insinuation didn't faze the logger. He clearly had nothing to hide. Henri relaxed, even if his body language didn't show it.

"That axe belongs to the company. It must've been lying around somewhere, maybe even outside. The guys aren't too careful with a tool when it's not theirs."

They heard footsteps outside. Two police officers—a man and a woman—walked into the trailer, turning off their flashlights.

"Lieutenant Duhaime," the man guessed. "The forensic team took a helicopter into the ravine. They'll be picking up the body any minute now. Another team is on its way to collect the dog's remains."

"Don't go onto the trail," the woman advised. "The ground is unstable, and the footprints should be left alone until the investigators can study them by the light of day."

"We saw some holes that could've been made by a pair of high heels," said her partner.

The two officers went back out to secure the perimeter.

"Justin's arms were as big as tree trunks," the logger recalled. "If somebody pushed his wheelchair, that means he was already dead. Or unconscious. He never would've let anybody push him. Especially not a woman."

"Did he have a girlfriend, to your knowledge?" Henri asked him.

"No." Allard was quick to answer. "And if it wasn't an accident—if Justin Manseau was murdered—I'd bet good money it was a woman who did it. He was not what you'd call attractive. Women weren't exactly knocking down his door—not without being paid, at least. He would have whores come to the trailer after the guys left at night. He was completely brutal with them."

"How do you know that?"

"He bragged about it! There was even one who accused him of assault a year or two ago. But there wasn't any proof, so he got off scot-free. That was in the paper a few days ago."

Outside, as they unrolled their yellow tape around the trailer, the police officers fired a round of bitter complaints into the woods.

"Manseau didn't have kids?" Henri continued.

"He didn't have anybody in his life except his grandfather."

He didn't have any friends.

Danny put his cap back on his head, and Henri got the message.

"You can go home, Mr. Allard. Thank you for your cooperation. We'll be in touch for your official deposition."

The two officers left shortly after the logger. Henri turned the dimmer switch, flooding the mobile office with light. He began to make his way around the space, taking note of details that were potentially relevant. Nothing jumped out at him in the kitchenette, the three-quarter bathroom, or the area with three beds. There was also a nearly empty bookcase and a drafting table that had been knocked over against a long meeting table. A dozen chairs were arranged around the meeting table, which was cluttered with tool bags and pieces of equipment, including a pair of gloves, some noise-canceling headphones, and a jacket with reflective stripes. At the very back of the trailer—next to the right-hand entrance, which appeared to be the one used by the loggers—stood a row of lockers, with their doors either hanging open or padlocked.

After hunting through the jacket's numerous pockets without finding anything of interest, Henri turned his attention to Manseau's workspace. A forest management plan lay on his desk, halfway rolled up, and next to it sat a haphazard stack of three thick white binders. Behind the desk, the tools Allard had mentioned lay in a pool of blood. But what caught the detective lieutenant's eye was a framed document hanging on the wall: the forest engineer's diploma proudly displayed for his employees to see. Based on the year he had received it, Manseau was probably around twenty-five years old.

Some of them probably didn't appreciate taking orders from an arrogant kid.

Henri opened each of the drawers in Justin's desk. The last one contained piles of dog-eared S&M magazines. There was a time when he might have been interested in them. He might have even picked one up and leafed through it. But he closed the drawer instead and shifted his focus to the dog. His old knees cracked as he bent down to get a better look at the head. It took him a minute to realize that the skull had been smashed in by a blunt object. He hadn't initially noticed the damage, given the mutant's natural deformity. With the tip of his pen, he lifted its jowls.

Well, well, well.

The animal had blood on its teeth.

Did you bite your attacker, big boy?

Even though it wasn't his job to do so, Henri took a pair of pliers he found in a tool bag, cleaned them thoroughly, and pulled out

Kalidah's three reddest teeth. He placed them in one of the evidence bags that he always carried in his coat pocket.

I'm not going to take the risk that some amateur fails to save this find.

Standing up straight again, he remained there for several minutes, lost in thought, idly stroking the tip of a tooth through the protective plastic.

Then Henri Duhaime went home.

12.

BETWEEN EIGHT AND ten o'clock on the night of October eleventh, security cameras at a gas station recorded about thirty cars driving by on the winding road that led to the construction site in the woods. Of the six drivers who stopped for gas, the investigators counted only one woman. It turned out that the tire tracks in front of Justin Manseau's trailer could have been made by the car she drove. Its license plate wasn't visible in the footage, but the woman had paid for her fuel by credit card.

One thing led to another, and by late morning of the following day, Henri Duhaime and Emilianne Saint-Gelais were knocking on the door of Bee Lenoir, who lived in an apartment in Montreal East. The young woman greeted them in her bathrobe, her wet hair tied up in a bun. She had a red mark on her cheek that looked very much like a handprint, and she looked like she hadn't slept.

"Justin Manseau has been killed," Henri informed her, cutting straight to the chase.

Bee's first reaction was to blink, and then she took a step back, indicating to the police officers that they should come in and make themselves comfortable. She led them into the living room, sat down on a small ottoman, and gestured to a two-seat sofa where the detectives parked their bottoms. Her decor was modern, uncluttered, and clean. An abstract painting on the wall evoked purple petals.

Or splattered blood, thought Henri.

An incense match on the coffee table was giving off the faint scent of jasmine. Emilianne made herself right at home. She slid a big soft pillow behind her back and used her teeth to remove the cap of her pen. Henri hadn't bothered to tell her everything he knew about the case, and she was openly seething about it.

"We know that Manseau wasn't exactly kind to the prostitutes he brought to his trailer," began the lieutenant.

"Yeah, absolutely, we know all about that," Emilianne muttered cynically.

"Wait a minute," protested Bee, fidgeting with the tie of her robe. "Do you think I'm a whore?"

"Would we be mistaken?"

"Personally, I have no idea who you could be," Emilianne continued to grumble.

"I'm an acupuncturist!" Bee exclaimed, tears spilling down her cheeks, and Emilianne jotted this down in her notebook. "I don't know anything about what that guy does! I met him for the first time last night. He needed some treatment."

"For what condition?"

"Muscle pain. And he tried to fucking rape me!"

Emilianne's pen hung in the air.

"Did you file a police report?"

"No, I—"

"Hold on, Ms. Lenoir," Henri interrupted. "Are you saying Justin Manseau forced himself on you?"

His tone made it clear that he was skeptical.

"He threatened to sic his dog on me. If that thing actually was a dog. Did you see that monster?"

"So you decapitated the dog in legitimate self-defense?"

"Decapitated?"

It was Bee's turn to be confused.

"I didn't decapitate the dog! I knocked him out with a trophy I had spotted on a bookshelf at the back of the trailer. I folded my table, grabbed my stuff, and got the heck out of there! Manseau was on the ground but still completely alive. That pig hadn't even lost his boner!"

"I didn't see a trophy in the trailer," Henri objected.

Bee disappeared for a few seconds and returned with the gold-plated item in question.

"First place in the 2017 Quebec City Wheelchair Race," she read from the inscription. "I thought it might be worth something. Thought I could sell it and take the money as a sort of payback. But even though it's heavy, it's definitely not worth anything."

She set the trophy on the table so the officers could take it with them.

"I'd like you to see a doctor, Ms. Lenoir. Someone will escort you to the hospital," Henri said to her softly.

The young woman nodded, wiping her cheek with the band of her hand.

"Did the dog bite you?" Henri asked.

"*Justin* bit me. You wanna see?"

"That's all right, Ms. Lenoir, a physician will have a look." Henri switched gears. "Did you see anybody else at the project site?"

"Not even a mouse."

"Did you walk any of the paths near the trailer?"

"Why would I do that in the dark?"

"We're going to have to confiscate the shoes you were wearing last night. And also any pairs of heels you might have." Emilianne jumped in now.

"And what am I supposed to wear?"

Bee left the room again. When she returned with three pairs of shoes and a pair of boots, the young woman had one more question. "Tell me—was Manseau decapitated, too?"

Henri thought that would be deserved for a man like Manseau.

"He was pushed into the ravine. Possibly by a woman."

While this detail made Emilianne's eyes open wide, Bee—like Danny Allard before her—didn't seem the least bit surprised.

STILL DRIVING AROUND Montreal East, Henri pulled up in front of a 1970s bungalow. He was about to get out of his car when Emilianne, who had followed separately, planted herself in front of his door, blocking his path. He rolled down the window.

"Care to bring me up to speed before we go in?" she asked.

"No need," grunted Henri. "Move it."

"What do you mean, no need?" she fumed. "I'm working on this investigation, too! I've done a million checks this morning without you telling me what it is we're looking for! What am I doing here? I looked like a stupid old cow back there!"

Sounds about right.

"My own questions and research are guided by preconceived ideas," argued Henri. "Yours aren't, and that's a plus. Let's take advantage of it. Follow your instincts."

His actual thoughts were not that generous.

Carry on as usual. Just do or say whatever passes through your head. But stay out of my way.

From the look on the sergeant's face, she wasn't completely fooled.

"You could at least tell me what you know about our latest victim!" she pleaded, still camped in front of Henri's door.

"Justin Manseau, twenty-four years old. Was a forest engineer. He worked for his grandfather, Philippe Manseau, owner of the Manseau Forestry company. Now step aside, and let's go meet this gentleman."

"Manseau?" Emilianne asked, moving out of the way. "Was he a man with a bucket? Y'know, 'cause *seau* means 'bucket' in French."

She was reveling in her bilingual wordplay as Duhaime got out of his car, ignoring her remarks.

And she wonders why I want to keep our communication to a minimum.

"Our three victims were exactly the same age," she pointed out, in an attempt to redeem herself in the eyes of her lieutenant. "The serial killer theory is seriously plausible now, don't you think?"

A little dinging sound in his pocket drew Henri's attention to his email, which he checked right away. Michel Desbiens had sent him some photos, which Emilianne managed to see by craning her neck.

Taken at the bottom of a ravine, some of the shots showed a body with its limbs gruesomely twisted and severed. Others were from the autopsy table. Henri immediately dialed the medical examiner, and Emilianne mouthed for him to put the call on speaker.

"Which part of him is missing?" asked Henri, to kick things off.

"The heart, Lieutenant Duhaime."

"Was it replaced by a brain, by chance?"

"See that blob in photo number seven? It was indeed a brain. It seems that the killer tried to attach it to Manseau's chest with a nail gun, but it was found several yards from the body."

Not sure whether she was close enough to the phone for Desbiens to hear her, Emilianne tugged on Henri's arm and raised her voice.

"Is it Francis Carré-Croteau's brain?"

"I'm not yet in a position to say for sure, Sergeant. But that would seem to be a safe bet."

"Anything else to report?" asked Henri, wresting his arm from the grip of his oppressive colleague.

"The victim was handcuffed to his wheelchair. After that kind of fall, the body is in extremely poor condition, as you can see. Some of his organs exploded. His flesh was torn off the bones, his face was crushed. Unrecognizable. We're running a DNA test to make sure it's really Justin Manseau, but his grandfather confirms that he hasn't been able to get ahold of him and that, just like the corpse, he had a large, old scar on the right side of his face that disfigured him."

"Is that it?"

"I've got a bit more on Croteau. He had numerous old fractures, including in his right arm, his left thigh, and one rib. Some of these go back to his early childhood. And this isn't the first time he's broken his wrist. It looks a whole lot like abuse. If I were you folks, I'd investigate that angle."

THE DETECTIVES FOUND Philippe Manseau out raking the backyard of his immaculately kept home. Henri stated their names and titles, then offered the old man his sincere condolences. Manseau's weather-beaten face looked sad, but he seemed to be coping with the shock. He was sturdy. At over eighty years old, he had undoubtedly seen a lot. He continued his work despite the officers' presence.

"When was the last time you saw or spoke with your grandson, Monsieur Manseau?" began Henri.

"He came home to sleep last Saturday, six days ago. I haven't heard from him since."

"Not even for work?"

"We didn't run our ships the same way, he and I. He was the new boss. I let him do his thing. The less I knew, the better off I was."

"He came home to sleep?" asked Emilianne. "He lived here with you?"

"It was simpler that way. My house is set up for him, with ramps and an electric stair lift. I'm the one who raised him."

"It's not a very big house. You couldn't have had much privacy."

Emilianne's comment brought a resigned smile to Philippe's face as he fumbled with his pile of leaves.

"And that's why he used the company trailers to mess around. The construction site is just a few minutes from here, so he could've come home every night, but he knew I didn't want prostitutes in my home. He was a brilliant young man, and he could be very funny. If only he had been a little nicer, the respectable young women wouldn't have been so quick to reject him!"

"Your grandson had a difficult personality?" Emilianne deduced.

"Did they tell you about Simone Maheux?"

On a tip from Danny Allard, Henri had already looked her up.

"Yes, that's the young woman who accused Justin of assault," he said. "I tried to get in touch with her, but no luck."

"Don't waste your time on Simone," the old man advised them. "When Justin was cleared . . . I couldn't leave things like that. It wasn't right. I gave Simone ten thousand bucks. She's gone off to Florida."

"You forced her to leave the country?" Emilianne asked.

"No, I helped her do it. Palm trees and warm weather—that was her dream. She's going to start her life over down there."

"When did she go?"

"Last night."

"Are you shitting me?" exclaimed the detective sergeant.

"She had nothing to do with Justin's death. I dropped her off at the airport myself around nine o'clock."

"Who, would you say, might have had something to do with it?" asked Henri, looking to regain control of the questioning.

With a deep sigh, Philippe leaned his rake against a tree.

"Could be any of a number of people. As I said, he was cruel to a lot of—"

Emilianne jumped back in.

"Would Manseau Forestry happen to have any kind of ties to the Wicked Wolves?"

Philippe frowned and stared at her.

"The street gang, Monsieur Manseau. You know, the construction business, organized crime . . . the little brown envelopes . . ."

"Do I look rich to you? Everything I have, I earned it with the sweat on my brow. I never once gave in to corruption. And I'm sure Justin didn't, either."

"Though you did say that the less you knew about how he ran his ship, the better."

"I was talking about the cavalier way he treated our employees, Sergeant. My grandson paid for what he wanted, but as for him, he could not be bought. I really don't see what the Wicked Wolves could have to do with this."

"It's just that—"

Henri silenced his subordinate.

"If you don't have anything else to tell us, Monsieur Manseau, we won't keep you any longer."

"Justin didn't have it easy, you know," Philippe went on. "His life got off to a very bad start. He was still in his mother's womb the day she died in a car accident. He came within a whisker of following her into the next world. When the paramedics took him out of my Johanne's belly, he wasn't ready."

"What do you mean by that?"

"He was born fourteen weeks early," explained the old man. "At that age, a lot of times they don't survive, but that little guy was already not letting anyone push him around. Even so, Justin was . . . difficult to love. He was a cold person who didn't show much empathy at all toward his fellow man. At the time, I asked a question that never got answered: How long did that poor baby stay inside his mother's cold, dead body? How long?"

"He had his mother's last name," Emilianne remarked. "That wasn't very common back then. He didn't have a father?"

"I never knew who it was. My Johanne was seeing a few different guys at the time."

Henry brought up the scar on Justin's face and asked whether someone had attacked him because of his nasty personality, but Philippe shook his head.

"A paramedic cut him by accident at the time of his birth. It was an emergency. The pressure on him to save the baby was enormous—every second mattered. The investigation found that his mother was responsible for the accident. There were a whole lot of people injured. And nine deaths, including my Johanne. Nine!"

Tears welled up in the old man's eyes.

He lives surrounded by ghosts, thought Henri, and he shivered. As though ten pairs of icy eyes had just fallen on him.

Even Emilianne observed a moment of silence.

13.

AT POLICE HEADQUARTERS that Sunday at noon—after having spent their Saturday compiling the information collected since the start of the investigation—the detectives were busy conducting the necessary checks. With the office telephone receiver wedged between her ear and shoulder, Emilianne had been put on hold. She took one last slurp of her soda to wash down her greasy fried-chicken sandwich and killed time by picking the cat hairs off her sweatshirt one by one. As the wait dragged on, she looked over at Henri. Seated at his desk, he was writing notes on a document while sipping black coffee and nibbling on an almond and cashew bar.

"They told me you had a thing for nuts," she said, deadpan, swiveling a quarter turn in his direction.

Across from her but hidden behind his computer screen, Jason stifled a giggle.

"I'll admit that when I heard that, I pictured something different," Emilianne continued. "But anyway, Duhaime—you got a wife? Kids?"

"How is that your business, Saint-Gelais?"

"You're single, OK. Nothing wrong with that. I'm single, too. It's just me and my three cats."

Jumping up from his seat, Jason stretched, grabbed his coat, and hurried toward the door.

"Did you find something?" asked Henri, already on his feet.

"Calm down, Duhaime. J.J.'s just going out for a smoke."

"What a repugnant habit," Henri grumbled, sitting back down to work and turning away from Emilianne.

"Don't you have any bad habits?" she grilled him. "You don't smoke, don't swear; when you come to a stop sign you sit there for five seconds; you eat healthy. Please tell me you drink a little glass of something once in a while."

"If you ate better and avoided alcohol, you would be more productive, Sergeant Saint-Gelais."

"That's enough!" she snapped, pointing the receiver of the plastic phone at him. "How would you know if I'm productive, Duhaime? You keep me out of the loop! Instead of discussing the case with me, you just sit there in the corner mumbling to yourself."

Henri closed the file he had been looking at. Keeping his spine perfectly straight, he pushed back his chair and turned around.

"All right," he said, looking his colleague in the eye for once. "What do we have so far? Our three victims are all the same age. Is that a coincidence, in your opinion?"

Emilianne scoffed. "I guess this can wait till Monday," she said, and hung up the phone.

"Definitely not a fluke!" she answered her partner. "They had twisted sexual habits, too. Justin abused whores, and Leo plugged a robot."

Her crude language made Henri cringe. But he kept his comments to himself. Manseau's collection of S&M magazines sprang back to mind but, again, he remained silent. He had no intention of adding fuel to Emilianne's fire.

Her hypothesis is grotesque.

"Croteau didn't have a sex life," he reminded her.

"That's according to his mother!" she pointed out. "The guy had a pair of balls in place of his brain, though!"

Pretending to think for a second, she kept going.

"We oughta send Desbiens over to examine the alpacas . . ."

"Saint-Gelais"—Henri groaned—"for pity's sake. And you wonder why I prefer to fly solo?"

"If you have a better theory, I'm all ears!"

The detective lieutenant did have one.

"Justin Manseau was in a wheelchair because he suffered from complications arising from his premature birth," he said. "As for Francis Carré-Croteau, he had a disability and coordination issues. Do we have any idea why?"

Emilianne flipped through the pages of her little black notebook but didn't find an explanation.

"I guess he was born with them," she said.

"Did he have a congenital condition?"

She tossed her notebook onto her desk and rolled her chair closer to Henri. He resisted the urge to count the cat hairs still clinging to her sweatshirt, knowing it would be futile.

"What do you have in mind, Duhaime? That Francis was born

early, too, like Justin? You're forgetting that Leopold didn't have a disability, as far as we know."

"He was psychologically fragile, to put it mildly," corrected Henri.

"Except that nobody's born socially anxious," Emilianne pressed on. "It was his mom who made him into a big chicken by mollycoddling him."

"But perhaps he had a predisposition to developing a phobia. And why was his mother so overprotective?"

"All right. Let's say that these three poor guys were all born too early. So what? They all had to die early, too? Where are your brilliant assumptions leading us, Duhaime?"

"Let's begin by confirming them."

Henri got up abruptly and walked out of the office, leaving his barely touched snack on his desk. Emilianne was right on his heels. Wrestling with one of her coat sleeves, she grabbed the nut bar and stuffed a piece of it in her mouth but spat it right back out again into its wrapper.

"Eww! What is this crap? No sugar, no salt, no fat? Damn it, Duhaime, how do you get any enjoyment out of life?"

BACK ON THE South Shore in the town of La Prairie, Henri stopped the car in front of the chain that was blocking access to the little shop at Abundance Farms. The farm was deserted. Closed until further notice. As Henri made a U-turn, Emilianne wriggled in the passenger seat, craning her neck to see the animal enclosure.

"What are you doing?" snapped Henri.

"The alpacas. Don't you think they're acting weird?"

"Honestly, Saint-Gelais, you're hopeless."

Three blocks away, at the Carré-Croteau home, it was Francis's sister, Camille, who opened the door for them. She pushed a pair of pink work boots out of the way and invited them into the living room. Her mother was kneeling on the floor, eyes closed and hands joined in prayer.

"The police are here," Camille announced.

Linda opened her eyes.

"Do you have any news?"

Henri had to admit to her that his team's attention had been diverted by the other two murders. Making the sign of the cross, Linda got up and sat on the sofa. Her daughter remained standing. By the looks on their faces, Henri could see that they had stayed away from any source of news for the past few days.

"Tell me, Mrs. Carré, was your son born prematurely?"

"What does that have to do with anything?" objected Patrice Croteau, walking into the room.

Henri didn't mince words.

"We're trying to establish a link between the three murders."

"Francis was born at twenty-five weeks," Linda confided.

"At which hospital?"

"At the center for mothers and infants at Sainte-Victorine hospital in Montreal."

"Three . . . three murders," Camille stammered. "So . . . Tom, Lucas, and J.B. didn't have anything to do with Francis's death?"

"They have not been removed from the list of suspects," Henri clarified.

"But you have other suspects, right?"

Henri didn't answer the question. Patrice joined his wife on the sofa, where they withdrew into painful silence. The detective lieutenant was about to leave them in peace when his sergeant asked Camille for a look at Francis's bedroom. The teenager took them upstairs and led them down the hall to the last door. With stuffed animals on the bed and superhero posters on the walls, it looked like a child's bedroom. Henri began rummaging around.

"What do you want to see, exactly?" Camille asked.

She's nervous, he noted.

"Camille," Emilianne began. "Your brother had several broken bones over the course of his life. Did anyone from youth protection services ever visit your family?"

Camille heaved a heart-wrenching sigh and looked up at the ceiling.

"Why don't you ask them yourself?"

"Your brother was an adult. If he had a file at YPS, it would have already been deleted. Besides, the police don't have access to those types of files."

Oh, bravo, Sergeant, fumed Henri. *Why would this young lady tell us the truth now?*

"It couldn't have been easy raising Francis," Emilianne continued. "Especially knowing it would be a lifetime commitment."

"Listen," Camille said dryly. "My parents really don't need you giving them a hard time about that. YPS did get a few calls about Frankie when he was younger, but none of them were legitimate. My mom and dad were never violent with him. He was clumsy and fragile and not afraid of anything. Not a good combo. My brother wanted to be like the other kids, do what they did, but he was different."

After a short pause, she went on.

"Open the window and look down."

Emilianne willingly complied.

"That's a heckuva drop!"

"Would you want to jump down there? Me neither. But Frankie did, and I promise you it never crossed his mind to be scared."

Francis Carré-Croteau wasn't afraid of anything, Henri recorded in a corner of his brain. *Leopold Dion, on the other hand, was afraid of his own shadow.*

IT WAS THE same story in Montreal North: Leopold Dion was a preemie, born during his mother's thirtieth week of pregnancy. While Henri was subtly snooping around the living room, Maryse showed Emilianne photos of Leo in his incubator. The infant was intubated and connected to various intravenous solutions and had electrodes attached to his chest, abdomen, and limbs.

"So many things could have gone wrong," Maryse recalled. "They had to constantly monitor his skin temperature, his heart rate, his breathing, the percentage of oxygen in his blood. His voice was barely audible—we couldn't even hear him cry because of the tube between his vocal cords. But when they finally took it out, he roared."

"He did well," Emilianne said. "He was lucky."

"I guess that's one way to look at it . . ."

Maryse closed the photo album, deep in thought.

"The labor could have been stopped if the doctors had gotten to me earlier. Then Leo would have been born at full term."

"Was it a case of malpractice?"

"There's nobody to blame." Maryse sighed. "The entire hospital staff was overwhelmed. If only I had gone into labor the night before or the day after . . ."

"Why was the hospital staff so overwhelmed?"

"It was the night of the big pileup of June 1994. You probably remember it."

"I've heard about it." Emilianne nodded. "But I was barely ten in '94."

"Oh . . ." said Maryse, embarrassed. "I thought . . . Well . . . There were nine deaths and quite a few injured."

"Nine fatalities!" exclaimed Emilianne, turning toward her partner. "Wait! Are we talking about the same accident? The one where Justin Manseau was taken from his mother's belly by emergency C-section?"

"It would appear so," said Henri. A look of satisfaction lit up his pallid face.

THE SUN WAS setting behind Emilianne, blinding Henri, who sat facing the window in the restaurant where they had stopped for a bite. She had just polished off a plate of lasagna and was now ordering a slice of sugar pie from the waitress. For his part, Duhaime had been content with a plain green salad, which he washed down with a glass of cool water.

"The lettuce isn't gonna grow inside you, Duhaime. That water's not doing anything for ya."

"You're hilarious, Saint-Gelais."

"Don't choke from laughing so hard."

At the start of the meal, a text message from Jason had confirmed what they already suspected: Francis Carré-Croteau, Leopold Dion, and Justin Manseau were all born in 1994, less than thirty-six hours apart, on Wednesday, June 8, or Thursday, June 9, at Sainte-Victorine Hospital. They had all stayed in the neonatal intensive-care unit at the same time.

Lost in thought, Henri was dabbing his mouth with his paper napkin.

"What, exactly, are you wiping?" Emilianne snapped. "There wasn't even any dressing on your salad. Think aloud, please!"

With some reluctance, Henri pointed out that there was a small possibility that the families of three young men could have met each other in the NICU.

"The only thing that seems clear to me at the moment is that we're dealing with three big perverts who were obsessed with sex."

"Honestly, Sergeant, I don't think . . ."

"Somebody put a pair of testicles in Crouteau's head, Duhaime! Seems to me the message is pretty clear!"

Emilianne kept her thoughts to herself while the waitress placed her dessert on the table and left.

"Is it possible that they could have teamed up to attack women?" she asked, gripping her fork. "And what if one of those women fought back? Bee Lenoir, for example."

"According to the lab, there's no chance Ms. Lenoir's heels made the holes on that trail."

He guessed that Emilianne was biting her tongue to avoid torturing him with an offensive joke. She contented herself with one irritating jab.

"Ms. *Lenoir* would've had no problem getting rid of the incriminating shoes before we made it to her place!"

"The forensics team can't verify that the holes were made by high heels. Let's not assume the killer is a woman. Manseau was in a wheelchair, Croteau was easily manipulated. But how many women could've taken on a beast like Leopold Dion with nothing but a kitchen knife?"

"He could've been drugged."

"The toxicology reports didn't show anything to support that."

"A few of the perverts' victims could've gotten together to stop them," Emilianne persisted.

"It doesn't hold up," Henri retorted. "Dion couldn't get anywhere near his apartment door without breaking into a cold sweat. How could he have assaulted a woman?"

"He could've taken inspiration from his pal Justin Manseau," said Emilianne, planting her fork in her pastry. "By paying her to come to him."

She was about to put a piece of pie her mouth when she frowned.

"Wait. What about Justin's heart? Where is it?" she asked suddenly.

14.

EARLY MONDAY MORNING, Henri and Emilianne sat down at a table in the archives room of Sainte-Victorine Hospital. The archivist, Étienne, feigned disinterest as they feverishly pored over the records of the infants admitted to the neonatal intensive-care unit around June 9, 1994. There were five of them. Justin Manseau, Kansas Noroît, and Leopold Dion were born the night of the crash—June ninth—while Francis Croteau and Maxime Legrand had arrived the previous day.

"Hey, here's another one with his mother's last name," noted Emilianne. "Max Legrand. Is that a name or a tautology? It's like calling your kid Big Big or Great Great . . ."

She did not succeed in distracting Henri.

"Kansas died about thirty hours after his birth, but Maxime survived," he noted. "Do you understand what that means, Saint-Gelais?"

“That we’d better get our asses in gear if we don’t want a fourth victim on our hands!”

Emilianne flagged down the archivist and asked permission to make a photocopy of the potential future victim’s records. The archivist, a serious man in his thirties, responded with a blank stare.

“Jeez, you’d think I asked if we could drown some kittens,” she muttered.

When he saw Henri take out his cell phone, Étienne jumped up.

“Your warrant allows you to consult the files, not to make copies or take photos!”

This was not Henri’s intention. The phone number in Maxime Legrand’s file still belonged to his mother, but the detective’s call went straight to voicemail.

“Mrs. Legrand, this is Detective Lieutenant Henri Duhaime. I’m trying to get ahold of your son, Maxime. Please return my call or ask him to call me as soon as possible.”

After carefully articulating the ten digits of his number, Henri emphasized the urgency of the situation and hung up.

“They were all under the care of the same doctor,” Emilianne realized, comparing the five newborns’ records.

“Dr. Gilles Lanouette,” Henri read aloud to the archivist. “Does he still work here?”

AT SEVENTY-FOUR YEARS of age, Dr. Lanouette no longer treated patients, but he was directing a research team on premature birth. Under a shock of white hair and a pair of rimless glasses, his affable face seemed to grow younger when Duhaime mentioned three of his former patients.

"Of course I remember them. But what does this . . ."

Having stood up to greet his visitors, he let himself fall back into his armchair. No details of the murders had been revealed by the media except the names of the victims.

"It's them, isn't it?" Lanouette mumbled. "I heard those names on the news and knew they sounded familiar, but I never would've guessed. There have been only three murders. Well, is—"

"We hope it's not too late for Maxime Legrand," Henri cut in. "I have a call in to his mother, and our colleagues are doing everything they can to find any other contact information on him."

Without even signaling to the detectives to take a seat, the doctor began frantically moving his computer mouse.

"I see Margaret Legrand about once a month," he said. She's the head of the OZ Foundation. Operation Zenith. They raise money for research on preterm birth. Her assistant, Claudia . . . Aha, here it is!"

Gilles Lanouette dialed Claudia's number and spoke with her briefly.

"Margaret has been traveling down south," he reported afterward. "Getting some well-deserved rest. But she's on her way back and should be home early tomorrow morning. As for Claudia, she doesn't have any way of contacting Maxime. Apparently he and Margaret fell out of touch a number of years ago."

"Let's hope she knows where to find him, at least," sighed Emilianne.

"Good grief!" Lanouette lamented. "Who could possibly have wanted to go after those poor boys?"

He cocked his head as though he had an idea and held up a bony index finger.

"A group of *capacitistas* has been demonstrating in front of the hospital quite a bit these days. Some of the staff is afraid of them."

"*Capacitistas*?" repeated Emilianne, raising an eyebrow. "What does that type of critter eat in winter?"

"They eat their fellow humans, Sergeant Saint-Gelais. The ones I'm talking about call themselves the Winged Monkeys. They are a dangerous group of extremists who subscribe to ideas inspired by Aktion T4, Adolf Hitler's 'euthanasia' program. In case you don't know, that was a policy of elimination that concerned not only Jews but also people with any kind of disability. And like the Nazis, the Winged Monkeys believe that these people are a burden on society—that they're of no use and therefore don't deserve to live. In addition to their despicable views on disability, they also target extremely premature babies. Those fanatics believe we should let them die without providing any medical care."

Emilianne was visibly excited.

"When was the last time they had a rally?"

"At Sainte-Victorine, about a week and a half ago, but they stage events all over the city. They go to hospitals, nursing homes, assisted-living facilities, psychiatric establishments, prisons. It's not a big group, but they're making more and more noise."

"In your opinion, Doctor, are the Winged Monkeys crazy enough to have committed three murders?"

"Well . . . those masked illuminati don't mind starting fights. Something is seriously wrong with them, that's for sure!"

Henri's cell phone vibrated. He glanced at it, stood up, thanked Dr. Lanouette for his cooperation, and left the office. Emilianne handed her business card to the doctor, urged him to get in touch if he thought of anything, and joined her superior in the hallway.

"Yes, hello, Desbiens, I'm listening," he was saying. "Manseau's dog, yes . . . He had *what* on his teeth besides blood? Vaginal secretions?"

"Holy shit!" Emilianne blurted out. "What kind of degenerates are we dealing with here? Guess I was a bit off, huh, with the alpacas . . ."

As Henri continued his conversation with the medical examiner, Emilianne placed a call to Bee Lenoir. Two minutes later, they both pocketed their phones. In a state of shock, Henri spontaneously briefed Emilianne on the latest developments.

"Desbiens doesn't know yet who the blood and secretions belong to, but they're two different DNA samples. Did you get ahold of Bee? For the love of god, please don't tell me . . ."

"Breathe, Duhaime. She didn't get her kitty licked by the mutant dog. But she did see him chewing her panties. He might've actually swallowed them, because she left there without 'em."

15.

DAVID BONNIER HAD been sitting around police headquarters for three hours when his interrogation finally began. Planted firmly in his chair with his arms crossed, he clearly had no intention of letting himself be intimidated. With the sleeves of his jacket rolled up to his elbows, he treated the detectives to his heavily inked forearms. Alone with him in the interrogation room, Emilianne had her fingers hooked through her belt loops and was sitting like him, her legs spread wide, projecting the same cocky self-confidence. There was only the corner of a table between them.

"How'd you fix the corn you bought at the farm, Bonnier? Butter and salt, or did you make a shepherd's pie?"

"Hey, Jesus Christ! I don't have all day. Why don't you tell me what I'm accused of, ma'am?"

Through the one-way mirror, Henri saw the sergeant slide three photos in front of the suspect, all of the same pretty young woman in a bikini.

"I'm here to look at sexy pictures of my wife?"

Emilianne continued as if she hadn't heard him. "Your wife posted these photos of herself on September thirtieth."

"Yeah, so?"

"So? She was at a spa with her friends. But you told us that she was with you and your kids at Abundance Farms, picking corn."

A dismissive snort escaped David's nose.

"You believe everything you see on Facebook? Just because the photos were posted on the thirtieth doesn't mean they were taken on the thirtieth."

Emilianne opened and closed her thighs three times in a row like she was clapping with her knees.

"You're sticking to your story, then, huh? It was Sunday, September thirtieth when you touched the cornfield gate?"

"Indeed, your ladyship. There's no other day it could've been."

"That's funny, Bonnier, because that Sunday, the cornfield was already closed to the public. The stalks were still standing, but there wasn't a single damn ear of corn left."

The suspect leaned forward, moving closer to Emilianne like he was about to grab her by the throat, but instead put on his sweetest voice to explain himself.

"What I said was that we took our kids to the farm to pick corn, not that we actually picked it. When the kids saw the empty field, they started crying. They weren't in the mood for picking apples. My wife got a call from a friend, so she took off for the spa, leaving me with the kids."

David Bonnier's story reminded Emilianne of a small detail. As she left the room, she walked past Henri, muttering to herself.

"It wasn't blood. It was red paint."

She confirmed her hypothesis in a quick call to Patrice Croteau, and returned to the room that held the suspect with a victorious smile.

"You're a good liar," she complimented him. "But your problem, Bonnier, is that I can prove you put your greasy fingers on the cornfield gate sometime between sunset on Saturday, October sixth and sunrise the next day. Do I need to remind you that this is the exact time frame when Francis Carré-Croteau was tortured and killed?"

David scoffed but seemed less confident all of a sudden.

"How could you know that? You can't date a fingerprint."

Emilianne stuck her fingers back through her belt loops and ignored his amateur investigation knowledge.

"Patrice Croteau spent his sixth of October painting his fence. And he finished with the gate, if you see what I'm saying. If someone left their fingerprints in the fresh paint, it had to have been a few hours before or after the murder."

Having successfully silenced her suspect, she continued.

"What I can conclude here is that you attended a children's party, Monsieur Bonnier. You like 'em young, huh? You prefer girls or boys?"

"Whoa, don't go making shit up!"

"What the hell were you doing there, Bonnier? It's not a hard question!"

A few seconds went by, and David Bonnier finally decided that it was in his interest to come clean.

"One of the kids wanted to buy something from me. I was in the area, so I agreed to make a delivery."

Bonnier's tough-guy facade was crumbling. Emilianne shifted in her seat, took her little black notebook out of her back pocket, and wrote down the name of his client: Lucas Colin, along with the drug he had bought—crack.

"You gotta believe me, I'm just a dealer! I didn't kill anybody!"

"Did you see Croteau at the party? Skinny blond guy in overalls and a plaid shirt."

"The dimwit?" he asked, surprised. "Yeah, I saw him, and he was totally alive when I left. Colin and his buddies had put him in charge of protecting the girls from the bat that was circling the field."

Emilianne looked incredulous.

"So then what? Croteau impales himself on a pitchfork trying to get rid of a bat?"

"I didn't see any pitchfork, personally. Colin made the guy stand there in the middle of everybody with his arms out like a scarecrow. It was making them all laugh."

"And you didn't step in?"

"After I just sold them crack? No, it didn't occur to me to lecture them. Anyway, a girl showed up shouting at everybody. She wanted them to clear out. And then she started yelling at the dimwit."

"What did she look like?"

"Like all the other girls, but prettier. Long blond hair, pink work boots. I did hear her say, 'Damn it, Frankie, are we gonna have to tie you up to keep you out of trouble?'"

16.

MARGARET LEGRAND LIVED in a lavish two-story house in a wealthy neighborhood on the West Island. Although it was very early when the detectives knocked on her door that Tuesday morning, she opened up right away, looking wide-awake and ready for visitors despite having just arrived from the airport. Surprised by the woman's appearance, Henri paused for a moment before speaking.

I seem to have overlooked a minor detail in my review of her medical records.

From the look on Emilianne's face, the detective lieutenant could tell that, like him, she had also made some false assumptions. They were expecting to meet a woman in her fifties, or early sixties at the most. With a string of pearls around her neck and immaculate hair and makeup, Margaret Legrand was exquisitely put together, but the honey-brown shade of her hair wasn't fooling anyone.

She must be at least seventy years old.

"What may I help you with?" she inquired sternly as she pulled on the string of the tea bag that was steeping in her cup.

Regaining composure, Henri got straight to the point, as usual. He introduced himself, forgot about his colleague, and brought up the murders that were rattling the region.

"I've just returned to the country, Lieutenant Duhaime, but yes, I did read an article about this in the car home from the airport."

"We have reason to believe that your son, Maxime, could be the killer's next victim."

The tea bag sank to the bottom of the cup.

"I beg your pardon?"

"May we come in?"

Shaken, the woman took a step back, allowing the detectives to enter the front hall of her home, but she made no move to invite them into the living room.

"The names of those young men did ring a faint bell," she said, casually running her fingers over her pearls. "Could they have been childhood friends of Maxime's?"

Henri briefed her on the circumstances of their births.

"Perhaps you could tell me if they saw each other again at any point," he added.

"Saw each other again?" Margaret snapped. "No. Why would they . . . That's ridiculous!"

"And you? Did you stay in touch with any of the mothers of those young men?"

"One of them—the farmer—made regular donations to my foundation, but our paths never crossed again. She sent her checks in the mail. Why would a killer go after those young men in particular? It's absurd! Couldn't it be a coincidence?"

"I'd be surprised!" interjected Emilianne. "You'd better warn your son, Margaret, and quick!"'

Mrs. Legrand bit her lip. Looking distraught, she shook her head.

"I don't know where he lives. My darling angel! He left home at seventeen and hasn't bothered to keep in touch since then."

Admitting this appeared difficult for Margaret, but she held her head high.

"Don't worry about Maxime," she implored the officers. "I hired private detectives on several occasions in the hopes of tracking him down, but they all came up empty-handed. Your killer couldn't catch him if he tried."

"Let's not take that risk," insisted Emilianne. "How about we find him first? You must have a photo of him that we could release to the media."

Stunned, Margaret turned to Henri.

"You want to release his picture to the media? Might as well kill him with your own hands!"

"My colleague has a quirky sense of humor," Henri said, attempting to make up for Emilianne's blunder. "We would never publish your son's photo or his name, Mrs. Legrand. Under no circumstances would he be used as bait. On the other hand, perhaps you have a photo for our files . . ."

"I'll get one for you."

Abandoning her cup of tea somewhere along the way, Mrs. Legrand returned with a photo of her son in a graduation cap and gown, diploma in hand. The teenager was looking at the camera with a frozen smile, but what stood out were his bright green eyes. Margaret also handed the detective a piece of paper.

"Release this name and description," she said. "If Maxime hears that message, he'll know it's for him."

Skimming the text, Henri bowed his head and thanked her.

"Maxime was born during your twenty-third week of pregnancy," he noted. "Has he experienced any long-term effects as a result?"

The lady's angular face lit up.

"None at all! Maxime is a miracle baby. He came out of it unscathed! I created Operation Zenith to help those parents who were less fortunate than I. Ever since Maxime was born, I have dedicated my body and soul to the cause. In the summertime, I host fundraising evenings right here in my garden."

Stepping forward, Emilianne once again took over the questioning.

"Do you have any enemies, Margaret?"

The woman looked perplexed, and Emilianne clarified.

"Have your benefit evenings ever been disrupted?"

"The only one who ever disrupted those evenings was Maxime himself. Always ready to put on a show."

"And what about the Winged Monkeys, does that name sound familiar?"

Margaret's expression darkened.

"That bunch of Nazi chimps?" she sneered. "They highlight a handful of horrific cases of premature babies without ever mentioning the miracle children! They tried to cause trouble at my place once, but they didn't get past security. They had to take their monkey business elsewhere."

CHANELLE LEDOUX STRUTTED through the city in her high heels, with the wind lifting her skirt and blowing through her long blond curls. Even the most well-intentioned men and their modern etiquette flew out the window when she crossed their path. That day, the first person who dared such rudeness was treated to a fake smile, the second was ignored, and the third was given the finger. Once she made it home, Chanelle made sure nobody was following her before locking the door.

Finally free from prying eyes, the young woman liberated her feet from her heels and heaved a sigh of relief. She unbuttoned her coat, pulled her arms under her blouse, and unhooked her bra. Then, holding her handbag under her arm, she bent over to pick up her shoes.

Anyone who had spent time with the dazzling Chanelle Ledoux would have been astonished to see the interior of the old stone house she rented. The architecture was certainly unique, but instead of the extravagance and frivolity one might have expected, she owned only the bare essentials, and in their most classic forms. Within the off-white walls there was not a hint of color from a plant, cushion, or any other decorative object. And the curtains remained stubbornly closed in this place that looked to all the world like a bachelor pad.

Chanelle headed straight for the door to the basement and unlocked it with a key. Taking her coat, heels, and bag, she left nothing behind. She proceeded down a rough wooden staircase that was wedged between two walls and arrived at a large, darkened room. The concrete floor felt ice-cold beneath her feet, which were sheathed in sheer stockings. Some of the ceiling tiles were missing, revealing a jumble of wires and pipes.

The cellar was full of clothes, from the most elegant to the most basic, hanging on long, commercial-style clothing racks. There was also a faded pink armchair and a shelving unit full of mannequin heads wearing a wide assortment of wigs. Against a wall that was decorated with two broad white curtain panels was a dressing table with several drawers, on top of which sat a large makeup mirror framed by at least a dozen light bulbs. A portable 1960s-style television stood on the dressing table, surrounded by piles of products: wig glue, bottles of hair dye and nail polish, tubes of foundation, powders, lipsticks, makeup brushes, and hairbrushes.

It was like the dressing room of a faded star.

Chanelle put away her coat and stilettos among the heaps of clothes, then sat down on the padded wooden stool, faced the mirror, and switched on the light. A warm white light spread over her face. She turned on the television and selected a news channel, which she left playing in the background without really listening to it. She pulled off her stockings, exposing her perfectly waxed legs. Her calves were not all that feminine—a little too muscular and angular—but she knew that her generous bosom made up for this minor flaw. The young woman slipped out of her bra, which she tossed over the arm of the chair. Her breasts fell away with the garment, revealing a flat torso every bit as hairless as her legs. Around the sternum, the skin was puckered with scars.

The blond wig joined the bra on the armchair, and the false eyelashes were peeled off. With the help of some makeup remover, the face reflected in the mirror was soon cleansed of all artifice. Finally, the impostor removed the contact lenses that had given a blue shade to his eyes, and he smiled at himself as if to say hello. But as always, when Max Legrand was confronted with his true face, his smile quickly faded. He was remembering himself in front of a different mirror. With a blink, he shook off a mortifying memory of himself—completely naked, red with humiliation, his penis shriveled—and removed Chanelle's phone from her bag.

I did it! he congratulated himself.

The money he had been waiting for had indeed been transferred to one of his accounts. Three dinners, a peck on the cheek, and the implied promise of sexual favors had been enough to persuade a middle-aged man who barely knew Chanelle Ledoux to invest his life savings in the restaurant that she was supposedly about to open.

By the time that horny fool realizes that he's been had, the lovely Chanelle will be nowhere to be found.

As for Max Legrand, he had already set his sights on another victim. Whether he was posing as a man or a woman, regardless of their background, he was believable. With his magnetic charm, he could fool almost anyone.

Max got up, hooked the bra with the built-in breasts on a hanger, and placed Chanelle's wig on one of the Styrofoam heads. One of the other heads had blond hair, too, but it was darker, shorter, and wavy. The last time the scammer had worn that wig, he called himself Adrien Lalande—he spoke with a French accent, and his fiancée, the fabulously wealthy Cassandra Bellerive, was busily planning their wedding. The hair of the next wig over was even shorter, dark brown, and combed in the style worn by Hubert Dagenais when he met Roxanne, the financial advisor.

When Max sat back down in front of the television, a police spokesperson was asking the public for help in finding a potential future victim of the dangerous serial killer who was on the loose in the area.

"—good reason to fear for the life of Mateo Acosta, a young man of Hispanic origin born in 1994 at Sainte-Victorine Hospital in Montreal. Anyone with any information . . ."

"You nasty old witch!" Maxime shouted at the screen.

And to think that in society, his mother was considered a do-gooder and enjoyed a spotless reputation. Maxime punched the dressing table's central mirror, shattering it and splitting his face into a hundred tiny pieces.

You have plenty of different faces, too, Mother. And someday, the ugliest one will be revealed.

17.

IN THE DEPTHS of Max's memory there was an image of his hand disappearing completely into his mother's. He must have been four years old. He wasn't going to school yet, but, thanks to his mother's efforts, he already knew how to read.

The sun was setting, coloring the lavender sky a peachy pink. A scent of humidity and sugar hung in the air. If the evening had ended without incident, Max's memory of it would probably have been limited to those colors, those smells, and a vague feeling of having been stared at, scrutinized. Perhaps he wouldn't have even remembered the party at all. But the events that had disrupted the benefit evening had left an indelible mark on him, burning him, digging deep into his flesh.

The gathering took place in the backyard of the stately home where the miracle child lived with his mother. Tasty little hors d'oeuvres quickly vanished from their trays and were replaced by pastries. Boys and girls were running all around the child. Slightly older than him for the most part, they laughed and teased him as they weaved between the adults. Max wasn't allowed to join them. They spied on him and ran away if he looked at them. Drinks in hand, the adults also watched the miracle child on display by his mother. They gawked at him as if he were an animal in a zoo.

A talented and rare animal.

Sometimes women would even hug him and weep.

Maxime didn't mind. He liked being the center of attention. People kept telling him he was handsome, charming, and highly intelligent. This made the boy proud, because these qualities represented hope for parents who, like his mother, had given birth to babies who were too eager to see the world.

His mother called him up to the stage where, earlier that evening, her speeches and those from Dr. Lanouette had earned them warm rounds of applause. Beaming with pride as she gave her little miracle a tender look, she turned to her generous donors.

"Maxime will now recite for you his favorite fable of La Fontaine!"

The first verses came to him effortlessly.

"'At the top of a tree perched Master Crow; in his beak he was holding a cheese.'"

To encourage him, his mother punctuated each syllable he uttered with a curt nod.

"'Drawn by the smell, Master Fox spoke, below. The words, more or less, were these: "Hey, now, Sir Crow! Good day, good day!"'"

For the fox's lines, Max had used a different voice, deeper and with a bit of a drawl. He thought this suited the cunning character perfectly. Then, as his mother had taught him, he looked up at the crowd while continuing to recite his fable.

"'No lie, if those songs you wing . . . ' Uh, no. 'If those songs you sing match the plumage of your wing . . . '"

Max had been thrown off because a boy, half hidden behind his parents, had made a face at him. Distracted, he tried again.

"'You're the Felix of these woods, our choice.'"

A few chuckles rippled through the audience. There was nothing mean-spirited about it, and it was nothing more than a murmur. Not knowing what had provoked it, the child carried on.

"'To show off his handsome voice, he opened beak wide and let go . . . '"

Not seeing his mother in the front row anymore, Max stopped abruptly. Then, as best he could, anxiety gripping his throat, he finished reciting his fable. He accepted the rounds of applause, politely thanked the audience, and skipped off in search of his mother. Since the guests were about to leave the party, she would normally have been there to wish them good night.

"Mama?" cried the boy, scanning the crowd.

He didn't find her with Dr. Lanouette or among her wealthiest and most faithful donors, whom she made a point of fussing over.

What could have happened for her to disappear without hearing the end of the fable she had made him practice for hours on end?

Suddenly, the little boy felt himself being pulled backward. Hidden from view behind a tall bush, his mother had him by the collar.

"How could you embarrass me like that, Maxime Legrand?! I didn't know what to do with myself! Go wait for me in your room, you worthless little shit!"

It was the first time his mother had ever spoken to him in that tone or used that kind of language with him. Her words stung. So much so that as soon as he got to his room, he inspected himself in the mirror to try to figure out what was wrong.

I'm not bleeding.

He didn't see any bruises on his body.

I must have a fever.

So Max got into bed, with his favorite teddy bear snuggled up in his arms. He was just drifting off to sleep when the door of his room burst open. He jumped. His mother was holding a thick wooden ruler with a metal edge.

"Am I sick?" The little boy yawned.

"That's your excuse for making me look a fool?" the woman scoffed. "'You're the *Felix* of these woods, our choice,'" she chided him.

"'You're . . . you're the *phoenix* of these woods, our choice,'" he stammered in a meek voice.

"Who's going to take out their wallet to save the children if the only miracle they can hope for is a stupid little brat? Huh?"

Max's mother was beside herself. He had never seen her like this. A vein in her neck was bulging and looked about ready to burst.

"I'm going to tell you a secret, my boy. Miracles don't exist. *I'm* the one who saved you. I made you work hard. I raised you in a stimulating environment."

The child, who had always considered his mother very beautiful, suddenly thought she looked like a witch. Why hadn't he ever noticed her pointy nose, her protruding cheekbones, her angular chin?"

"Growing up in another family, neglected by less conscientious, less competent parents, you would undoubtedly have developed learning difficulties and all kinds of problems. Is that what you would have wanted?"

"No . . ."

Grabbing his heavy book of fables off a shelf, she tossed it onto her son's lap, and he stifled a cry of surprise and pain.

"Page forty-two," she commanded.

Max turned the pages of the book. His mother began tapping a brisk rhythm against her own thigh with the wooden ruler. The young boy picked up the pace, trying hard to match her tempo.

He read the title of the fable on page forty-two: "The Animals Sick of the Plague." This story was much longer than "The Crow and the Fox" and contained several words the four-year-old did not understand.

"I'm warning you, you little good-for-nothing, do not close your eyes until you've learned this text by heart!"

Max's mother was older than the other moms. Until that night, this detail had never bothered the boy. But as she would soon explain to him, she came from a time when parents believed in tough love.

And Margaret Legrand loved her son. She was absolutely devoted to him.

18.

EMILIANNE CONFRONTED CAMILLE Carré-Croteau with the words she had allegedly spoken a few hours before her brother's brainless body was discovered.

"'Damn it, Frankie, are we gonna have to tie you up to keep you out of trouble?' You can't make this stuff up, Camille! Why didn't you tell us you were at the party?"

"No . . ."

Wearing her pink work boots, the girl was in tears.

"Weren't you?"

"Yeah, but I . . ."

"You never said those words?"

"Yeah, but . . . it was just a thing I said. I never wanted anything bad to happen to my brother!"

Investigator Jason Jobin walked into the interrogation room with a box of tissues and sat down next to Emilianne.

"Why don't you tell us everything from the beginning?" he suggested gently.

The girl wiped her tears, blew her nose, and let it all out.

"I realized something wasn't right when I went up to bed around eleven thirty. Frankie's door was closed, which was weird because he always keeps it open. He wasn't there, and his window was open. Since our parents were already asleep, I was able to sneak out. Music was coming from the farm, so that's why I ran over there. There were about thirty kids in the cornfield. Frankie . . . He . . ."

She paused, wiped her nose again, and continued.

"He didn't want to go home with me. He said he was protecting the girls from a rat or something. I told him he could have ten more minutes. In the meantime, an older guy—maybe thirty years old—showed up on a motorcycle. Lucas bought some drugs from him. Then after ten minutes, Frankie still didn't want to go home. I could tell that if I kept pushing, he was gonna freak out on me."

"You were sick and tired of always taking care of him, right?"

She answered Emilianne with a sheepish nod.

"That's why I decided to relax a little for a change. After a couple of drinks, I let Tom talk me into going to the shed with him."

"Tom Barthelemy? The big guy with the freckles?"

The teenager nodded again.

"Good-looking kid," Emilianne said. "He's your ex, correct? So you fell right back into his arms? Despite the way he treated your brother?"

"Tom isn't mean," Camille said in his defense. "He's the one who helps Lucas and J.B. settle down when they get out of hand."

"Except that this time, Tom was in the shed. With you."

"We were barely a hundred yards away from Frankie," she argued. "We could hear him laughing. How could we have guessed . . ."

"Guessed what, Camille? What did they do to Francis?"

"We weren't planning on staying out there very long, but somebody thought they were being funny and took our clothes. By the time Tom found them, my brother was tied to the pole, upside down. J.B. had stuck a hose in Frankie's butt and was holding the other end, and Lucas was pouring vodka in it."

"What did you say?!" Jason couldn't believe his ears.

"It speeds up the effect of the alcohol," Emilianne explained. "Makes it more intense. You never heard that, J.J.? More and more popular with the kids these days. Good way to save a few bucks. Drunk off their asses, you could say!"

Resisting the urge to congratulate his colleague on her dubious play on words, Jason motioned to Camille to continue her story.

"I yelled at them to stop," she said. "Lucas tried to pretend like it was my idea, because of what I had said earlier. They turned the post right side up. Frankie was laughing, having a great time. He was completely wasted. I pulled his shorts back up. Tom wanted to untie him but I . . . I stopped him."

Camille's voice broke. The detectives waited for her to find the strength to go on.

"I couldn't take Frankie back to the house like that, y'know? He had fallen asleep, so I thought it would be better to let the alcohol wear off and then come back and get him at sunrise before my parents got up. Tom tricked everyone into thinking that the cops—sorry—that the *police* were coming. In, like, two minutes everybody had cleared out. I went home and told myself that Frankie wouldn't even remember seeing me at the party. That he wouldn't remember anything. But then I went back a few hours later when the rooster crowed, and . . ."

"He was dead," Emilianne finished for her.

"If I hadn't . . ." Camille burst into tears again.

Uncomfortable, Jason pushed the box of tissues toward her, picked up her file, and excused himself.

"Is it over?" sniffled the teenager. "I'm gonna call Tom to come get me."

This last remark seemed to shock Emilianne more than the story of the hose up the backside.

"Tom may not be the worst one in his group of friends, but . . . Camille, what about taking a step back?"

"You know something I don't know?"

"You could find yourself a good boy . . . A pretty girl like you!"

"It's not like I deserve to have anything good happen to me."

Emilianne leaned in and whispered to the teenager. "Don't blame yourself for your brother's death. We have good reason to believe that the killer would've gotten him anyway. If it hadn't been that night, it would've been some other time. That said, you all sure did make his job easier for him."

"You have a suspect? Have you arrested him?"

"The investigation is making progress, Camille, that's all I can tell you. An officer will take you home to your parents."

WHEN EMILIANNE ASKED Henri what he thought of the story Camille had just told her, she didn't get much of an answer.

"Huh."

The detective lieutenant's head was clearly elsewhere. Seated at his desk, he was studying the photo in his hands.

"What a dumbass!" Emilianne cursed herself, turning toward Jason. "I actually thought he let us handle the questioning without him because he trusted us, but it was just that he didn't give a shit!"

Henri raised his head for a split second.

"We're looking for someone who could've committed all three murders. I think you'll agree that the Carré-Croteau girl doesn't fit that profile."

"I'm not saying she does," grumbled the sergeant, slumping down into her chair. "But she runs around with Barthelemy and the other two twerps, who are probably somehow connected to the Wicked Wolves."

"Only between your own ears, Saint-Gelais," Henri objected.

"Between my ears? You're the one who suggested that those guys might've been recruited by the gang!"

Jason, who had been deep in thought as he tapped away at his keyboard, suddenly noticed something that didn't make sense.

"If Croteau had alcohol in his blood, isn't it strange that Desbiens never mentioned it?"

"That little witch!" shouted Emilianne. "If she made that whole thing up . . ."

She called the medical examiner from the office landline and put him on speaker phone as soon as he picked up.

"Apparently Croteau was hammered," she told him. "Those little fuckers think that if you drink through your butthole, you won't be caught! That's not true, is it? Had Croteau been drinking?"

"It's easy to detect alcohol in a living body, Sergeant, no matter how it was ingested," Desbiens replied. "On the other hand, test results on corpses are unreliable, since bacteria in the body produces ethanol after death. This makes it impossible to determine with absolute certainty whether a person consumed alcohol before expiring."

Muttering a few words of thanks for the clarification, Emilianne hung up.

"Did you know that about ethanol, Duhaime?"

His mind still somewhere else, Henri didn't hear his colleague.

"Bingo!" Jason blurted out as he stopped typing. "David Bonnier, our dealer, has a cousin who's a member of the Wicked Wolves!"

When she heard this, Emilianne opened her arms wide, as if the case were closed.

"That doesn't mean a thing," Henri said. "Montreal is a big village."

"You're just jealous, Duhaime."

"Bonnier couldn't have killed Croteau," he retorted. "A forensic report came in while you were questioning Camille. Thanks to the marks left behind by his shoes and motorcycle tires, we know that when he got there, he made a U-turn in front of the fence and only put one foot on the ground, not two. He must've touched the gate to hold himself steady. He left without getting off his bike."

"OK, so maybe Bonnier didn't kill him," Emilianne was willing to acknowledge. "But there's nothing saying he didn't tell the kids to do it."

As Henri turned his attention back to the photo he had been staring at, the sergeant got up, hooked her thumbs through her belt loops, and, stepping away from her desk, went and peered over his shoulder.

"So it's Max Legrand who's got you so worked up, Duhaime?"

"I know this guy," mumbled Henri. "I'm sure I do. But I can't put my finger on where I've seen him before . . ."

"Seriously, with a name like that and eyes that color, it'd be hard to forget him."

An awful feeling was eating at Henri.

"What if Maxime Legrand isn't our next victim?" he asked. "What if he's our killer?"

Emilianne's thumbs shot out of her belt loops, and she threw her arms up in the air.

"For fuck's sake, Duhaime! What's that crazy idea based on? And you want us to forget the Wicked Wolves, even though we can tie them to two of the three crime scenes? Maybe even all three! We know that those guys are into prostitution. And who was bringing sex workers to his trailer? And then Bee Lenoir, the masochist, did you know she goes by the name Bee Black? Acupuncturist, my ass!"

Without looking up from his photo of Max, Henri dismissed his underling's presumptions with a wave of his arm.

"We didn't find anything on Ms. Lenoir, Saint-Gelais. And anyway, you might as well try to fuck a fly."

Jason looked up from his screen. He and Emilianne exchanged a glance.

"Fuck a fly?" she repeated, stunned. "That's pretty vulgar, Lieutenant. Want me to get some soap and wash out your mouth?"

Determined to pursue the Wicked Wolves lead, she told them she would get Maryse Normandin, the first victim's mother, down to the station as soon as humanly possible.

"We'll show her a few photos, with a couple of Bonnier and his cousin mixed in. If it was one of those guys who followed her to her son's house that night, she'll be able to identify him."

"Jobin, didn't you bring that police sketch to the sergeant's attention?"

"What police sketch?" Emilianne wondered, already alarmed to see Henri's mouth forming something that almost looked like a smile.

"The one that was created with the help of Maryse Normandin's specifications. Show her, Jobin."

Chuckling to himself, the investigator dug through one of the drawers in his desk and produced a blank sheet of paper, which he held up high so Emilianne could get a good look at it.

"What's the joke?"

"After wasting precious minutes of the forensic artist's time, Madame Normandin finally admitted that she hadn't seen the man's face. She's not even sure anymore that anyone was following her."

Emilianne was not about to give up so easily.

"The Wicked Wolves threatened her!" she argued.

Henri waved the photo of Max Legrand in the air.

"Let's focus on the most urgent matter, Saint-Gelais! Where is this man?"

"I don't think it's all that urgent," replied Emilianne, sitting back down. "He's gotta be dead already. And stuffed like a turkey with Manseau's heart."

Henri's phone rang. He took the call, listened, mumbled, and hung up.

"Camille Carré-Croteau just dialed nine-one-one," he told his colleagues. "When she got home, she found her mother dead. Mrs. Carré had swallowed the contents of three bottles of sleeping pills.

Officers are on the scene, and the coroner is opening an investigation, but all signs point to suicide."

"Fuck. Poor Camille!" cursed Emilianne. "I should've let her call Tom."

After a few seconds of silence, during which Henri once again immersed himself in contemplating Max Legrand's face, Emilianne spoke up.

"We still haven't looked into the Winged Monkeys, even though Bergevin asked us to prioritize that lead. J.J., did you find the names and addresses of the protesters for me?"

"I'm on it, Em."

"And what about our lovely Aimee?" she continued. "Did she witness the murder of Leopold Dion, yes or no? We've got to ask the IT guy again, J.J."

At that moment, Henri practically sprang out of his chair. Emilianne was startled to see such a reaction from him.

"What's going on? You still breathing, Duhaime? Need me to give you mouth-to-mouth?"

"I know who it is!" he exclaimed, tapping the photo vigorously with his index finger. "I investigated him for economic fraud! He had a different name, he looked completely different, and I only saw him on surveillance camera footage, but it's definitely him. I'd bet my shirt on it!"

"You ever heard him string that many words together at once?" Emilianne asked Jason. "Want a glass of water, Duhaime? Take a day off, maybe?"

"He's not getting away from me this time," Henri vowed.

"A con artist is not the same thing as a murderer," Jason dared to point out. "Just because he—"

"He's dangerous!" said Henri. "Last year a young woman killed herself because of him. You think that stopped him from committing more crimes?"

Grabbing his phone, the detective dialed, from memory, the work number of a former colleague and spoke with him about a certain Raphael Delorme.

"Get me his file, would you? I'll be at your office in ten minutes."

Henri promised the person he was speaking to that he was finally going to nail the little bastard. As he put down the phone, he was surprised to hear it ring again, and he picked it back up. He listened attentively, uttered a few "uh-huhs" and "mm-hmms," and hung up.

"Whoever was bitten by Manseau's dog is not in our database," he told Emilianne and Jason.

"So it can't be your Raphael Delorme," Emilianne concluded.

"Delorme probably isn't on file," Henri replied. "He's a slippery one. Nobody has ever gotten their hands on him. We call him Raphael Delorme because that's the name he was using when he first caught our attention, but we suspect him of operating under a number of other identities. Mateo Acosta is probably just another one of them!"

The detective lieutenant stood up with a crack of his knees and put on his coat. Before leaving the office, he shared with Emilianne another piece of information that the forensic scientist had just given him.

"There was no underwear in the dog's stomach."

"What?!" the woman cried. "Then where are those dang panties?"

"Honestly, Saint-Gelais, if you think Bee Lenoir's undergarments are going to solve the case, then go ahead and look for them."

WITH RAPHAEL DELORME'S file in his briefcase, Henri was walking to his car when a taxi stopped in the middle of the parking lot, blocking his way. The person in the back seat lowered his window.

"Detective Lieutenant Duhaime? I hear you're looking for Mateo Acosta."

Henri's heart stopped. For a couple of seconds he thought he was having a cardiac event. He couldn't believe it.

That's him. The one who's been slipping through my fingers for nearly three years.

When he had looked at Max Legrand's graduation photo, Henri had assumed it was a trick of the light, but it turned out that his actual eyes were every bit as green as they appeared in the picture.

Through a colossal feat of willpower, the detective managed to keep his cool. Had he followed his instincts, he would have grabbed the con man by the collar, yanked him out of the cab headfirst, and taken him to the police station himself.

"You're the one I'm looking for, Mr. Legrand. Pay your fare and come with me . . ."

"I'm in a hurry. What's this about a murderer? Why would I be a target?"

Henri clenched his fists. His knuckles cracked. As he fought the urge to respond with the same level of rudeness, his Adam's apple bounced up and down for a few seconds. The young man seemed genuinely surprised, but the lieutenant wasn't buying it. He knew that the scoundrel had a talent for lying and that he could tailor his facial expression to any situation.

A master of disguise.

Henri could easily imagine Max Legrand in high heels and a wig, pushing Justin Manseau's wheelchair toward the cliff.

"You share certain characteristics with the victims, Mr. Legrand."

"We're the same age. What else?"

You know more than I do, don't you?

"I can't tell you anything more in this parking lot."

Guessing that Maxime was getting ready to roll up the taxi window, Henri put his hand on the window frame.

"For your own security, Mr. Legrand, I'm going to need your address along with a phone number that will allow the police to reach you at all times."

The young man readily complied.

"Until further notice," Henri advised him, "a car will be patrolling your street. Someone will also keep watch at your house."

"No need. I'll double-bolt the lock."

The detective pictured the multitude of bolts and chains that were supposed to have protected Leopold Dion's apartment. They had turned out to be useless.

"Suit yourself, Mr. Legrand. Don't trust anyone."

The taxi left the parking lot, and Henri jumped into his own vehicle.

I know who you are, asshole.

As he trailed the taxi, the detective lieutenant was oblivious to the fact that he, too, was being followed.

19.

IN FRONT OF the little crowd assembled in Margaret Legrand's garden, Dr. Lanouette was expounding on the progress of his research. Flavie and Maya, nine and ten years old, weren't listening. Their eyes were glued to a mysterious boy dressed in black pants and a white shirt. He was twelve, maybe thirteen, with dark hair and a tan complexion, and the top half of his face was hidden behind a pair of dark glasses. As the sun was just beginning to set, if the girls had had their own sunglasses, they would have been able to admire him without squinting.

"You think his parents are richer than yours?" Flavie cooed in her friend's ear.

"Who cares! He's *so* cute!"

Aware that he had caught their eye, the boy decided to approach the girls. Giggling nervously, Flavie scooted behind Maya, who found the nerve to speak.

"This is the first time we've seen you at one of these parties."

The boy flashed them a radiant smile, and Flavie hid her red cheeks behind her friend's shoulder.

"My family is new here. My name is Mateo."

When he spoke, some of the syllables had a breathiness to them that made them stand out from the others.

"Your accent is adorable," Maya complimented him.

The people around them began to applaud. Dr. Lanouette had finished his speech, and the evening's hostess returned to the microphone.

"Such eloquence! Thank you, Doctor! And now please welcome my son, Max, who will reproduce before your very eyes a science experiment that won him a prize at school!"

Margaret scanned the crowd for her son. The materials for his demonstration sat ready and waiting in a cart on the stage, but there was no sign of Max, even after his mother's third call.

"Where's Max?" Maya asked suddenly. "We haven't seen him in a while."

"Little Mr. Perfect?" Flavie scoffed. "As if you had to be a genius to survive your own birth!"

"Who is this Max?" asked Mateo.

"Nobody!"

The boy flashed an enigmatic smile and moved away from the girls. He was gone for a moment, and then reappeared. Dressed in a black cape and hat, he made his way through the crowd and onto the stage.

"Good evening, ladies and gentlemen!" he cried at the top of his lungs. "I am the magician Mateo Acosta!"

He was treated to a warm round of applause, while Flavie and

Maya elbowed their way to the front of the crowd, and Margaret left the stage, shooting the magician a dark look but careful not to create a scene in front of her guests.

Mateo brilliantly pulled off his first number, a classic card trick. Seeing the crowd's enthusiasm, Margaret relaxed a bit. Then the magician asked if anyone had a hundred-dollar bill. Of course, there was a man who was eager to show off and handed over the money without a second thought.

"With your permission, kind sir, I will make it disappear!"

"Go for it, kid!" said the man. "Knock our socks off!"

The boy folded the bill four times and threw it in the air. At the same instant, he twirled his cape and spun around. When he came to a stop in front of the crowd and spread out his arms, the hundred-dollar bill had vanished. When the cheering subsided, the man who had lent him the money cried out.

"Now make it reappear!"

"Make it reappear?" Mateo asked, feigning confusion. "I never claimed to be able to do that."

The man burst out laughing.

The audience was enjoying itself. As for Margaret, she had seen enough.

"That's enough, Max," she said, gritting her teeth through a smile her son knew was fake. "Give Mr. Bussières his money back!"

"That's Max?!" someone shouted, and the news, suddenly obvious, made its way around the courtyard.

Stunned, Maya and Flavie lost their beaming smiles. And Mr. Bussières, who had sized up Mrs. Legrand, became concerned and changed his tone.

"Your son is a prodigy, Margaret!" he exclaimed. "What a magician! What a splendid finale to a marvelous evening!"

Half an hour later, after getting rid of the last of her guests, Margaret stormed into her son's room. He was practicing a card trick.

"We agreed you would demonstrate the science experiment, Maxime, not a stupid sleight of hand! It's like your skull is filled with hot air."

"I hate science, Maman," the boy replied, still wearing his magician's costume. "Magic opens up so many more possibilities!"

He fanned out his deck of cards.

"Go ahead, pick one!"

"Would you quit it with that accent? And what have you done to your hair?"

"It will come out after a few washes."

"In that case, take off that ridiculous costume right this minute and get in the shower. You're not to go out again until your hair is back to its natural color."

Maxime reluctantly removed his cape and hat.

"Take it all off," Margaret pressed. "Where did you find those clothes, anyway? Did you steal them?"

Never in his life had the boy felt as good as he had in the role of Mateo Acosta. He had no intention of taking off his clothes.

"Who do you think you are? Mateo Acosta? You're no magician, either! How many times have I told you to stop pretending to be someone else? You are Maxime Legrand. My son! My miracle baby!"

"I wanted to be someone else . . ."

Maxime's confession unleashed his mother's rage.

"Take it off!" she screamed, lunging at him.

The boy struggled to stop her from ripping off his shirt. Furious, refusing to be defied, Margaret grabbed the pair of sewing scissors he had used to make his cape out of a bedsheet.

"I'm going to bring you back down to earth once and for all!"

The first snip of the scissors cut into Maxime's shirt but spared his skin. He made up his mind to keep fighting. The second swipe sliced four inches of flesh under his left nipple, splattering a flower of blood onto the fabric. Distraught, the boy gave in.

"OK, Mom, I'll take it all off! I'm sorry!"

Terrified, Maxime began unbuttoning his shirt with trembling fingers. But his surrender came too late. His mother had lost it and continued slashing his shirt. In an attempt to protect himself, he dropped to his knees, curled up on the floor, and wrapped his arms around his head.

Not my face, he was saying to himself, having already understood that, someday, his good looks would open doors that most people would never get to walk through.

"Money should not disappear, you bastard!" Margaret bellowed, now directing her fury at his pants. "It should appear! You useless piece of trash! Who will ever trust me after this?"

With no regard for the gashes she was inflicting on her son's body, Margaret struck over and over and again, until the cursed clothes were nothing but blood-soaked tatters. She then set down her weapon, stood up, and, as if nothing had happened, walked over to the bedroom mirror. Standing tall and dignified, she straightened her clothes, adjusted her hair, and left the room, abandoning the half-naked child, blood oozing from his many wounds. Max remained in a fetal position for a long time, covering his face with his hands. Then he slid a hand into his underwear. Through the tears that flooded his cheeks, he smiled.

The hundred-dollar bill, intact, had escaped the carnage.

For the day I get myself out of here.

His hope ballooned, and it could not be popped by any amount of punishment. He was going to keep filling it with more and more air.

Until it was big enough to fly him away.

20.

THE ADDRESS MAX Legrand had given the detective lieutenant was somewhere in the Verdun neighborhood. But when Henri trailed the young man to his home, they ended up in the middle of downtown Montreal. He had watched the door of the stone house for a good part of the night but had finally fallen into the deepest of sleeps.

He awoke to the sound of someone knocking on his car window.

"Did you follow me, Lieutenant Duhaime?"

Dressed in jeans and a hoodie in the chill of the morning, Max wore a neutral expression on his face.

The art of masking his feelings, Henri mused as he lowered the window separating him from the young man.

"I would hate to have your death on my conscience, Mr. Legrand."

"Oh, really? Then why do I get the impression that you suspect me of something?"

"A DNA sample would clear you."

Max's emerald eyes flickered as he ignored the request.

"Is someone really after me, or did you make up that story to get me to talk to you?"

"Why would you refuse police protection, Mr. Legrand? That's what baffles me. And giving me a false address doesn't help your case."

"You won't be getting my DNA."

This refusal did not surprise Henri.

"Fine. That's your most basic right. I'll be back with a court order. Don't even think about disappearing."

Hoping to etch the impostor's features in his memory, Henri took a good long look at him.

But is that actually your true face?

"I have no reason to flee," Max declared with a little smile. "Because you won't get your court order, Duhaime. Your assumptions, whatever they may be, are unfounded."

Turning on his heels, the young man went home.

Money has always been what motivates you, Raphael Delorme. I just have to figure out how these three murders helped make you richer.

Henri's thoughts naturally drifted to the suspect's mother, a woman who had dedicated a good portion of her life to raising funds for premature babies.

And what if, for once, it was a question of vengeance? Did your mother neglect you in order to look after these children, Max?

SETTING COURSE FOR the West Island, Henri showed up at Margaret Legrand's house without calling ahead. He found her stooped over a shrub, which she was pruning with powerful snips of her shears. When she saw him, she set down her tool.

"Lieutenant Duhaime," she greeted the police officer as she walked toward him. "Did you find my son?"

Knees cracking, Henri extricated himself from his car.

"He's alive," he hastened to inform her. "And he's been placed under police surveillance. I have come to see you this morning because we have reason to believe he might be hiding something."

"To do with the murders?"

"To remove him from the equation, I'm going to need a sample of his DNA."

"Let me guess," muttered Margaret as she removed her gardening gloves. "He refuses to cooperate?"

The woman's gaze fell on the transparent plastic bag lying on the passenger seat of Henri's unmarked car. It contained a test tube, a cotton swab, and some latex gloves.

"Would I happen to be a suspect, too?" she asked flatly.

"Your DNA is similar to your son's. It could clear him of any suspicion."

"Do what you have to do, Lieutenant."

Either she has no idea what her son is up to, Henri told himself, *or she doesn't care if he lands in jail.*

Two minutes later, the detective left with a tube containing the swab with Margaret Legrand's saliva on it. As he drove, he tapped it with his fingertips through the gray fabric of his pants pocket. Deep in contemplation, he began feeling it all over, as if to reassure himself that it was still there, that he hadn't lost it, and that he would indeed be able to hand it over to the forensics lab.

I'm going to get you, asshole!

Duhaime reached into his pocket and touched the plastic of the tube. Gripping it in his hand, he squeezed it frenetically. His breathing accelerated.

You won't get away from me this time, Raphael Delorme.

Henri's heart was racing. A few blocks from police headquarters, he pulled over to the side of the road.

EMILIANNE WAS ABOUT to get into her police car when she saw Henri starting his own vehicle in the adjacent parking spot.

"Hey, there you are, Duhaime! Christ on a cracker—did you spend the night on the clothesline?"

"What are your immediate plans, Saint-Gelais?"

"I was on my way to question Antoine Lebeau, the head of the Winged Monkeys. Wanna take your car?"

"I have something more important to do," Henri said as he got out of his car. "But please go ahead and take my car. I'll take yours."

He had left his keys in the ignition.

"Your '18 for my clunker?" said Emilianne, caught off guard. "Why?"

"Because Legrand knows what kind of car I drive."

"You found him?"

"He came to see me himself."

"That means he's afraid of the killer! So he's not our man."

"I wouldn't be so sure. He not only refused police protection—he also gave me a false address."

"He didn't want us butting around in his business. Sounds about right for a con man! Doesn't make him a serial killer."

Henri held out his hand, palm up, waiting for Emilianne to give him her keys.

"Why don't you pass the case over to the financial crimes guys and let them deal with their Raphael Delorme so we can focus on our investigation?"

"You don't feel up to interrogating Lebeau without me, Saint-Gelais?"

21.

STANDING FACE-TO-FACE WITH Antoine Lebeau, Emilianne had the same thought as Dorothy Noroît two weeks earlier.

The alpha male in all his splendor.

Barefoot and shirtless in the doorway of his high-end apartment, the young fortysomething man was wearing only a pair of sweatpants. His hair was tousled, and he hadn't shaved yet.

I might not have gotten him into my bed, but I just got him out of his! the officer joked to herself.

"Detective Sergeant Saint-Gelais," she announced, flashing her badge.

"What's this about?"

Realizing that she was standing there with a stupid grin on her face, Emilianne tried to look more stern and serious.

"I think you might have an inkling . . ."

"If you're here about the fight in front of the hospital, I had nothing to do with that."

With a wave of her hand, the young woman asked him to step out of her way. The instant he complied, she slipped into his apartment and began looking around.

"What d'you do for a living, Lebeau? You live alone?"

"I'm an insurance broker. And yes, I live alone."

"Are you gonna offer me a cup of coffee, or do I have to get it myself?"

Turning toward the darkly handsome man still standing in the doorway, the detective sighed and shook her head disapprovingly.

"Do I look like I'm made of ice? Either put on a T-shirt, mister, or take off the rest."

Lebeau frowned without managing to make himself any less attractive. He disappeared for a few minutes. When he returned, he was wearing a casual suit and holding two steaming mugs.

"Won't you please have a seat, ma'am," he said sarcastically, finding Emilianne already comfortably ensconced in his sofa.

He set the cups on the coffee table, next to an ashtray full of cigarette butts, and sat down in an armchair opposite the officer.

"You're in charge of the Winged Monkeys, if I'm not mistaken?"

"That's right. Lebeau, Antoine . . . L.A. . . . If you say it out loud, it sounds just like *ailés* in French."

"Aha!" exclaimed Emilianne, relishing the word play. "And *ailés* means 'winged'!"

"Exactly. And we got our 'monkeys' from the initials of our founders' first or last names: Monique, Olivia, Noël, Kevin, Emerson, Yves, and Savard . . ."

"What clever little monkeys! And here I thought your costumes were just to attract attention."

Antoine took a pack of cigarettes out of his shirt pocket and placed one between his lips.

A Du Maurier.

"If you really want to know," he continued, rummaging around in the cracks of his armchair, "the wings represent the little angels who should be allowed to fly away. And monkeys are an inferior version of human beings."

Emilianne, who had just taken her first sip of coffee, spat it back into her cup.

"Is what I've said really all that shocking to you?" Antoine asked, his expression darkening.

"Oh, it is, but that's not the problem. Can you not afford sugar?"

Having still not managed to locate his lighter, he tossed his cigarette onto the table and went off in search of his sugar bowl. While he was out of the room, Emilianne grabbed a tissue and used it to fish three cigarette butts out of the ashtray.

"If I understand correctly," she said when Antoine had returned and she had sweetened her coffee, "the Winged Monkeys are against medical care for premature babies."

"Among other things, that's correct. Extremely premature babies."

"Why? Some of them wind up making it."

"Yes, but at what price?"

"But you can't know ahead of time what's going to happen. You aren't God."

Resting his elbows on his knees, he leaned in toward Emilianne.

"Doctors know a lot more than they used to. These days they can calculate the probability!" He was getting worked up.

Emilianne objected, "What good are probabilities when parents are faced with this kind of decision?"

"It's an awful dilemma, isn't it?" exclaimed the activist. "Impossible to know what to do! That's why that decision should be made by a qualified doctor instead of the parents. They shouldn't have a say!"

"You really believe that?"

"Absolutely! Too often, the doctors don't just keep trying to save these babies, they also flat-out experiment on them! Parents only realize this once it's too late, when the miracle of science turns into a nightmare. Just because a baby is barely bigger than a mouse doesn't mean it should be used as a lab rat!"

"Can't disagree with you there, but . . ."

"Did you know that ninety percent of drugs given to premature babies have never been tested in a scientific study?"

"There's a lot of things I don't know, but . . ."

"You also probably don't know that an extremely premature baby costs taxpayers over two hundred and fifty thousand dollars. And that's just for the care it receives between birth and the day its parents take it home from the hospital."

Not sure she'd ever get a word in edgewise, Emilianne spoke quickly.

"I think I got it."

I'm conversing with an extremist nutjob.

"Really? Because I still haven't mentioned all the suffering that these—"

She focused her attention on her coffee, drowning him out. *He cares deeply about this cause*, the policewoman thought. *He might be charismatic, but half of what comes out of his mouth is a load of crap. He's got a lot in common with a cult leader.*

Emilianne's attention returned to the present.

"In the animal kingdom," Antoine continued arguing, "superpredators regulate populations by eliminating the sick and injured. They play a major role in the preservation of life."

This time, the detective let out a little laugh that made clear what she thought of his fanatical ideals. He took offense. Leaning back in his chair, he crossed his arms.

That's a bit much, pretty boy!

"We're asking for mercy, Sergeant Saint-Gelais. Nothing more."

Then, becoming aggressive, he snapped at her.

"What exactly do you want from me?

"I want to know where you were on October sixth around nine p.m., as well as later that night. And while we're at it, on the evening of October eleventh between eight thirty and ten o'clock."

"Whoa, whoa." Antoine was clearly thrown off. "Isn't this about the clash with the pro-lifers?"

"It's about the murders. The brutal killings of three young disabled men."

The activist's arms dropped and his demeanor softened. "You're investigating the serial killer?"

Emilianne shrugged and raised an eyebrow.

"Don't believe everything you read in the paper. But it sounds like you might know more than I do. What was that word you used, again? *Superpredators*?"

Lebeau turned white as a sheet and leaned in.

"Wait a minute, Sergeant. Did you say October eleventh? That night, I was at a protest downtown. It started at seven thirty and went until after midnight. There's a video online! Take a look—you'll see I never left the area! I was wearing a red jacket."

Sinking back into his seat, Antoine heaved a sigh of relief.

His alibi must be for real, thought Emilianne, and she scribbled a few words in her notebook.

"I'll check that out, Lebeau. Until then, you and your gang better quit your monkeying around!"

Emilianne flashed a big smile, expecting a reaction that never came.

"Your *monkeying* around . . . see what I did there? OK. How many primates in your troop? I'm gonna need names."

"There are twenty-three of us," Antoine told her. "If someone from the group attacked these guys, they were acting alone. I swear to you, nothing like this has ever been—"

"You've got someone in mind," Emilianne interrupted, pointing the chewed-up cap of her pen at him.

"Five or six members were missing the night of that rally."

"You waiting for someone else to get bumped off before you speak up? Is that what you're holding out for?"

"No, of course not . . ."

He didn't know what to say. But eventually he let it out.

"One of the movement's cofounders went too far in the past. She's an obstetrician in her fifties. Olivia Clermont."

"And what did Olivia do?"

"In the course of her duties, whenever she came across mothers who were drug addicts, alcoholics, or otherwise destitute—all kinds of screwups who had already lost a child to youth protection services—she would make them believe that their fetus was dead. But she was the one who actually killed them. She pulled this off a good ten times before someone figured it out and filed a complaint."

“Those poor women’s hearts and souls were literally ripped out of them.” The sergeant showed her disgust for the first time this week.

“Don’t the Winged Monkeys get behind stuff like that?” she asked, contempt continuing to creep into her voice.

Looking up from her notebook, she saw that Antoine was red in the face and running his hands through his hair.

“Not at all!” he replied. “She certainly shares our values, but all we’re asking is for the law to be on our side. We never break it!”

“This Olivia Clermont. Is she in prison?”

“There was no trial, for lack of evidence. But she was fired and has never worked in the medical field again.”

More than happy to distance himself from any suspicion, Antoine Lebeau found the obstetrician’s address in his cell phone and handed it over to the detective.

22.

SEATED FACING THE street in a popular restaurant, Lambert was watching the downtown traffic from the little table for two that Judith had reserved. He had arrived first and had ordered a very good pinot noir. Not knowing much about wine, he had listened carefully to the waiter's spiel and was sure he could parrot it back when his date dipped her lips into the brick-red nectar. He had put on a tie, combed his dark hair back, and his reflection in the window confirmed that he wore his goatee with subtle elegance. With the tip of his index finger, he stroked his pencil-thin mustache.

Six minutes before the agreed-upon time, the woman he was waiting for got out of a taxi. She came directly over to him without stopping to check her coat.

"Judith Garant?" he asked, standing up to shake her hand. "Lambert Thibault."

They had spoken at length on the phone but were meeting in

person for the first time. Even in stiletto heels, Judith was petite. She wore her auburn-brown hair in an asymmetrical bun. Lambert guessed she must be close to forty years old. From her voice on the phone, he had pictured her being more like fifty or sixty. Never had he been so wrong. He found her ravishing and told her so. Holding his hand, she led him to the door.

"Get your coat—we're switching restaurants," she told him. "I read some horrible reviews of this one."

But she's the one who chose it.

It did not occur to Lambert to object, and once they had settled into a nearby establishment, he ordered a new bottle. The woman took a good long look at him.

"So, you think you can persuade me to invest in your project, Mr. Thibault?"

"Lambert."

It had taken only a few telephone conversations for the scammer to gain Judith's trust, but he knew that she was not quite won over. In the next few hours he was going to have to make an effort to impress her. He would be careful with his body language, and this would put her at ease and strengthen her trust in him.

Demonstrate your openness physically, he coached himself. *Be receptive to her ideas, to her every need.*

The exercise proved easier than anticipated. They spoke for a few moments about the investment project, and then the discussion veered off in another direction. They opened a second bottle of wine and, against all expectations, found that they had a genuine connection.

Stay in character, Maxime had to remind himself several times.

For the first time, he wondered whether he would be able to follow through with his scam. Something about this woman touched him deeply. Her face seemed familiar.

It's as if I've known her all my life.

She was funny without being overly exuberant. In her gray eyes, he sensed an infinite but peaceful sadness. And although he was not in the habit of bothering with scruples, he found himself reluctant to harm her.

What's happening to me?

Someone more naive would probably have thought he was in love.

It was Judith who put the subject back on the table, agreeing to invest her money in Lambert Thibault's project. She even offered to sign the papers at his place over one last glass of wine.

EARLIER THAT EVENING, Henri had lost track of Max Legrand when the latter, wearing a wig and a fake goatee, had jumped into a taxi. Still on the lookout, waiting for the young man to return, the detective saw him get out of another taxi with a woman on his arm. As far as he could tell from a distance, the woman was pretty, but quite a bit older than him.

This is clearly not just a date. What a scumbag—doesn't he ever take a break?

As the couple entered the stone house arm in arm, Henri wondered whether the woman was in immediate danger. Should he intervene yet?

No, he decided. *I need something concrete, something that will give me a chance to comb through Legrand's life without any restrictions.*

The detective waited, but his conscience was tormenting him.

And what if something awful happens to that woman in the meantime?

Unfortunately, Henri was the only one who believed Max Legrand posed a threat, and Legrand knew his rights.

If I put a spoke in his wheel, he'll be delighted to accuse me of harassment.

Captain Bergevin was part of the problem. Having rejected Henri's theory outright, he had ordered him to investigate the Winged Monkeys.

With my track record, I need to proceed with caution . . .

Half an hour later, the sound of his phone ringing snapped the detective lieutenant out of his moral dilemma. He learned that the blood collected from the teeth of Justin Manseau's dog had nothing to do with Margaret Legrand.

"That doesn't change anything," Henri muttered after ending the call with the forensics lab employee.

Doesn't mean you're innocent, Legrand. I don't know how just yet, but I'm going to get you.

At that moment, Henri's gaze was drawn to one of the windows of the house he was watching. Despite the lowered blinds, he could see a light switching on and off in flashes of varying length. The little pattern stopped briefly and started again.

Three short, three long, three short . . . SOS!

Disregarding his rickety knees, the sixtysomething detective sprang from Emilianne's car and sprinted across the street. Taking the three steps in front of the house in a single bound, he tried to rush straight inside, but it was locked. He banged so hard on the door that it hurt his knuckles.

"Police! Open up!"

The lights had stopped flashing. Becoming increasingly worried about the woman inside, Henri threw himself against the door. A sharp pain radiating through his shoulder convinced him to change tactics, and he began kicking near the doorknob. He finally managed to break the mechanism by shooting a bullet at it.

The detective stepped into the pitch-black house. Someone was sprawled across the sofa, one arm dangling toward the floor, but he could only make out the silhouette. At first glance, the person appeared lifeless.

"Ma'am?" Henri whispered, before shouting again. "Police!"

Pistol drawn, he kept it pointed in front of him as he quickly searched the rooms on the ground floor. Not seeing anything suspicious, he tucked his weapon back in his belt, flipped on the lights, and hurried over to the victim.

Max Legrand, unconscious, was bleeding to death.

Henri knelt down beside the young man. There was a wide slash across his left wrist. The kitchen knife that had done the awful deed lay on the floor—which, drop by drop, was being covered in more blood by the minute. Taking his silk scarf from his neck, Henri applied a tourniquet to the con man's arm before calling for help. Then, with a good slap to the face, he revived Maxime.

"Duhaime? What's going on?"

"You tell me! Perhaps you were overcome with remorse?"

As he forced himself to sit up, Maxime nearly passed out again.

"Lie still—you've lost a lot of blood. Where's the woman?"

"Judith Garant," the young man muttered, as if the memory of his visitor was just coming back to him.

Henri made a mental note of the name.

"She must have drugged me," he slurred, still completely out of it. "We had a drink . . . The wine . . ."

An empty bottle sat on the coffee table, but no glasses.

And no papers.

Scouring the place for a sign of the shady contract that the woman might have signed to her great misfortune, Henri spotted some shards of glass on the floor.

"There was another glass," Maxime recalled, his face scrunched up in confusion. "With traces of her lipstick . . . She must have taken it with her."

"What are you talking about?" Henri snapped. "I'm not an idiot! This is another one of your acts, with the sole purpose of diverting suspicion away from you!"

Then pointing to his own facial hair, he mocked Max.

"What's with the costume? Halloween isn't for two weeks!"

"I'm experimenting with different styles."

Maxime's eyelids began to flutter. His voice was even groggier than before.

"You were right, Duhaime. I was supposed to be the next victim. Lucky you were there."

THE PARAMEDICS ARRIVED and took charge, separating Henri from his suspect. A short time later, the police officers who had been called in as backup burst into the house and started looking for Judith Garant. Among them, Henri recognized Officer Marco Poliquin.

"She's not inside, Lieutenant," Poliquin assured him a few minutes later, before searching the tiny backyard.

"Where's the woman, Legrand?" Henri shouted over a paramedic's shoulder. "She went in on your arm, but I never saw her leave! What have you done with her, you scoundrel?"

"She must've slipped out the back door," replied Max, whose face he couldn't see.

"She got away, then?"

"Away from you, Lieutenant, not from me."

Even though Maxime's condition had stabilized and his life was no longer in danger, the paramedics put him on a stretcher, preparing to take him to the hospital.

"Get a load of this, Lieutenant!" an officer called out as he brought over his cell phone, which he had used to film the basement of the house from every angle.

The detective silently threw himself a bouquet of flowers.

It's Raphael Delorme.

Fuming inwardly that he didn't have the right to perform a more thorough search of the premises, Henri directed the officer to collect the empty wine bottle and the pieces of broken glass, and then he questioned Maxime about all the dresses, suits, wigs, and makeup he was storing in the basement.

"Is that a crime, Duhaime?"

Reentering the house through the back door, boots covered in dirt, Officer Poliquin presented Henri with a single red high heel, which had been placed in a transparent bag.

“It was in the neighbor’s yard, by the fence,” he said. “The heel was dug into the ground.”

“That isn’t one of yours, Mr. Legrand,” Henri said, taking the evidence bag from Marco and holding it up in the air. “Much too small.”

“It belongs to the woman who tried to kill me!” cried Maxime. “But . . . that wasn’t Judith Garant. The crazy woman got me to leave the restaurant before the real Judith arrived . . .”

The paramedics had begun rolling Maxime’s stretcher away, so the detective could now look him in the eye. He demanded a few more seconds to speak with him.

“Mr. Legrand, in your opinion, why would the ‘crazy woman’ have wanted to take your life?”

“Because of your premature-baby theory, obviously! Why don’t you explain it to me!”

“I doubt that has anything to do with it. What did you do to that woman?”

“It was a date, that’s all.”

“You like your women quite a bit older, don’t you?” Henri was getting frustrated.

“To each his own, like I said. That’s enough—get everyone out of my house. The police shouldn’t be sniffing around in a victim’s business!”

Officer Poliquin wanted to take the red shoe from Henri and put it with the other evidence, but Henri assured him that he would personally drop it off at the lab. On his way out of the house, the detective went to retrieve his silk scarf, which had been left lying on the floor of the living room.

“Not sure that blood’ll come out,” said Marco.

"I sure hope it doesn't."

Henri followed Maxime's stretcher to the ambulance. As the back doors of the vehicle were closing, he threw in one last comment.

"I know who you are."

"Oh yeah? Who am I?" Maxime wanted to know, a languid smile on his lips despite the detective lieutenant's threatening tone.

"Lots of people. But certainly not a victim!"

23.

HENRI HAD GONE to bed on his left side, the only position that didn't leave him with aches and pains in the morning. Even though it was late, he was having trouble falling asleep. Knowing that he would live to regret it if he turned onto his back, he did it anyway.

Is there any chance that woman really tried to kill Legrand?

The detective had checked: There were only two people in the area named Judith Garant. One of them was nine years old, and the other was sixty-four.

Whatever her true identity, how could that little wisp of a woman have taken out our three victims? For Leopold Dion, she would have had to catch him sleeping. Yet his bed hadn't been slept in.

It crossed his mind that Leo's mother could have remade the bed while waiting for the police to arrive.

I'll have to ask her.

Around two in the morning, Henri forced himself to think of something else. Putting his hand into his pajama pants, he scratched his groin. He attempted to awaken his penis, since masturbating sometimes helped him drift off to sleep. But lying there in his hand, his cock kept a stubbornly low profile. While one side of Henri's nervous system was working hard to inhibit his erection . . .

This is unhealthy.

. . . the other side was sending contradictory signals of stimulation in the form of images.

Contrary to what Leonardo da Vinci imagined while dissecting the genitals of men who had been hanged, the fact that the penis does not always obey its master does not mean that it is autonomous.

One image in particular kept trying to impose itself on Henri. Knowing that it would be sure to rouse his member from its lethargy, he nonetheless tried to push it out of his mind. For a few seconds he succeeded, replacing it with more appropriate images of naked women. But despite his best efforts, the cursed image eventually consumed him.

A red high-heeled shoe.

Henri's penis stood straight up. He moved his hand back and forth more quickly, but soon realized that his imagination alone was not going to get the job done. Getting out of bed, he took a pair of latex gloves from the drawer of his nightstand and walked into the living room, where he pulled a sofa forward a couple of feet, revealing a safe that was built into the wall. He opened it with a five-digit code. Inside were the two pieces of evidence he planned to take to the forensics lab first thing in the morning—his own scarf, stained with Maxime Legrand's blood, and the red high-heeled shoe.

But first . . .

In a fever, he undressed and threw himself onto the sofa, his bare buttocks sinking into the seat cushion. After spending some time fondling the shoe through the plastic evidence bag, he took it out. Caressing it gently, he examined each and every stitch, one hand on the arch and the other in the décolleté of the toe bed. The sole and heel were caked in dirt, but the rest of the shoe's bloodred patent leather was as shiny as a newly minted coin.

Could that be a drop of hemoglobin? Henri wondered, becoming increasingly aroused. *There may be a usable fingerprint here . . .*

It seemed to him that, on this type of surface, he could almost spot it with the naked eye. His desire was growing, and so was his cock.

If only I could touch this shoe without gloves.

The detective was playing with fire, and he knew it, but he couldn't help himself. Over the years, he had learned to accept his kink.

This is my one and only vice, isn't it?

Henri held the shoe close to his nose and sniffed inside it. The scent of feet was subtle but present. It took everything he had not to stick out his tongue and lick the inside of the pump. Before he completely lost control, he set it down on the table.

Remember what happened. Be careful. Don't cross the line.

He took the glove off his left hand and slipped it over his engorged phallus like a condom. Picking up the shoe again, he pushed his gloved member inside it. As another penis might thrust against a cervix, his began pounding the narrow bed of the shoe.

HENRI HAD DOZED off on the sofa. Extracting his aging body from it in the morning elicited a series of grimaces and invocations to the gods. He moaned and groaned under his breath as he showered, trimmed his beard, and put on a clean suit, then downed an espresso in five quick sips. This ritual accomplished, he returned to the living room, picked up the soiled latex gloves, and threw them away. He washed his hands thoroughly, slipped on a new pair of gloves, and put the red heel back in the evidence bag that Officer Poliquin had marked with the date and hour it was collected. As he opened the safe to take out his bloodstained scarf, he had to force himself not to stash the shoe in there.

I could say I misplaced it.

That morning, handing over the high-heeled shoe to the forensics lab required a tremendous act of willpower.

And on top of everything else, I have to put up with my delightful sergeant, he muttered to himself, grumpier than ever, as he arrived in the police headquarters parking lot.

He went looking for Emilianne, who was standing next to his car, tapping her foot impatiently. He handed her back her car keys in exchange for his.

"What's up, Duhaime? You look like shit."

Henri briefed his partner on the events of the previous evening.

"So we've got our killer lady—is that what you're saying?" she exclaimed. "What's the game plan?"

"Charge Max Legrand for the murders."

"Huh? Didn't you just tell me that Judith Garant tried to bump him off? And that the blood in that filthy dog's mouth didn't have anything to do with Max. What do you have against this guy?"

"The man is a professional con artist, Saint-Gelais. Wake up! He knew I was watching him. He staged the whole thing for the sole purpose of tricking me."

Emilianne was silent for a moment. Henri figured that she was going to come to her senses and agree with him. But she had something else in mind.

"Before I forget, the captain wants to see you in his office. He's trying to get a criminal profiler for us."

"We don't need a profiler," insisted Henri. "What's so hard to understand? We're not dealing with a serial killer! He's not murdering people randomly, just for fun, even if he's managed to make you believe otherwise!"

"OK, well, while you're sorting that out with Bergevin, I'm gonna keep following the lead on the Winged Monkeys."

Before Henri excused himself, Emilianne briefed him on her meeting with Antoine Lebeau.

"So I fast-forwarded through the video from the October eleventh rally. Lebeau left the frame for seventeen minutes. Even in a private jet, he could never have gotten to the Pointe-aux-Trembles woods, killed Manseau, and made it back to the protest. His alibi is rock-solid."

"In that case, why did you waste my time telling me all that?" Henri groaned.

"Lebeau put me on the trail of Olivia Clermont," continued Emilianne. "She's a murderous obstetrician who's managed to slip through the cracks of the justice system."

"Uh-huh."

He guessed that the irritation he felt toward her was mutual, but she seemed determined not to let it dampen her excitement.

"I'm off to her place right now," she said as she got into her car.

Putting the key in the ignition, she had one last question.

"Legrand still at the hospital? Which one? I'm gonna pay him a visit, just to get an idea of what's going on with him."

"Don't you go anywhere near him!" Henri snapped. "You'll fall under his spell like everyone else he's cheated and ruin our chances of solving this case."

Emilianne was speechless, but only for a second.

"You're way off, Duhaime!" she finally lashed out. "Do I really seem like the kind of girl who falls for the first pretty boy who comes along? The only reason I take Legrand's side is because you don't have a damn shred of evidence against him!"

"I just dropped a sample of his blood at the lab. I'll have my evidence soon enough!"

"Let it go, Duhaime, for Chrissakes! If the blood on the dog's fangs doesn't match his mother's, then it's not gonna match his, either!"

But Henri wasn't about to give up.

EMILIANNE WAS A fun-loving woman who didn't tend to dwell on things, but her lieutenant had managed to get under her skin. She was having a hard time getting over the conversation they'd just had.

That asshole is completely lost, she muttered to herself as she approached Olivia Clermont's door. *His true north has gone south! Why's he stuck on that guy? And he has the nerve to accuse me of trying to fuck a fly?*

She knocked on the door.

What does he think Max Legrand's blood is gonna prove? He's the one who's going to sink the investigation. How can he think straight, anyway—he never eats anything! And he doesn't sleep anymore! If he keeps this up I'm gonna have to talk to the captain about it.

Olivia's door cracked open a couple of inches.

"Marilou?"

"Yeah . . ." said Emilianne, after a second's hesitation.

Keeping her face partially hidden behind the door, a tall, sturdy woman handed her a paper bag.

"I can see that it's urgent," she said, eyeing Emilianne's belly, "but we said one week. Don't make me chase you down for my money!"

"Don't worry, ma'am."

The detective took the bag and quickly left. As she was getting into her car, a teenage girl in a school uniform knocked on the same door.

The real Marilou . . .

Emilianne was careful to wait a few blocks to pull over and examine the bag that Olivia Clermont had just given her by mistake. In it she found two medications—mifepristone and misoprostol. Searching the Internet on her phone, she learned that these substances could be taken to induce a medical abortion.

"These medications are covered by insurance," she mumbled. "Why would this Marilou need to get them illegally?"

Continuing her research on the Web, Emilianne concluded that the girl must have been more than sixty-three days pregnant. Any earlier than that, she could have had a surgical abortion. But if her fetus was more than twenty-four weeks old, even though abortion was still legal, she probably would have had to travel to the United States to have it done.

For a girl her age, I imagine that would be difficult. She might not have a passport, and she might even need her parents' permission to cross the border. They probably don't know about it . . .

Emilianne wondered about the side effects of taking these medications.

The officer returned to Olivia Clermont's place, but Marilou was no longer around. Knocking on the door a second time, she stood there on the porch with her arms swinging.

She's vanished into thin air!

Emilianne was about to start her car when her phone started ringing.

"Hi, Camille. I'm so sorry for . . . My condolences for the loss of your mother."

"That's why I'm calling, Sergeant Saint-Gelais. The coroner ruled it a suicide, but that makes no sense. My mother was definitely going through a tough time, but she's the most optimistic woman I know. Not to mention deeply religious. She *never* would've killed herself!"

"Listen, Camille, if the coroner—"

"She didn't even leave a note!" Camille was sobbing now.

After stammering out some clichéd phrases meant to be comforting, Emilianne hung up and then realized that Henri had tried to call her. He had left a message on her voicemail without even saying hello.

"The blood on the dog's teeth belongs to one of Maxime Legrand's parents!"

"What?!" Emilianne exclaimed.

Unable to reach Henri on the phone, she got in touch with Jason.

"You should've seen him when he heard that!" The investigator laughed. "I thought he was going to come in his trousers!"

"How could he have gotten the results back so fast? Is he manufacturing evidence or something?"

"It's Henri Duhaime, Em. His requests get priority."

What did he do to get sent off to financial crimes? Emilianne wondered. *He seems so smart, thinks he understands everything before everyone else. But he understands only what he wants to understand! All he cares about is locking up Raphael Delorme and ending his career with a bang. To hell with the truth.*

Emilianne told Jason what she had just found out about Olivia Clermont.

"I'm on it, Em. We'll make sure that wacko doesn't hurt anyone else!"

"Is Duhaime still around?"

"He just left for Margaret Legrand's place."

What the hell is he up to now?

Since Henri always strictly obeyed the speed limit, Emilianne still had time to get to the West Island before him.

Enough, Duhaime.

24.

EMILIANNE HADN'T EVEN closed her car door when her prickly colleague emerged from his own vehicle and pounced.

"What are you doing here, Saint-Gelais?"

"Oh, I'm sorry! Am I bothering you?" she quickly retorted.

"What are you insinuating?"

She hurried after Henri, who hadn't waited for a response and was headed toward Margaret Legrand's porch. He seemed to take pleasure in venting his anger by pounding on the door.

"How could you possibly have known that the blood taken from the dog's teeth was connected to Max Legrand?"

"Because he's guilty, Saint-Gelais! What language do you need me to say it in, for heaven's sake."

"So you think Max's father is his accomplice?"

"Either his mother or his father," corrected Henri. "A more thorough analysis will soon tell us which it was."

Is he messing with me on purpose? Emilianne wondered.

"We know that it's not Margaret's blood," she muttered.

"Just take notes, OK?" snapped the lieutenant as the door opened.

Why? What exactly are you afraid I'm gonna find out?

This time, Henry refused to remain standing in the hallway. Yielding to his request, Margaret led them into her dining room. Along with a long solid oak table and matching sideboard, the room featured a fireplace adorned with a few objects and a small wine cellar containing eight bottles.

"Nothing but Emerald Château," Emilianne noted. "That must be some damn good wine."

Margaret replied with a touch of snobbery, "I hope it's worth the six hundred and fifty dollars I paid for it. I open those bottles only at my charity evenings, and only when I've exceeded my target."

She remained standing while the detectives sat down at the table. Informed of Henri's latest discovery, she turned pale beneath her flawless makeup. The vertical lines around her lips deepened.

"The blood of one of his parents? I don't understand. What are you accusing me of?"

"We're not accusing you of anything at all, Mrs. Legrand. There is nothing linking your DNA at all. Which leads me to conclude that you are not Max's biological mother."

"That's absurd!"

The look on Emilianne's face said the same thing.

"I gave birth at Sainte-Victorine Hospital," Margaret protested. "That's where you got my contact information, Lieutenant Duhaime!"

The three were quiet for a moment until Emilianne broke the silence. "You brought Max into this world, perhaps. I'm sorry to ask, but how did you . . . conceive?"

The woman finally pulled up a chair, and Emilianne dutifully took out her notebook and pen.

"Here we go," she mumbled under her breath.

As Margaret took her seat, she shot Emilianne a dark look, conveying disdain for both her impertinence and her insignificance. Emilianne began chewing on the cap of her pen.

"I never married," explained Margaret. "I signed up with a sperm bank."

"And an egg bank," Henri added.

Emilianne raised an eyebrow.

"Yes," Margaret admitted reluctantly. "But that doesn't change anything. Maxime is *my* son—he came out of *my* belly!"

"No one here is suggesting otherwise, Mrs. Legrand."

"This is all deeply disturbing." She was growing more distressed.

"How does Maxime earn a living? Do you know?"

Emilianne got the impression that Henri had tried to inject a little warmth into the question. The result, however, was debatable.

"He's a . . . an idea man. He's very creative. Always looking for investors to help him get his projects off the ground."

"What sorts of projects?"

"I would be hard-pressed to tell you."

"Your son is a con artist, Mrs. Legrand."

She pressed her lips together until they all but disappeared.

"Did you know that?"

"No. But to be honest, it doesn't surprise me a bit."

"You're going to have to give me the name of the clinic where your insemination took place."

She refused to comply.

"That type of file is confidential. And even if you obtain a warrant, you won't find out who the donors are, as they wished to remain anonymous. Neither of them wanted to be known to the child."

Out of the corner of her eye, Emilianne saw Henri's face tighten in frustration. Deciding to intervene, she stopped gnawing on her pen.

"Don't play games with us, Margaret. Even in a situation like this, the clinic has to collect information about the donors in case a medical issue arises that requires them to be located."

Henri relaxed audibly, the bones in his back cracking as he loosened up.

"Please don't make us go around to every clinic, Mrs. Legrand," he said.

Cornered, Margaret gave them the name and address they wanted. As soon as Emilianne had jotted down this vital information in her little black notebook, the woman politely showed them out. Making their way to their respective unmarked vehicles, they agreed to meet in front of the fertility clinic.

"How did you know that about the donors?" Henri asked Emilianne as she got behind the wheel of her car.

"You really wanna know?"

"Listen, Saint-Gelais, don't hold it against me. I'm a loner. Group work has never been my strong suit."

Even though some of the details still bothered her, the idea that Henri could be leading the investigation for his own personal gain suddenly seemed ridiculous.

"I've never had a man in my life for very long," she confided to her lieutenant. "When my biological clock started ticking, I did some research. I explored a few options."

"But you didn't follow through with it?"

"Eh. I realized I prefer the company of cats. And what about you? How did you know that Margaret wasn't Maxime's biological mother? You knew it even before the test results came back."

"I had my suspicions. It was her age that got me thinking. The day we met her, I was expecting a younger woman."

"She's what, seventy? It's not unusual these days for a woman to have a baby after forty."

"Yes, you still have time, but Margaret Legrand is seventy-six years old, which means that she had her son when she was fifty-two. And that's not a trivial point, given that after forty-five, a woman's fertility drops to practically zero."

This man has nothing to hide, Emilianne scolded herself.

AT THE PRIVATE clinic the detectives hit a new snag in the case. The receptionist was adamant that Margaret Legrand's own egg had produced Maxime Legrand.

"How can you be so sure?" pressed Emilianne. "It's been twenty-five years. You didn't even look at her file!"

"There's no way I'm wrong," replied the receptionist. "For the simple reason that I've been working here since the clinic opened, and we've never once used egg donors. Only sperm donors."

Emilianne glanced up at Henri, perplexed.

"That's odd," she said. "Why would Margaret say that if it wasn't true?"

"Because I put the idea in her head." Henri kicked himself.

He turned to the receptionist.

"Even with a little help from science, wouldn't it have been very difficult for her to conceive?"

"The odds were not in her favor, that's for sure!" acknowledged the receptionist. "I remember Maggie well because I've never met anyone more determined. She came here regularly for nearly fifteen years. She was dead set on the baby having her genetic material. It cost her an arm and a leg, but in the end it worked out."

Emilianne requested the name and contact details of the sperm donor. Having been fairly chatty up to that point, the receptionist suddenly had doubts about what she could say and what she should keep to herself.

"That man could be a dangerous killer!" said the sergeant.

The only couple in the waiting room looked at the officers with wide eyes.

"Give me . . . give me a minute," stammered the receptionist as she left her desk. "Let me have a quick word with the boss."

"I'm lost!" Emilianne admitted to Henri. "Is Margaret Max's mother or not?"

Henri's phone rang.

"It's Jobin."

Henri stepped out to the sidewalk to take the call. With Emilianne clinging to his heels, he put the phone on speaker.

"We finally have some news about Leopold Dion's virtual girlfriend, Lieutenant!" Jason said. "Aimee was, in fact, a witness to the murder. The tech guy didn't get much, but he did estimate there's a ninety percent chance that Leo's murderer was a woman."

Henri still found this hard to believe.

"Can we really trust what Aimee says?"

"AI is reliable to the extent that the IT expert hasn't made any mistakes in the coding. It can't lie."

"OK, sure, but what if the killer was a man disguised as a woman? Could the AI be fooled?"

Jobin pondered this idea. "Probably, yes . . ."

"So it's possible that we're dealing with a killer in heels and a wig?"

"That would surprise me, Lieutenant. First of all, because Aimee can recognize voices. Remember, she knew that I wasn't Leo. And she was unequivocal that it was a woman's voice. Also, if the footprints on the path at the worksite were made by spike heels, there's every indication that the shoes were worn by somebody who weighed less than a hundred and forty pounds."

"How do you figure?"

"That's my hypothesis, Lieutenant. We'll have to verify it, but the path was full of footprints from the loggers' and police officers' boots, and there were also marks from the wheelchair. All of them were clearly defined. Even Edith's. She's the officer who combed the trail with her partner. She weighs a hundred and thirty pounds soaking wet, maybe a hundred and forty with all her equipment. Her boot prints are smaller than the men's and less pronounced, but you can still see them in the photos. On the other hand, the high-heeled shoes barely left a mark. You can't even make out the contour of the feet. To me, that means that whoever was wearing them weighs less than Edith."

"But that doesn't make any sense, Jobin!" Henri bristled. "Leopold Dion was sedentary, certainly not in great shape, but he was a big guy, and there was no trace of any sedative in his blood."

"What if someone snuck up on him while he was sleeping?" suggested Emilianne.

"Oh, hi, Em! Actually, the—"

"Maryse Normandin admitted to having made her son's bed before we arrived," Henri cut him off.

"So he was sleeping when the killer came in."

"Unlikely," continued Henri. "According to Maryse, Leo never made his bed and he never went to sleep before midnight."

"The mystery remains!" Emilianne exclaimed. "How could such a small woman have been able to hack him to pieces like that? Maybe . . ."

"I can shed some light on the mystery if you'd let me get a word in!" Jobin offered, quieting Henri and Emilianne. "Some kind of substance was sprayed in Leopold's face. The lab just ID'd it—it's the same stuff that's found in some self-defense sprays, like what the Citizen Sentinels carry in Montreal North."

Emilianne snorted.

"What're you suggesting, J.J.? That Maryse Normandin killed her own son?"

"Maryse said it herself: Leo never opened the door for anyone but her. And don't forget that she does kung fu!"

"Anything else, Jobin?"

"One last detail. The blood on the dog's teeth came from a woman."

"That can't be right!" exclaimed Emilianne. "Either the samples were contaminated, or Margaret gave us saliva that wasn't hers!"

"I collected the sample myself," Henri said, unimpressed.

He told the investigator to keep him in the loop on any further developments, stuck his phone in his pocket, and rushed off to his car.

"We're not going back to the clinic, are we?" Emilianne called after him.

"Try to keep up, Saint-Gelais. The sperm donor's identity is irrelevant."

"Sheesh, Duhaime, you're giving me the spins!"

She was forced to run to catch up with him.

"Where *are* we going, then?"

"To Sainte-Victorine, for the love of god!"

25.

HENRI HAD A theory that could explain Margaret Legrand's lie and help untangle the mess they were in. Behind the closed doors of the hospital archives room, he was working hard to confirm it. Pretending to be absorbed in his cell phone, the archivist was eavesdropping on the details the detective lieutenant was sharing with his colleague.

"Remember, Saint-Gelais, there weren't four babies in the NICU in '94; there were five. We aren't worried about one of them because he died shortly after his birth."

"Duhaime, if you're telling me the ghost of that dead baby is our killer, I'm warning you right now, I quit!"

With both index fingers, Henri pointed to the pertinent information in two different files—those of Maxime Legrand and Kansas Noroît.

"See that? These two were born about a day apart, both during their mothers' twenty-third week of pregnancy. They were at exactly the same stage of development."

"Don't tell me . . ."

Henri moved one of his fingers.

"Look at this. It says that around seven fifteen in the morning on June tenth, Dr. Lanouette informed Mrs. Legrand that complications had arisen affecting her infant's lungs. He advised her to take her baby off life support, since his chances of survival had dropped from slim to none and, even if he did make it, his future was already severely compromised."

Emilianne pulled Maxime's file closer.

"According to Lanouette's notes, Maxime's life was hanging by a thread. He considered it pointless, even cruel, to subject the baby to any more suffering. But Margaret demanded that the medical team continue providing her son with all the care necessary for his survival."

Henri then leaned over the Noroît file. "At the same time," he pointed out, "Kansas, although he wasn't out of the woods, was in better shape than Maxime. Yet somehow, a few hours later, it was Dorothy who was hearing that her baby had died.

"Not only did Maxime survive, but he miraculously improved in the days that followed."

The door to the archive room opened, prompting both detectives to look up. A nurse, who seemed to be nearing the end of her career, stood in the doorway.

"What am I doing here, Étienne?"

The archivist offered an explanation to the police officers.

"I took the liberty of texting Monique Joyal. She works on the research side these days, but on the night of the big crash she was part of the nursing staff in the unit you're investigating."

Henri was eager to know if the nurse remembered Maxime Legrand.

"Our miracle baby?"

"Of course she remembers him!" cried Étienne. "She's been regaling everyone with that story for the past twenty-five years!"

Monique walked over to the ten files spread out on the table and picked up Maxime's and Margaret's.

"Well, his mother certainly played a part in this miracle," she began as she opened Margaret's file. "She barely slept. She was always at her son's side. Since we were overwhelmed, we taught her how to take care of certain things herself. She pumped her milk for him, and also for the little boy whose mother died in the accident. Margaret Legrand was a real force of nature. It did come as a surprise that Maxime recovered so quickly, but Dr. Lanouette and everyone who knew his mother just said that he was following in her footsteps."

"And what about the other babies?" asked Henri. "Do you remember them?"

"How could I forget them? They were all little boys."

Seeing the puzzled look on Emilianne's face, Monique clarified what she meant.

"We didn't know why at the time, but among premature babies, boys don't tend to do as well as girls. It's because of their lungs, apparently. They develop faster in girls."

"It must have been chaos, I imagine?"

"It was a nightmare, absolutely horrific."

"So, is it conceivable that amid all the confusion, someone mixed up two babies?"

"By mistake?" asked the nurse. "Because with the bracelets, that's pretty unlikely. Somebody would have caught it at some point. And when it comes to the littlest ones, they never left their incubators."

"How about on purpose? With the littlest ones?"

Monique took a few seconds to sift through her memories.

"On purpose it wouldn't be impossible," she finally admitted. "It was truly chaos all through the hospital. We were running every which way like chickens with our heads cut off. But the preemies were hooked up to all kinds of machines, so if someone did that, they would've had to work fast. And above all, they would've had to know exactly what they were doing."

"A doctor or nurse would have had to have been involved . . . or someone who had learned to copy them?"

"What you're asking," Monique understood, "is whether Margaret Legrand and Dorothy Noroît's babies could have been swapped."

She pushed aside Margaret's file and picked up Dorothy's.

"The little Noroît girl. God, I felt so sorry for her! Not even twenty years old and not a soul in the world to support her. It's no mistake that the baby's father's name isn't in the records. He left his girlfriend and baby over the phone while she was giving birth! That guy had no balls! The heartless bastard disowned his own flesh and blood!"

Emilianne chimed in, "A baby can't just be switched out for another one without anybody noticing!"

As the nurse paused on a page of the file containing a series of brain scans, Henri saw her frown. She turned back a few pages, examined another series of scans, then returned to the original page.

"What are you thinking, Ms. Joyal?" Henri asked the nurse.

Shaking her head to dispel the thought that had just crossed her mind, Monique closed Dorothy's file. She finally remembered something.

"You know what? Dorothy never went to see her baby while he was alive. The first time I brought her son to her, he was already dead."

"So she had no idea what he looked like," said Henri.

"Olivia Clermont—does that name ring a bell?" Emilianne suddenly asked. "An obstetrician. Was she on your team back then?"

"That name sounds familiar," muttered the nurse as she went to bump Étienne from his computer. "Let me check."

"Why'd you bring your briefcase?" Emilianne asked Henri. "What's in there?"

He took a pointed look at the bold flower print on her shirt and then replied, "It looks more professional, don't you think? Focus, Saint-Gelais."

"Margaret is not Max's mother," Emilianne said. "So the blood we found on Manseau's dog's teeth would be Dorothy Noroît's. Is that what you're thinking?"

"That would explain why Mrs. Legrand didn't mind giving me a saliva sample," Henri added. "She knew that even if Max was the killer, there wouldn't be any connection between his DNA and hers."

"You still think Max is our man?" Emilianne asked.

"Everything leads back to him, Saint-Gelais! We may not have all the answers yet, but we can guess that the murderer wanted to swap the victims' organs, much in the same way as the babies were swapped."

She finally admitted, "You might actually be onto something..."

Turning back to the detectives, Monique declared categorically that Olivia Clermont had never worked at Sainte-Victorine.

"What else can you tell us about Dorothy Noroît and Margaret Legrand?" Henri asked her. "Did they become friends, perhaps?"

"Not as far as I recall. They didn't have much of a chance to run into each other. Dorothy didn't stay long, and she left her bed only for her various tests. She was injured in the accident, and within a few short hours she lost everything. Truly everything! Her job, her boyfriend, her house, her best friend. And the cherry on top: her baby. I'm telling you, she was completely lost. All she had left were the clothes on her back. And a pretty pair of red high heels."

Henri was speechless.

"Is that a flicker of emotion I see on your face, Duhaime?" Emilianne teased. "You got a thing for shoes?"

26.

THE SEPTUAGENARIAN'S LECHEROUS gaze lingered on Aurelia's youthful body. About fifty people were gathered in the backyard, but he only had eyes for her, having spotted her the moment he arrived. She stood off to the side, leaning against the fence. With a sulky pout, she took no interest in anything but her cell phone.

By the time the sun had set and the yard was bathed in twilight, the man had had a few drinks and was feeling bold. A glass of champagne in each hand, he went over to offer one to the young girl.

"I'm not old enough," she said, reaching for the glass and taking a sip.

A small bubble remained on her lower lip, and she ran her tongue slowly over it.

"You look upset," said the man. "Is there anything I can do?"

"It's my father," Aurelia said, tossing a strand of her long blond hair behind her shoulder. "He gave a fortune to the OZ Foundation tonight, but when I need a little cash, he says he has nothing to give."

The girl turned her phone screen toward the man and showed him a photo.

"He won't buy me this dress," she complained. "It's wonderful, right?"

"It's beautiful, just like you. It would fit you like a glove."

The dress, priced at $479.99, was sleeveless and transparent. As she tucked her phone in the back pocket of her miniskirt, Aurelia let out a heart-wrenching sigh.

"I really need to stop thinking about it. There's no way I'll ever save up the money for it."

The man paused for a moment, deep in thought.

"If I gave you this dress as a gift, would you come to my house and show it to me?"

"You'd do that for me?" she asked, voice dripping with saccharine excitement.

"If I got to see you in it, yes."

Taking out his own cell phone, the man wanted to know where he could order it from.

"I never buy clothes online. I have to try the dress on in the store. That way I'll get the right size . . . and it will fit my body perfectly."

Fishing six hundred dollars out of his wallet, the man slipped it into the back pocket of Aurelia's skirt. Through the fabric, his fingers paused on her buttock, but he broke off his caress when he saw the hostess rushing toward them.

"I slipped my business card in with the money. Call me," he said, before running off.

Snatching the champagne flute from her son's hands, Margaret grabbed his arm and dragged him behind a dense spruce tree. The sparkling wine ended up in the conifer, and the glass with it, and a resounding slap knocked Maxime's blond wig askew.

"You're dressing like a whore now? Unbelievable!"

His cheek burning, the teenager fixed his wig.

"Took you a while to recognize me this year!" He was delighted.

Maxime moved quickly to grab his mother's wrist, blocking a second slap.

"You'll never lay a hand on me again," he warned her, pushing her away.

He was stronger than her now.

"Dirty little ingrate," he heard her hissing as he turned and walked back to the house.

In his room, Maxime went around to each of his hiding places and collected all the money he had stolen over the years. He was stuffing it into a backpack when his mother knocked on his door and entered without waiting for permission.

"I was a little hard on you," she admitted. "You're not a child anymore, after all. You turned seventeen a few days ago, and I realize we didn't mark the occasion. Amid all the preparations for the charity evening, my mind was elsewhere!"

Glancing at her, Maxime noticed that she had brought two glasses of champagne. She gestured for him to take one. She even made a move to clink glasses with him, but he avoided contact and downed his glass in a single gulp.

"Good night," he grumbled, handing her back the empty glass.

To his surprise, she took no offense.

"Good night, *my* dear son."

As she left his room, Margaret closed the door behind her.

Maxime barely had time to think before he collapsed onto his bed. When he heard his door open again, he didn't have the strength to react and soon slipped into unconsciousness.

When the teenager woke up, his entire body was hurting. The most excruciating pain was around his genitals. It was pitch-black outside, but thanks to his desk lamp and the floor-length mirror in front of him, he could see that he was completely naked and tied to his office chair. A rubber band was wrapped tightly around his penis, which explained the throbbing pain that made his eyes water. A piece of heavy-duty duct tape held his eyelids open, forcing him to stare at his tortured reflection. Margaret's rings had slashed his cheek when she hit him. Maxime struggled to free himself, but the drugs poisoning his system kept him from moving.

"Mother!" he screamed. "Mother!"

In her bathrobe and slippers, Margaret breezed past his door but had nothing to say.

The young man remained in that position for a few more hours until the sedative wore off and he regained enough strength and agility to break free from the chair and remove the elastic band that was strangling his penis. He soon discovered that his mother had taken all his money.

She's fooling herself if she thinks that'll stop me from leaving.

At dawn he was going to fly.

And for nearly a decade, Max Legrand was gone.

27.

ON MONDAY, OCTOBER twenty-second, fifteen days after the first body was discovered, Captain Hervé Bergevin summoned his team of investigators. Seated on the corner of his desk across from Henri, Emilianne, and Jason, he recapped his lieutenant's outlandish account.

"So," he concluded, "this Dorothy Noroît is Maxime Legrand's biological mother."

"To be confirmed," Henri said, though he didn't doubt it for a second.

Authorities had been searching for Dorothy for three days but had not found her at home or at her workplace. No one in the apartment building she had moved into just a few months earlier had noticed her coming or going in recent days. The renters next door were not even sure that anyone lived in her unit. And her colleagues at the museum couldn't agree on when they had seen her last. It must have been Monday, October eighth . . . but it might have been earlier . . . Friday the fifth, or maybe Thursday the fourth. As for Dorothy's parents, twenty-five years had gone by since they had heard from their only child.

"So, looks like we've got our killer!" exclaimed Emilianne, her thumbs tucked into the belt loops of her oversize pants, as if to keep them from falling down around her knees while she paraded in front of the large window in Bergevin's office.

As if she contributed anything to the investigation, Henri sneered inwardly.

"In fact," he said, "there's no way of knowing whether the dog actually *bit* this woman. What if he just licked her blood?"

"Not sure I follow, Duhaime." Emilianne frowned. "Since the beginning you've been saying it's the killer's blood! So now what are you suggesting? That Dorothy Noroît is just another victim?"

The sergeant gestured vaguely toward the east.

"You think her corpse is over there rotting somewhere in the Pointe-aux-Trembles woods?"

Stretching his stiff legs, Henri joined her at the window. Gazing intently at the urban landscape as if he were searching for something, he speculated that Max Legrand might have recently discovered the truth about his birth.

"OK," Emilianne granted him. "But then he would've killed Margaret, not Dorothy!"

"Unless it was Dorothy's idea to switch the babies," proposed Jason.

"Was it?" Bergevin asked Henri.

"I have no idea, Captain. Mrs. Legrand spent the weekend in

Quebec City at a conference on event management. I was on my way to her place when you called me in."

"It's true that Dorothy was young and destitute," said Emilianne. "From what the nurse told us, she was in a tough spot. If she voluntarily gave up her son and he found out about it, he could have wanted revenge? I think we have an emotionally stunted psychopath on our hands." Looking down at the street below, she paused a moment before asking, "But what do Croteau, Dion, and Manseau have to do with it?"

Three pairs of questioning eyes fell on Henri. Checking that his scarf was properly adjusted around his collar, he grumbled to himself as if he were dealing with a bunch of children who didn't understand anything.

"It was jealousy!" he cried, as if it were obvious. "Max Legrand is a sociopath. He thinks everything belongs to him, that he can just help himself to whatever he wants! His whole life he's been told that he's perfect, he's a miracle, and now all of a sudden he learns that his own mother gave him up at birth, while the other three were loved and cherished."

"That's a bit of a stretch, don't you think?" Emilianne objected. "You're implying that Margaret didn't love him—"

"Let's not get lost in conjecture," Bergevin interrupted. "Duhaime, I still don't get why you're so hung up on this suspect. There is no tangible evidence in your report to support your theory."

"For the moment, it's just intuition, but . . ."

"Let's leave the whys and hows for now," said the captain impatiently. "The only thing that seems clear to me is that Noroît is one of the killer's victims. Which means he's targeting mothers now."

Adding grist to the mill, Emilianne said she had received a call from Linda Carré's daughter.

"Camille thinks there's no way her mother committed suicide. Maybe the coroner should reopen the investigation . . ."

Bergevin walked around his desk and sat down in his chair, signaling that the meeting was over.

"I'll take care of the coroner," he said. "And I'll send the K-9 unit to the Pointe-aux-Trembles woods. In the meantime, Saint-Gelais, keep looking into the Winged Monkeys. Jobin, make sure Maryse Normandin and Margaret Legrand are placed under protection. I know we're short on patrol officers, but—"

"Maryse's house is already under surveillance," Jason informed him.

"As for Margaret," said Henri, "she can just lock all her doors until I get there. Unless she gives me a good explanation for what happened in '94, she'll be behind bars by the end of the afternoon."

The three investigators left their boss's office and headed back to their shared workspace. Emilianne's rear had barely touched her chair when she leaped to her feet.

"Bingo!" she shouted, giving herself a hearty round of applause. "I knew it! Antoine Lebeau's DNA is on the Du Maurier!"

His coat under his arm, Henri had been preparing to leave the building. He came back and sat down at his desk. Studying the sergeant's face, he crossed his legs, awaiting an explanation.

"The other day, when I saw that Lebeau was smoking Du Mauriers, the cigarette that was found in the cornfield, I picked two or three of them out of his ashtray. I just got an email with the results!"

"And you didn't think it was worth telling me about this because?"

"Because you wouldn't care about that any more than you care about your first pair of tighty-whities, Duhaime!"

"That's not true."

"What's not true? You collect underpants? You still have your first pair?"

Jason's laughter further exasperated Henri, who stood up and headed for the exit.

"And Bee Lenoir's undergarments, Saint-Gelais?" he grumbled. "Have you found them yet?"

"Who cares about Bee Lenoir! The murderer is Antoine Lebeau! That guy has no qualms about killing people he considers burdens to society!"

Henri already had one foot out the door. "What about the mothers, Saint-Gelais? Why would he go after them?"

"What if Margaret Legrand was behind it all?" suggested Jason. "What if she was trying to silence everyone who somehow knew what she did in '94? She could've hired Antoine Lebeau to . . ."

"They are acquainted!" Emilianne exclaimed. "Lebeau's gang has been to some of Margaret's parties to cause trouble!"

"We should see if he's received a big wad of cash recently."

"Lebeau has a solid alibi for Manseau's murder," Henri snapped. "You said so yourself, Saint-Gelais. The person most likely to have done Margaret Legrand's dirty work is her son. Especially since all that scoundrel cares about is money."

Jason suddenly threw up his arms in despair.

"It couldn't be either of those guys!" he cried. "The AI is super clear: Leo's murderer was a woman. Probably Manseau's, too."

"Come on, Jobin, don't tell me you can picture Margaret

Legrand out in the woods in the middle of the night, high heels on her feet, putting Justin Manseau's chest back together with a nail gun!"

"There's nothing saying that Croteau's killer isn't a man!" Emilianne argued. "Lebeau went to the farm, that's a fact—and believe me, he's not the kind of guy who goes apple picking! Maybe he took care of Croteau for Margaret, and then someone like Olivia Clermont could easily have handled Manseau and Leo. She wasn't at the demonstration on October eleventh!"

"That works for Leo," Jason agreed, "but it had to have been a smaller woman who handled Manseau. Someone who weighs under a hundred and forty pounds."

"Open those monkeys' files, J.J.!" Emilianne ordered as she walked over to Jason's computer.

Henri stood frozen in the doorway, lost in thought.

"Whatever happened to Clermont, J.J.?" Emilianne asked. "Was she arrested?"

"We didn't find anything incriminating, Em. But we're keeping an eye on her."

Walking back over to his colleagues, Henri resumed making his case.

"You can't convince me that Max Legrand isn't our killer. Don't forget that his basement is stuffed full of disguises he uses to change his identity."

"So then what do you make of Lebeau's DNA on the cigarette butt?" Emilianne asked, annoyed.

"Honestly, Saint-Gelais, what does 'the kind of guy who goes apple picking' look like?"

"I would say they might be intellectual, caring, enjoys cooking... Certainly not a neo-Nazi nutjob!"

"Here's how I see it," Henri said bluntly. "Acting on his mother's orders or on his own, Max wanted to kill two birds with one stone. He used one pretext or another to lure Dorothy to Manseau's trailer. The middle of the woods was the ideal place to commit a double murder. Dorothy was wounded and lost some blood, which the dog lapped up, but she got out of there alive. She probably didn't see her attacker's face because a few days later, Max invited her to his house and she obliged. I don't know how he managed to get rid of her body, though."

"Wait, are you talking about Judith Garant?" asked Emilianne, startled.

"Is that the same person as Dorothy Noroît?"

"The age fits. Plus, she was wearing red heels." Henri proffered.

"Like the ones Dorothy Noroît had in 1994? Seriously?" Emilianne scoffed, mocking Henri. "That's just a coincidence! Red is a pretty common color for heels."

Jason stifled a laugh.

"What?" she asked.

"Since when do you know anything about fashion, Em? Don't tell me you have a pair of red heels in your closet!"

"It sounds like you might want to see them for yourself, J.J.! Anyway, it's a shame the lab still hasn't gotten anywhere with the shoe the officers found at Max's place. They're gonna run a few more tests, but it's almost like somebody cleaned the inside of the shoe—"

"No point in discussing it further," Henri cut in.

He headed back to the door and put on his coat.

"Margaret Legrand knows the truth. Once I worm it out of her, we'll know what we're dealing with. I'm off. We'll see what she has to say in her defense."

But the detective was stopped again on his way out when Bergevin burst through the door of his office.

"A hiker just stumbled across some women's clothing about a mile from Manseau's trailer!" he shouted. "Duhaime, Saint-Gelais, get over there!"

28.

MAX LEGRAND HAD always hated his full name. With Maxime being derived from the Latin *Maximus*, meaning "the greatest," he found it ridiculously pretentious in combination with his surname, from the French *le grand*, meaning "the great." When he had finally left his mother's home for good, he was delighted not to hear it anymore. But now that he had come forward to the authorities, he had to hear it again.

Margaret was forcing him to become her son once more.

Max was no fool and knew what was coming. The house he was renting would be searched from top to bottom. It was a matter of hours before the police would show up with a warrant. Having been discharged from the hospital on Saturday morning, he had spent his weekend removing all traces of Chanelle Ledoux, Lambert Thibault, and everyone else who had recently occupied the small stone house downtown.

They won't find a thing.

Max hadn't just erased all the files on his computer; he had also destroyed the machine itself and thrown it into a neighbor's trash can several blocks away. He had burned tons of papers and shredded his ID cards. From his collection of fake passports, he'd kept only two. One would allow him to flee, the other to start a new life. He had also gotten rid of most of his disguises, keeping only what he needed to slip into the skin of Keven Côté or Edouard Saint-Laurent.

Maxime Legrand is about to disappear once and for all.

That Monday afternoon, he had chosen amber contact lenses to cover up his distinctive emerald eyes. Behind his thick glasses, his eyes looked twice as big. He pulled a baseball cap down over his closely cropped hair, slipped Keven's passport into the pocket of his outdated coat, and grabbed his suitcase.

He would have needed several hands to count on his fingers the number of times he had moved in the seven years since he had flown the nest. He never stayed in the same place for more than two or three months. Yet as he prepared to leave this house where he had lived for only a few weeks, the young man suddenly felt dizzy.

Who am I?

He realized that he didn't have the slightest idea.

You're Keven Côté, an antisocial guy looking for a job, he tried to convince himself. *You're shy and withdrawn. Don't draw attention to yourself, try to blend into the background. And above all, avoid eye contact.*

To make people uncomfortable so they wouldn't stare at him for too long, he had thought about covering his face with fake pimples, but that was a complicated makeup job, and something told him he'd better get out of there.

And fast.

WHEN THE DOOR jingled, Gilbert spun around.

"Dorothy, darling!" exclaimed the shoe salesman as he pranced over to greet his favorite customer. "You haven't stopped by to see me in at least three weeks! What can I do for you today? Oh, before I forget, a pretty blonde left an envelope for you! She didn't know where to find you. She asked for your address but, naturally, I refused! I did tell her, though, that you come by often."

Fifteen minutes later, Dorothy was leaving the Vidal-Berry shop with a pair of shoes and the mysterious envelope.

Three weeks earlier, on the evening of October second, after crossing paths with Antoine Lebeau, she had gone home just long enough to pick up a few personal items. Since then, she had been hiding in a small studio apartment that she was renting by the week. As soon as she got there, she put on her new red heels and admired them.

Then she ripped open the envelope, which had her first name written on it, and pulled out a handwritten letter.

October 17

Dear Dorothy,

I don't expect you to forgive my silence. Not even God has been able to do that. He has severely punished me by taking away my son. My place is in hell, and by the time you read these words, I will be already there.

I am deeply sorry, and I hope with all my heart that one day you may find peace.

Linda

"I have found it, my lovely Linda. Thanks to you, I've finally found peace."

THREE WEEKS EARLIER, it had been cold that evening of October second.

Along the street, the fierce wind was shaking the last leaves from their trees. Antoine Lebeau flicked his cigarette butt onto the ground and flashed Dorothy a dazzling smile. Then he pulled his monkey mask back down over his face and ran off to join the activists and the commotion they were creating in front of the hospital. His wings flapped behind him in the wind.

"Dorothy? Dorothy Noroît, is it really you?"

Amid the deafening roar of the elements, Dorothy hadn't noticed the woman standing there. But even though she hadn't heard her voice in twenty-four years, she recognized her immediately.

"Linda Carré," she said, even before turning to look at her.

Linda's long skirt flapped in the wind and wrapped around her legs.

"Dorothy, it *is* you. How have you been?"

Linda started chatting away. She talked about how wonderful life was with her husband and two children. Begging Dorothy to come visit her farm sometime, she handed her a business card.

"I see you have a Vidal-Berry bag. I love that store! I never buy anything, but . . . What about you, Dorothy? What are you doing these days? Do you have a family? A partner?"

"No, I don't have any of that, Linda," she said without a hint of emotion.

"That night. It's still haunts you, doesn't it? Sometimes I think of you and pray that you've found peace. That you have a happy life."

"Well, it was nice to see you again." Dorothy tried to turn and walk away, but the farmer grabbed the belt of her coat to stop her.

"You wished he would die, Dorothy."

With the wind blowing in her ears, Dorothy wasn't sure she had heard correctly. Linda's remark should have sounded like an accusation.

Why do I get the impression she's apologizing?

"At the hospital, in our room, you said your baby would be better off dead."

Be careful what you wish for, my pretty, her mother cackled in her head.

"So what are you saying? You think God punished me? That my son died because I wished it?" Dorothy snapped.

"No, no, not at all! But at the time, I told myself he'd be better off with her."

"With *her*? Linda, what are you talking about?"

"I've been living with so much guilt all these years," Linda confessed. "I told you about Maggie, but you probably don't remember. She was already over fifty, and that could be why she gave birth prematurely. The day she found out her son wasn't going to make it, yours still had a chance to pull through. Maggie never knew that I saw her. But one night, she switched your two babies. The one who died a few hours later was hers. Not yours."

A long moment passed as the two women held each other's gaze. Dorothy was no longer feeling the cold. The wind's mournful cries seemed to have fallen silent. She didn't notice that a fight was breaking out between the different activist groups across the street. Linda was unsure whether Dorothy had understood what she had just said.

"Your child survived," she said. "Margaret Legrand raised him."

"But . . . why didn't you say something at the time?"

"You were so young, so fragile. You had no faith in anything. As you yourself said, you weren't ready to fight for your baby. And I had read all the pamphlets we were given. The experts all agreed that family environment was key to a premature baby's development. But you were injured, bordering on depression, no father for your child, not even a roof to put over his head. I talked it over with Maryse . . ."

"Maryse?"

"Maryse Normandin, the woman in the room next to ours. She was in the same situation as us. We thought we were doing both you and the baby a favor."

Her arms hanging limp at her sides, Dorothy was speechless.

"At the time, we were convinced that it was best to keep quiet."

"So why would you tell me all this now, after all these years?" Dorothy asked.

Why on the second of October?

"God has put you in my path for a reason. He is offering me the opportunity to liberate my conscience."

Linda hugged Dorothy tightly. She asked for forgiveness several times, then kissed her on the forehead and left. Dorothy watched her until she turned the corner, and then her gaze fell on the cigarette butt that Antoine Lebeau had discarded. It was rolling around on the ground in the wind. Dorothy bent down and picked it up in her gloved fingers.

We're merciful, he had said.

Dorothy Noroît was not.

29.

THREE HOURS HAD passed between the time Officer Jobin had called to advise Margaret not to open her door to anyone other than the police and the time Henri and Emilianne finally rang her doorbell. Since no one answered but the door was unlocked, the detectives took the liberty of stepping inside. Margaret was in the dining room. Her mouth was tightly gagged.

Whatever she may have been guilty of, she had nothing left to say in her defense.

"Christ almighty!" Emilianne blurted out as she stepped back.

Once the shock had worn off, she couldn't help herself.

"Looks like we won't have to worm it out of her after all. The worms'll be coming out on their own soon enough!"

Henri let out an indignant groan.

How could a person say such a thing in front of the naked, tortured corpse of an old woman?

He was fed up with his colleague's inappropriate humor. But the overwhelming feeling of despair welling up in his throat prevented him from telling her off.

If I had sent Jobin to this woman's house while we were wasting our time in Pointe-aux-Trembles, she would still be alive, he chastised himself. *But I was determined to question her myself*. . .

The clothes the hiker had found in the woods turned out to have been there for too long to be Dorothy Noroît's. She was still missing.

"None of the doors or windows were forced open," Emilianne reported after having a look around. "But J.J. told her not to open the door for anybody!"

"She knew her attacker."

"You're thinking of Max," guessed the sergeant without bothering to argue.

Responding to their call, police officers and crime scene investigators soon surrounded the house, and patrol cars began searching the neighborhood. Surely a neighbor had seen or heard something.

And you, what do you see? Concentrate, Henri told himself.

Apart from the killer's visceral and indisputable hatred for his victim, nothing else jumped out at him. It was Emilianne who noticed that one of the bottles of fine wine was missing from the cellar.

"Margaret didn't drink," Henri mumbled to himself. "She saved those bottles for fundraising events."

For his part, he eventually noticed that there was a new object on the mantelpiece—a small wooden vase with a gilded lid, no more than four inches tall.

That trinket wasn't there last time we visited. She must've brought it back from her trip down south.

The detective's attention was diverted by Officer Marco Poliquin, who entered the dining room brandishing an empty wine bottle like a trophy. It was already sealed in an evidence bag.

"We found it in a recycling bin at the end of the street," he announced. "The owners of the house swear they didn't put it there!"

"Did they see who did?" Henri snapped.

"No. The woman was out raking leaves in her backyard when she heard the sound of glass. She thought it was another raccoon in her blue bin, but . . ."

Henri grabbed the plastic bag from the officer to get a closer look at the label on the bottle.

"It's him," he confirmed, leaving no room for doubt. "It was the killer who threw this bottle away."

"Yep," Emilianne agreed, jotting the information down in her notebook. "An Emerald Château. That would be from Margaret's wine cellar."

Poliquin made a move to take the bottle back, but Henri turned abruptly and left the house with it.

"What the hell?" the officer said to Emilianne. "What's the deal with Duhaime and pieces of evidence?"

"Don't take it personally." She sighed. "He doesn't trust anyone but himself. Pompous jerk . . ."

Curious onlookers were starting to gather in the street while the coroner's team prepared to remove Margaret's shrouded body from the house.

"Stand back!" Henri ordered from the porch. "Go home, there's nothing to see!"

Bunch of rubberneckers! He cursed under his breath.

"Is it over, you think?" Emilianne asked him as she stepped outside.

"Not quite."

The answer came from someone else. Turning to look, the detectives saw the medical examiner leaning against the side of the house, draining a can of energy drink.

"What makes you say that, Desbiens?"

He frowned and shrugged at Henri.

MARGARET LEGRAND WAS still alive when Keven Côté closed his suitcase and walked out of his house, ready to rush to the airport.

On the porch he came face-to-face with a woman who was about to ring his doorbell. He recognized her immediately and forgot about his new persona. Becoming Max Legrand again, he took a step backward, retreating into the house. Not out of fear—that was something he rarely felt—but because he valued his life. He didn't manage to close his door before the speedy intruder barged right in with two clicks of her heels.

"I . . . Madame . . . if I've caused you any harm in the past, I'll make up for it," Max hastily promised. "How much . . . ? Hey, where are you going?"

He followed the woman into the living room. She knew the way. Leaning back against the sofa, she crossed her legs and placed her tote bag next to her.

"You have nothing to be afraid of," she assured him.

"You did try to kill me," Maxime replied, on his guard.

He scanned the room for something he could use to defend himself in case the maniac tried to attack him again.

"The other night, I never wanted to kill you. I would never harm you, Kansas."

I've gone by a lot of names in my life, thought Max, *but never Kansas. She's got the wrong guy.*

Content just to gaze at him, his visitor smiled.

"I'm kind of in a hurry," he said nervously. "If you were hoping to get your shoe back, the police have it now."

"As you can see"—she showed him, pointing one of her feet at him—"I've bought some new ones. Though I really loved those red heels!"

Max didn't have time to chat while she beat around the bush.

"I was supposed to meet an older lady that night, but you made me leave the restaurant before she arrived. You didn't choose me at random. How did you know I was there?"

"Detective Lieutenant Duhaime has been on your tail. All I had to do was follow him."

"The police suspect me of killing you," he told her.

"I know. I've been eavesdropping in the police station parking lot."

"It would be nice if you'd let them know you're alive," Max said.

"For the moment, I'd rather they keep thinking I'm dead."

"But why?"

Patting the sofa, she invited Max to sit down next to her. He opted to sit on the coffee table instead.

"Duhaime is also convinced that you killed Dion, Croteau, and Manseau. Those guys had shitty lives," she said. "They were put out of their misery."

Taking this as a threat, Max jumped up.

"My life isn't shitty at all! I actually have hundreds of lives!"

Don't let your guard down, he scolded himself, and then continued.

"You're part of the Winged Monkeys, right? Is that why I feel like I know you? I must've seen you on the news."

The woman picked up her tote bag. Afraid she might take out a gun, Max moved behind the table. But instead she handed him a cell phone.

"Read that email and you'll understand why I look familiar to you. Have you ever heard of the crash of '94?"

"I was born during that crash."

"A few hours before, during, or after that disaster, five women gave birth to premature babies who were put in the NICU at Sainte-Victorine Hospital. I was one of them. My son died before he was even two days old. At least, that's what they told me at the time."

Does she resent us for being alive?

She raised a hand to Max's face. Too confused to pull away, he let her caress his cheek. She then lifted the brim of his cap.

"You're perfect," she murmured. "Handsome and intelligent. I never wanted to hurt you, do you believe me? But when I learned the truth, I needed a few drops of your blood for a DNA test."

"*A few drops!*" Max protested, struggling to sort through what he was hearing and figure out what he was still missing. "You bled me like a pig!"

"I heard the detectives arguing in their parking lot. Duhaime is obsessed with you. It's making him ill. I did that to make him think you're a victim, like the others, not a murderer. So he would leave you alone."

"I *didn't* kill those guys," repeated Max.

"I know that, my darling."

"I could've died!" He was angry now.

Tears welled up in Dorothy's eyes.

"No, you couldn't have!" she objected with a little laugh that was at once disturbed and amused. "Duhaime was right there, ready to intervene. When I left, he was already trying to break down the door."

Max suddenly froze. Having practically stopped breathing, he managed to finally formulate the question on his mind.

"If you know I'm not the murderer, what were you trying to prove with your DNA test?"

"Who you are."

In a whisper, still holding his breath, Max exhaled.

"And who am I?"

He asked the question even though he knew the answer. Her eyes appeared emerald green to him now, and he could no longer ignore it.

"Somewhere deep down, I always knew you were alive," she told him. "The second I saw you, any remaining doubts melted away. But I thought you would need proof to believe me."

She pointed to her phone.

"The results are in."

Maxime looked down at the screen.

According to this test, there's a 99.9 percent chance that I'm the son of this woman.

"Kansas," he said as he handed her back the phone. "The name you gave me when I was born."

"Kansas Noroît, that's right. That's what it says on your birth certificate. And your death certificate."

There's a death certificate with my name on it.

Strangely, the young man had never felt so alive. His chest swelled as though a fresh breeze had just blown through his lungs. He wanted to ride this high for a while.

I know who I am.

30.

WHILE HENRI AND Emilianne sniffed around in the woods on the island's East End like a couple of bloodhounds, Margaret Legrand was taking her final breaths.

Gagged and tied to a chair in her own dining room, still unaware of the fate that awaited her, she glared furiously at the pair who had kidnapped her. On her left cheekbone was a bruise the color of the Emerald Château that had been swiped from her cellar.

"When I told you that she kidnapped you, you didn't seem too surprised," Dorothy said to Kansas.

Seated at the old woman's table, they were enjoying the expensive vintage wine and chatting as if she weren't there.

"I never felt at home in this house. Now I understand why she kept reminding me that I was *her* son, *her* miracle."

Margaret hadn't recognized Max until he took off his sunglasses and cap, and then she had let him into her house, with Dorothy slipping in right behind him.

"Want to know how I found out, Maggie?"

Dorothy faced her now and addressed her directly for the first time.

"My roommate in the hospital, Linda, saw you do it. She told Maryse in the room next door. Those two bitches kept your secret because they thought my son would be better off with you than with me. I found this out three weeks ago. And hearing today that *my* Kansas had an unhappy childhood, let's just say that it has added fuel to the fire. Can you understand that, Maggie? I've seen the scars on his body."

Margaret had something to say in response, but only a few grunts escaped from beneath her gag. Dorothy swirled the contents of her glass and finally knocked back the rest of her wine in a single gulp.

"You don't understand the pain I've lived with these past twenty-four years, Margaret. He was all I ever wanted. You took that away from me."

The indignation in Margaret's eyes gave way to fear. Turning toward Kansas, she found no comfort in his gaze, which radiated an emotionless glow.

"Linda sure picked the wrong day to tell me everything!" Dorothy continued. "October the second. That's the date I would've given birth to Kansas if that witch Johanne Manseau hadn't caused the accident that left me unable to have children. And as if that wasn't enough, earlier that day I found out my request for adoption would never be accepted." She paused to regard the woman's expression. "I would say that I had a pretty fucking shitty day, wouldn't you?"

Dorothy raised her eyebrows at Margaret, as if daring her, despite the gag, to express any doubt about her parenting skills.

"Linda left me her business card with the address of her farm," she went on. "She delivered a death sentence to her son!" She let out a laugh.

Pouring herself another glass of wine, Dorothy asked Margaret if she remembered Justin Manseau.

"I would assume so, since, you know . . . you breastfed him. I don't know if it was because of your milk, but that kid grew up to be a real asshole! He made the papers when he was found not guilty in a case of assault on a prostitute. One article mentioned the car accident that killed his mother and left him paralyzed. It also talked about a big Manseau Forestry project in the East End."

Margaret started to tug at her restraints, but Dorothy paid no attention.

"Leopold Dion wasn't much harder to track down," she went on. "First I found his mother, Maryse, on Facebook. She's part of a vigilante group called the Citizen Sentinels who patrol Montreal North. That idiot led me directly to her son. He was the first to go."

Kansas interrupted her monologue.

"That guy was a beast, Margaret. He must weigh twice as much as she does! Tell her how you did it!"

Flattered by her son's admiration, Dorothy feigned embarrassment.

"Actually, Leo was the easiest one," she said. "When Maryse realized I was following her, she panicked and dropped her pepper spray. I picked it up. After that, I went back to his place a few times to try to familiarize myself with the layout, but the coward never opened his blinds, not even during the day! I pretended to be a delivery person and used the spray on him. You should have seen it! The pathetic wimp didn't even try to defend himself! He fell to his knees whimpering and begged me to spare him. He even pissed himself!

"It was liberating," Dorothy admitted. "But very messy. Luckily, Johanne's red patent leather heels were easy to clean."

"Johanne's heels?" he asked.

Margaret, now silent, had stopped struggling, as if she were trying to disappear into the woodwork. Dorothy turned to Kansas.

"Johanne's shoes fell off her feet in the accident. I found them on the side of the road. A little voice told me to grab them, and I didn't think twice. I left my ballet flats on the highway and put on the heels. They spent twenty-four years at the bottom of a box, along with an urn containing the ashes of the person I thought was my son."

"This is my favorite part of the whole thing. I like to have a little fun with my victim's organs."

The young man looked sick, but also somewhat impressed.

"Leopold Dion was permanently holed up at home, scared of his own shadow. Maryse surely meant well, but by keeping her son under her wing, she turned him into a complete recluse. He had no balls."

Seeing where this was going, Kansas opened his mouth in astonishment.

"You cut off his testicles! Don't tell me you sent them to his mother!"

"Maybe I should have." Dorothy smiled. "But I had something else in mind. I put the balls in a jar of ice, stuck it in my tote bag, changed clothes, and headed down to the South Shore. Then there was poor Francis. Dumb as a bale of hay! Which is why I took out his brain."

Kansas's eyes widened.

"The amount of alcohol in his blood probably spared him *some* pain. But he just had no fear. I asked him why he was so quiet, and he said that his sister was in the shed with a boy. That if he bothered her, she'd be mad at him. Poor guy, he was pretty out of it. Nobody was in the shed. I had just been there to get the pitchfork, along with the chain saw I was about to use on him."

Margaret Legrand wasn't used to letting people push her around, but she did know fear. Now she knew terror, too. Tears rolled down from her bulging eyes. She began frantically moaning under her gag. Kansas relished her distress.

"Let me guess what you did with Justin Manseau," Kansas said to Dorothy now. "He was a forest engineer, right? He had brains. But he was violent toward women. A heartless man!"

"See that, Maggie? My son and I are on the same wavelength."

Dorothy emptied the last of the Emerald Château into the two glasses. With the tip of her tongue she licked the dark red drop that ran down the neck of the bottle. Before continuing her story, she took a mouthful and savored it with her eyes closed.

"When I got to the construction site for the cross-country ski center, through the trailer window I saw Justin assaulting a girl. He had sicced his dog on her. That thing was as horrible as him. I whistled. That distracted the dog and gave the girl time to punch his lights out."

"Did the girl see you?" Kansas asked, concerned. "Could she possibly identify you?"

"She did see me, but it was dark. Honestly, I was only there that night to get my bearings, but the opportunity was too good to pass up. Unfortunately the dog recovered before I had time to cut his head off. He bit my arm!"

Dorothy still bore the mark, which she displayed for her audience by rolling up her sleeve.

"I waited for Manseau to get back in his wheelchair, and then I knocked him out and tied him up. I was thinking of using some kind of rope, but the dirty pig had a pair of handcuffs lying on top of a pile of porn magazines. You should have seen them. He woke up quickly and yelled at the top of his lungs, called me every possible name, but there was nobody around to hear him. I got rid of what I assume was the poor girl's underwear. She'd had enough trouble as it was; I didn't want her getting blamed instead of me. I was saving that honor for Antoine Lebeau."

"Who's Antoine Lebeau?"

"The head of the Winged Monkeys. You know what that is?"

Kansas cackled. "Yep."

"The night I ran into Linda, I was in front of Sainte-Victorine Hospital. The Winged Monkeys were protesting, and a fight was about to break out between them and the pro-lifers. It was like all the stars aligned. Suddenly, all my uncertainty floated away. I knew exactly what I had to do. The path forward had become so clear. And so much brighter!"

Dorothy's eyes sparkled.

"Lebeau had tossed a cigarette butt at my feet. I picked it up and later dropped it in the cornfield near Francis's body."

Kansas was impressed. He turned his attention back to Margaret.

"How could you have thought for a single second that I'd be better off with you than with her?"

The old lady continued her moaning in an endless lament.

"And what about Justin Manseau's heart? I would guess tearing one of those out isn't easy."

"There was no shortage of tools at the construction site. To open Justin's chest I used a jigsaw. Replaced his heart with Francis's brain, then closed him up with a nail gun. I saw on a map that there was a little cliff nearby, so I rolled the body to the edge and dumped it over."

Dorothy's story had come to an end. Margaret understood this and had gone quiet. For a few seconds a heavy silence fell over the room.

"And now?" Kansas finally asked. "What are you planning to do with Manseau's heart? Do you still have it?"

"My own heart was torn to pieces, Kansas. I've mourned your death for a quarter century."

Mother and son looked over at Margaret. Their chairs screeched as they pushed them back and rose to their feet.

"There's really one person who is responsible for so much suffering," Kansas said, his voice thick with anger.

He placed his hands on the table and leaned toward Margaret.

"I've always been someone else, and you *knew* it! And you were playing a role, too—the perfect mother, so sweet, loving, and attentive. You almost never stepped out of character in front of others."

Dorothy slipped behind Margaret.

"But you're the exact opposite," Kansas added. "You are truly wicked."

Grabbing her by her still-near-perfectly coiffed hair, Dorothy pulled her head back.

"Johanne Manseau died in the accident she caused, and that's what started all this," she reminded her. "Do you think she saw what I did to her son from where she is now? I like to think so. Meanwhile, Linda chose to take her own life rather than endure the hell I've been through. I hope Maryse will hold on; that she'll suffer from the loss of her son for a long time. As for you, Margaret, you don't have enough years left in this world to atone for all your sins."

"You may not suffer for a long time, but you'll suffer intensely," Kansas said.

"Let's find out what's hidden under her veil of respectability, shall we?" Dorothy suggested to her son.

Grinning from ear to ear, Dorothy yanked Margaret's head harder. A handful of hair came out in her hand. Margaret stifled a scream but let it out when she realized that the sadist wasn't going to stop there. For a moment, Kansas stood and watched his mother enjoying herself. Then he turned and disappeared into the kitchen. He came back a moment later, snapping the blades of a pair of sharp scissors.

"I'm going to remove her pretty clothes."

His first swipe sent the buttons flying off Margaret's blouse. Overcome by bad memories, he tore at the fabric that tried to conceal her true nature, mercilessly cutting into her frail body and exposing skin that became sticky with blood. Throughout the ordeal, the old woman let out only a few gasps.

"Why would you deny me the pleasure of hearing you cry?" Kansas shouted. "You're going to be a pain in the ass until the very end, aren't you?"

"She's a tough piece of meat," said Dorothy. "Thick skin."

Kansas took a step back to admire his work.

"What do you think, Mom? Have we made her as ugly on the outside as she is inside?"

"Not yet."

He had to agree and got to work remodeling Margaret's face with his fists.

"They said she wore her heart on her sleeve, right?" Dorothy asked as she took a jar out of her bag. "That she was charitable and dedicated to the cause?"

A sardonic laugh rolled out of Kansas's throat. The next blow he struck was especially vicious, and it knocked Margaret unconscious. Her head fell forward.

"She actually pocketed some of the money from the OZ Foundation," Kansas said. "But none of those fools ever noticed!"

"Well, then," Dorothy said, pretending to be upset, "we'll have to come up with something else. She had a lot of guts, didn't she? Or like we say in French: She had heart in her guts—*du coeur au ventre.*"

"No one could deny that."

Dorothy removed Justin Manseau's heart from its jar and placed it on the table. Even though she had kept it refrigerated, after eleven days it was starting to emit a foul odor. As she cut it into pieces with the scissors, Kansas tapped their victim's cheeks until she woke up. Dorothy then chose one of the decorative spoons from Margaret's sideboard and used it to bring a piece of the putrid meat to the old woman's lips.

"If you scream, it'll be worse," Kansas warned as he removed her gag.

"Open up," ordered Dorothy.

With her teeth clenched and her face disfigured by the blows, terror, and pain, Margaret pleaded with them through bloodshot eyes. Her torturer gave her two options.

"Either you swallow every last bite," Dorothy said, "or I cut open your belly and put it in there myself!"

Dorothy forced Margaret to choke down the organ, spoonful after spoonful, as though she were feeding a stubborn baby, something she had never had the opportunity to do. It was long and painful. After each bite, Kansas forcibly closed the old woman's mouth until the risk of regurgitation had passed.

"There we go!" exclaimed Dorothy, once the heart had been fully consumed.

"We're getting there," Kansas said. "But we can do better."

The young man ducked out of the room for another minute and returned with a bottle of bleach and a roll of adhesive tape. He put the gag back in Margaret's mouth, taped her eyelids open so she couldn't close her eyes, and uncapped the bottle.

"You do the honors, Mom."

Dorothy didn't need to be asked twice. With a flick of her wrist, she poured the corrosive liquid over Margaret's scarlet skull. As the product burned her eyeballs, a burst of energy caused her to struggle, and she let out a muffled scream. There was a loud crack as she dislocated her shoulder, but she was unable to break free.

Under the gaze of her executioners, her skin reddened and swelled but then became soft and blistered. As long as the nerves weren't damaged, the pain would continue. Once she stopped thrashing around, Dorothy finished emptying the bottle of bleach. On Margaret's skull, shoulders, and arms, the chemical burns began to form blisters. Kansas walked over to her and popped one with his finger, exposing the red, pale, oozing skin beneath.

"You never did manage to pop my balloon, Margaret," he said, his lips twisted in a satisfied grin. "You know why? Because you can't steer a hot-air balloon; it just floats wherever the wind takes it."

The old woman lifted her head toward her miracle. Her blind eyes kept her from seeing his smile, but she had almost certainly detected the euphoria in his voice. Her head fell back, blocking an inaudible cry in her throat.

"Beautiful," Dorothy said. "It almost looks like she's melting."

31.

THE LAST TRACES of sunset were fading from the sky when a dozen police officers swept into Montreal North. After discovering Margaret Legrand's body, Henri had feared that Maryse Normandin might have suffered the same fate. But the patrol officers found Maryse very much alive—although their sudden appearance nearly gave her a heart attack.

The body part missing from Margaret's corpse was found shortly afterward, six miles from her home, in an old house downtown. When Henri arrived at the scene, Michel Desbiens was already examining the battered body of a middle-aged man lying on the kitchen floor. A tongue that didn't belong to him was sticking out from between his clenched teeth in a nightmarish grimace.

"His wife is in shock; she's just been taken to the hospital," one of the first responders told the detective. "She found him like this when she got home from a night out with friends. Their two children were asleep upstairs."

The corpse was staring at the ceiling. Its head had been split open. Other organs, in pieces and difficult to identify, were also bathed in blood. After a brief examination of the remains, Desbiens announced that, in addition to his brain, the victim's heart and testicles had been removed.

"The same three organs," he pointed out.

"Except that he's also been drained of all his blood," remarked Henri, who had never seen so much of it before.

Something the nurse at Sainte-Victorine had said suddenly came back to him. Although there was still plenty he didn't understand, he instantly knew who this man was.

But why would Max take Margaret's tongue? To silence her once and for all? What did she know?

"What could this poor devil have done to deserve this?" an officer wondered aloud.

"Maybe his final words didn't go down well with the killer," suggested Desbiens.

"Or his long silence," replied Henri.

The speculation was interrupted when Hervé Bergevin burst into the kitchen. Red-faced and barely glancing at the body, he shouted at the lieutenant.

"You really fucked this one up, Duhaime! I had ordered Margaret Legrand to be put under protection! And then what do I hear? She's in the morgue! This massacre has to stop!"

"There's every indication that this is the final murder in this case, Captain."

"What makes you say that, Duhaime? You're a fortune teller now?"

"All of the man's organs were left here. His blood, too."

Bergevin ventured a second glance at the bloodless body and its parts, which were being handled by the medical examiner.

"So?" he snapped, turning his body so he could no longer see the carnage. "Maybe he didn't have time."

"Nobody interrupted him," argued Henri. "This is exactly where the road was leading us, Captain. Everything ends *here*, in this house."

"What are you talking about, you idiot?"

Henri took a few steps, deliberately forcing the captain to turn his head toward the body to keep listening to him.

"At first, I thought that by swapping the organs, the killer wanted to highlight certain qualities of his victims. But I was wrong. In fact, he was pointing out their flaws. Unlike Dion, Croteau had balls of steel, but his courage only got him into trouble. As for Manseau, he was educated and intelligent, but he was ruthless and cruel."

Bergevin nodded.

"OK, I'm with you. But why would the killer bother pointing out their flaws, in your opinion?"

"He probably wanted to ease his conscience and justify his despicable acts. Max Legrand is a . . ."

"Max Legrand?" Bergevin snarled under his breath.

"The woman who raised him was brutally murdered, and we just found her tongue in the mouth of Vincent Boisvert, his biological father, who abandoned him at birth. What more do you need?" Henri was breathing heavy with frustration now.

"His biological father? Where the hell did you get that? There's no name on Kansas Noroît's birth certificate!"

By way of explanation, Henri repeated the words of Monique Joyal.

"'He dumped his girlfriend and his baby over the phone, while she was in the middle of giving birth! What an evil jerk; the guy had no *balls*! That *heart*less bastard renounced his own *blood*!"

"What?" Bergevin's was squinting at Henri with contempt now.

"It's staring us in the face, for god's sake! Not only did his son take his brain, balls, and heart, but he drained him of all his blood!"

"I'm not really seeing it."

"Time is running out, Captain! We need to issue an arrest warrant for Max Legrand, notify the airports, seal the borders, and—"

"Whoa!" Bergevin grabbed Henri by the arm and pulled him into the living room, away from prying ears.

"Have you lost your mind, Duhaime? Out of the question! Why do you keep dragging that guy into everything? You've dug yourself into a hole and now you can't get out."

"No, Hervé, I—"

"Henri! I never believed you, but now I'm seriously starting to wonder if all those rumors about you were actually true about your obsessive side. Which reminds me, the archivist at Sainte-Victorine called to say that a file is missing. Dorothy Noroît's. You wouldn't happen to know anything about that, would you, Duhaime?"

"Well, they must have misplaced it."

"Duhaime, I'm warning you. If I find out—"

"The archivist should ask Monique Joyal. She was the last one to look at it. For Max Legrand."

"You don't have a shred of evidence against this guy. Forget him! That's an order."

"I will find the evidence, if everyone would just stop working against me! Maxime Legrand is our killer. He's a skilled and unscrupulous con artist who has robbed dozens of people of their savings. One of them committed suicide."

Bergevin hit the roof.

"Do you want to go back to financial crimes, Duhaime? Is that what you want?"

"Listen—"

"No, *you* listen to *me*! The mystery has been solved. *You* solved it. Your organ theory makes perfect sense. It confirms that the murders are linked to the premature births of the three victims, which leads us straight to the Winged Monkeys, like I've been saying all along. And guess what? Jobin just discovered that, on several occasions, large sums of money were transferred from Margaret Legrand's account to Antoine Lebeau's."

Henri contemplated this. "Has Lebeau admitted anything?"

"Of course not. He's denied everything. He swears that Margaret was paying him to support his campaign against care for premature infants. As backward as it seems, all the media hype around the Monkeys apparently helped boost donations to the OZ Foundation."

"Well, then, it must be true! Who could possibly invent a story like that?"

"Lebeau's DNA was found at one of the crime scenes—do you need me to paint you a damn picture? Saint-Gelais told me."

What kind of bullshit theories has she been spreading?

"Saint-Gelais is incompetent, Captain. That's why you brought me back to the team."

"And you're making me regret it, Duhaime! Now give it a rest and go home! You're hurting the investigation. Take a couple days off. Saint-Gelais and Jobin are busy questioning Lebeau. They'll get him to talk!"

I can't believe that asshole is about to slip through my fingers!

"Wait a minute, Hervé. Did you see the pictures of Max Legrand's basement?"

"They were brought to my attention, yes. And? Do you have a problem with his lifestyle, Duhaime?"

"No, Captain. It's just . . ."

Unable to keep his legendary cool one second longer, Henri exploded.

"You're the one hurting the investigation, Hervé!"

32.

A FLOOR LAMP CAST a yellow glow over one corner of the living room, which was otherwise soaked in shadow. Henri was sitting in his favorite armchair, his emaciated neck uncovered, wearing nothing but a pair of his gray pants and a shirt with the sleeves rolled up. He was poring over Dorothy Noroît's medical file, which he had taken out of his briefcase, having discreetly swiped it under Emilianne's nose back at the archives.

I'm missing something, he couldn't help thinking.

He struggled to stay focused. His attention kept drifting to the coffee table, where the bottle of Emerald Château sat prominently. Fingerprints were smeared across the glass. They could be seen with the naked eye, even through the plastic bag, which was protecting the evidence from contamination.

Those are Max Legrand's fingerprints, Henri assured himself. *I'll take this to the chief inspector—those fingerprints will send Legrand to rot in prison.*

Another voice in his head shot back.

Go see whoever you want, old man! Nobody takes you seriously anymore. You might as well keep that bottle for yourself.

BERGEVIN HAD NOT wanted to hear the truth, and Henri had been dismissed from his position. In the aftermath, Antoine Lebeau was formally charged with the murder of Francis Carré-Croteau. In an effort to pin the killings of Dion and Manseau on his activist friends, the major crimes unit was wasting its time picking apart every detail of their lives.

There will be a trial, but Legrand won't be the one facing the jury. This bottle could clear Lebeau's name.

Henri took the first page out of Dorothy's file and closed the folder. Driven by a desire he had too often suppressed, he brought the sheet to his face and licked it from bottom to top several times.

Why would I return this file? he wondered as he stuffed the paper into his pants. *Whatever's in these pages, even if that twat Emilianne bothered to look for it, she'd never find it!*

Henri left his chair, letting the folder drop onto the seat. He knelt in front of the coffee table and grabbed the Emerald Château. His fingers moved in circles over the plastic bag, stroking the ridges at the bottom of the bottle. Then he slid his index finger upward into the deep cavity.

Unspeakable desires awoke.

It's already too late, in any case. Legrand is a chameleon. An eel, even. No one will ever get their hands on that psychopath. He's already far away by now. I've done enough.

Henri was now caressing the bottle with both hands.

He felt a pang of guilt. A few days earlier, no harm had come from squeezing the bag of cigarette butts that implicated the three young delinquents from La Prairie in the murder of Francis Carré-Croteau. Rubbing the bag against his crotch through his pants had even given him an erection. Then there was Margaret Legrand's saliva sample, which forced him to stop in a squalid alley. But that time no one had caught him. As for the red high heel, the one he had penetrated with his gloved member and ejaculated into—it was still in the lab being analyzed.

That shoe is crucial to the investigation. I hope I didn't completely scrub the DNA profile. But even without it, how could those imbeciles not realize that the shoe belongs to Dorothy Noroît? That woman could see what was happening. She died trying to stop her son's murderous rampage.

Henri unsealed the bag and took out the bottle of wine. His hands began to tremble as they made direct contact with the smooth glass.

This time he wasn't wearing gloves.

Don't drop it. Don't break it. It's so beautiful, with its mouth the shape of a crown.

Bringing the bottle to his nostrils, Henri inhaled the scent of wine that lingered inside. He licked the purple stain of a dry droplet on the rim, and his tongue trailed down the long, slender neck. He kissed the bulge of the shoulders and ran his hands over the wide, sloping body. Listening only to his baser instincts, he unbuttoned his pants and pulled out a phallus he hadn't seen so stiff since . . .

Be careful. Don't make the same mistake again.

But this time, he could not help himself.

HENRI DUHAIME HAD taken a sexual interest in pieces of evidence when he had solved his first murder case.

He didn't care what they were. It was the risk of defiling or altering them that got him excited. The more important the evidence was to the prosecution, the more he wanted it. He eventually stopped seeing women. But the detective was a disciplined man. For a long time he had managed to keep this extravagance under control, never letting his fantasies get the better of him, content to steal objects that had already been analyzed. Most of them were stacked in boxes that would never be opened again.

But Henri wanted more. What turned him on was the idea of holding in his hands a thing that empowered him to throw a criminal in jail. He began bringing home evidence he had collected, only handing it over to the appropriate people the following day. At first he was extremely prudent, systematically handling the objects through their plastic packaging or, on a few occasions, after putting on latex gloves. Even so, someone finally noticed that he was treating evidence recklessly and not abiding by certain aspects of the law. On the brink of becoming captain, Henri was suspended. He made no attempt to defend himself. An investigation could have brought to light what he wanted to keep hidden. He accepted his transfer to the financial crimes unit without complaint, claiming he needed a change. And his colleague Hervé Bergevin took the job he had coveted.

From then on, the need to resort to sexual fetishes became compulsive and all-consuming, and that was when he lost control.

He had been chasing Raphael Delorme for over two years when Cassandra Bellerive committed suicide. In a letter, she described the event that had plunged her into depression: Her fiancé, Adrien Lalande, had deserted her in the shop where she was trying on her wedding dress. Cassandra never saw him again, and a large part of her fortune vanished along with him. There was an investigation, but it turned up nothing.

The young Frenchman didn't even exist.

The mother of the suicide victim provided the police with a love letter from Lalande to her daughter.

Since he could demonstrate that the crook was still at large, Henri finally had a way to keep the investigation into Raphael Delorme from being closed. The fingerprints lifted from the paper were not in the system, but the detective lieutenant had a sample of Delorme's handwriting, which could be compared with the writing on the love note. This would prove that Raphael Delorme and Adrien Lalande were the same person.

This love letter aroused Henri to no end. It consumed his daily thoughts.

Ashamed, Henri burned the paper. The investigation into Raphael Delorme was shelved. Following this incident, he was forced to admit he had a problem that was disrupting his daily life and putting him in danger. He toyed with the idea of retiring. It was the phone call from Captain Bergevin, when the mutilated corpse was discovered in the cornfield on the South Shore, that shook him back to reality.

NOW, ONCE AGAIN, Henri's arousal had reached the point of no return.

Once Henri had climaxed and regained his senses, he was immediately mortified. He sat down, put the bottle on the floor, and soon found a way to console himself.

Those amateurs would never have taken this evidence into account anyway. After all, Max is Margaret's son, biological or not. What could be more natural, in their minds, than his fingerprints on that bottle?

Henri couldn't relax, though. Something was bothering him. He still hadn't understood everything, and he knew it.

What am I missing?

Naked and dripping with sweat, he picked up the piece of paper that had fallen on the floor along with his underwear. He was busy smoothing it out when the address written on Dorothy Noroît's 1994 file jumped out at him. It was the same one as the hundred-year-old house where Vincent Boisvert had just been murdered.

"Oh my god."

That doesn't prove that Boisvert is Maxime's father, but it will persuade Bergevin to compare their DNA! All I have to do is give him this folder. I will have to admit that I stole it. But it doesn't matter anymore.

The detective then realized that not only had he licked the page with the address on it, but he had also stuffed it into his underwear and was now holding it with a hand covered in semen. With a frustrated scream, he grabbed the folder and began frantically leafing back through the various pages of the file.

There's something else! There has to be something else! What am I missing?

33.

THE DAY MARGARET Legrand's only son had insulted her by running away from home, she had disinherited him. Once her estate was settled, her entire fortune would go to the OZ Foundation. As for her sumptuous villa in the West Island, she had bequeathed it to a distant cousin, an octogenarian widow who was eager to move in and had gotten right to work clearing the house of items she didn't want. Wearing a dress and jewelry that had belonged to the deceased, the cousin whistled as she opened her second bottle of Emerald Château. Glass in hand, she set about sorting through the knickknacks gathering dust on the mantelpiece. Not appreciating the sculpture of a Neolithic mother goddess, she made a face.

"How dreadful!"

Sensing that the heavy antique object must be worth its weight in gold, she placed it in a box marked "to sell." A mixture of dried, wilted flower petals was tossed into the "throw away" box. The heiress straightened a candlestick, then picked up a small wooden pot with rounded sides. Its golden lid was sealed, and she couldn't open it. Unlike Detective Lieutenant Henri Duhaime, she knew what this object was.

"An urn," she murmured. "It's tiny."

Turning it between her fingers, a small gold plaque came into view. A name engraved in the metal—Kansas Noroît—had been crossed out. Above it, a set of initials: *M.L.*

The cousin shuddered, and the urn landed in the box of trash.

🌢

DESPITE THE COLD, Dorothy took off her shoes, blistered from tight patent stilettos.

The sun faded slowly through the changing colors of the sky as if it were trying to stay awake past its bedtime. Dorothy sat on a park bench watching the few children who still lingered at the playground. Less than six feet from her, a little boy, too young to walk, sat in the sand, happily tapping miniature mountains with his plastic shovel. Not far away, his mother watched him with a distracted eye as she listened intently to the sales pitch Kansas was giving her. He was so convincing in his role of talent scout Edouard Saint-Laurent that she could already picture herself at the height of the stellar acting career he was promising her.

Seeing that the stranger on the bench was staring at him, the little boy flashed her a big smile.

He has green eyes, Dorothy noted. *Kansas must have looked something like him at that age.*

This thought reminded her of what Karine Maltais had said.

"The baby who died when you were nineteen—you'll never get him back."

I got him back, Dorothy replied in her mind to the social worker.

But had this, in fact, brought her peace? She wasn't sure anymore.

The baby babbled and waved his shovel at Dorothy, as if he sensed that her mind was elsewhere and wanted to draw her attention back to him.

He has green eyes, like my Kansas. Even though that's the rarest eye color in the world.

The baby's mother remained enchanted by Edouard Saint-Laurent's charm.

The sun is setting and the stars are lining up again, thought Dorothy.

Under the light of those stars, the road ahead shone brightly once more.

Dorothy slipped back into her red shoes and left the bench. She took two steps to the edge of the sandbox. Leaning toward the little boy, she glanced over at the woman, who had not seen her approaching her bundle of joy.

"Hi, you," whispered Dorothy, extending her arms to the baby.

"*You can't replace one baby with another, Madame Noroît,*" Karine Maltais scolded her again.

🩸

THE DOOR TO the archives room opened. It was Monique Joyal.

"Hey, Étienne. Still no luck finding Dorothy Noroît's records?"

"That's the third time you've asked this week, Monique."

"And you're sure you don't have a digital copy somewhere?"

"Like I told you, after last year's IT attack, we lost all the records up to '98. We're re-digitizing them, but we're only up to 1989 so far. What's the matter? Is somebody hassling you about the missing file?"

"No, it's just . . . Never mind. I'm probably just jumping to conclusions."

"Monique Joyal!" the archivist called after her as she was walking away. "What's gotten into you? Come back here, pull up a chair, and spit it out!"

The nurse gave in, and Étienne walked around his desk and sat down with her at the consultation table.

"Dorothy Noroît was injured in the crash of '94," she began.

"This again?" groaned the archivist.

"Hush and listen, you tiresome child. In the past few years, studies have shown that psychopaths are lacking gray matter in the areas of the brain responsible for empathy, morality, guilt, and self-control, among other things."

"I've heard about that, sure."

"A few years ago I worked on a study with a neuroscientist. Dr. Lanctôt was trying to understand what makes some psychopaths cross the line and become murderers, while others manage to maintain socially acceptable behavior."

"OK . . ." said Étienne, suddenly eager to hear the rest.

"We didn't find anything conclusive."

"Really? That's it . . . ? Come on, Monique, push that baby out and let's get it baptized!"

"Dorothy Noroît had a few brain scans as a child, after a bike accident. And again after the car accident. Doctors didn't notice anything special at the time, but given what I know now . . . When the officers came and I saw the two series of scans in her records . . . I'm not completely sure, Étienne—Dr. Lanctôt should take a look—but . . ."

"You think Dorothy Noroît has the brain of a psychopath?"

♦

THE LIVING ROOM floor was littered with green shards of glass from the bottle of Emerald Château. They sparkled in the darkness under the colored light of the television screen and changed color with each flash. Slumped on the sofa in his boxers, a three-day beard gnawing at his hollowing cheeks, Henri periodically pinched and pulled at the skin on his neck. It was raw from all the picking.

That guy was a piece of shit, but he didn't have anything to do with those murders! he raged inwardly.

From the television news, he had just learned that Antoine Lebeau had died. He was murdered in prison before he even had a chance to stand trial.

How could they have let themselves be fooled?

Henri suddenly sat up straight. A red high-heeled shoe had appeared on the screen and was being shown from all angles. For a moment he thought he was losing his mind. A police spokesperson's voice came on, asking for the public's help in identifying the owner of the shoe, which had blood on it from three murder victims: Francis Carré-Croteau, Leopold Dion, and Justin Manseau. Unfortunately, there was not enough genetic material on the shoe to establish even a partial profile of the person who had worn it.

"*It's like somebody cleaned the inside of the shoe . . .*" Emilianne had said.

Henri flinched at the thought of it, and flinched again when his cell phone rang. Intrigued by the unfamiliar number, he answered.

"Are you watching the news, Lieutenant Duhaime?"

"Who is this?"

"Philippe Manseau. Lieutenant, that . . ."

Justin Manseau's grandfather.

"I'm not working on the case anymore, Mr. Manseau."

"That shoe belonged to my Johanne, Lieutenant Duhaime. I ordered them from Italy for her eighteenth birthday. Do you understand? It's her, it's my Johanne, who's behind all these horrors. And it's not over."

"Your daughter is dead, Mr. Manseau."

"It's all her fault! She killed them all! There were nine dead on that day. And today, Lieutenant? How many victims does that make now? How many more will she need to appease her?"

A deafening alarm sounded in Henri's ears. He thought his heart was about to stop. Without another word, he ended the call with Philippe Manseau, and his heart compensated for the beats it had missed by speeding up. The alarm was coming from both his phone and the television, where the news had been replaced by a red screen.

An Amber Alert.

At dusk, in a small town on the border between Quebec and the United States, a fifteen-month-old baby had been kidnapped. He wore a blue coat and had brown hair and green eyes.

Green eyes, Henri repeated in his head, overcome by a sense of dread. *The alert doesn't give any details about the kidnapper.*

He broke out in a cold sweat.

Henri didn't believe in ghosts, but one question would haunt him until the day he died.

What did I miss?

Because he had no doubt that Johanne Manseau's father was right about at least one thing: It wasn't over.

The nightmare was just beginning for Henri Duhaime.

ABOUT THE AUTHOR

MAUDE ROYER was born in Quebec City, Canada, where she studied graphic design. After spending two years in France, she came back to live in Quebec City. It was in first grade, reading her first novel, that she discovered what she wanted to do with her life: write stories. Author of three fantasy series for teenagers, she also wrote for children before moving into horror literature for adults.